Love and the Game

Love and the Game

Johnni Sherri

www.urbanbooks.net

Urban Books, LLC
300 Farmingdale Road, NY-Route 109
Farmingdale, NY 11735

Love and the Game

ISBN 13: 978-1-60162-228-0
ISBN 10: 1-60162-228-7

First Trade Paperback Printing July 2019
Printed in the United States of America

10 9 8 7 6 5 4 3 2 1

Distributed by Kensington Publishing Corp.
Submit Orders to:
Customer Service
400 Hahn Road
Westminster, MD 21157-4627
Phone: 1-800-733-3000
Fax: 1-800-659-2436

Love and the Game

by

Johnni Sherri

To my children,

When I look into eyes as beautiful and as innocent as yours, I want to protect you from the world. Reveal every piece of wisdom I have and have ever heard, in hopes of making your life's journey that much easier. But when I come to the realization that the journey will be yours and yours alone to make, I have three preliminary thoughts: remember to always follow your heart, live your dreams faithfully without fear, and know that God will handle the rest.

—Johnni Sherri

Chapter 1

Perri

"Fight! Fight! Fight!" the crowd around us cheered.

It was a hot, sticky day in May when I found myself straddled across little Ricky's body. I pummeled his face over and over again until I felt my arms finally growing weak and I was completely out of breath. Desperately he squirmed beneath me on the blacktop, trying to block my wild blows with his arms and hands. We were in the dead center of the basketball court, and I had just gotten through kicking his ass in a game of one on one. He owed me $3 from the bet we made, and now the little nigga was refusing to pay up.

"That's enough, Perri! That's enough," Plus yelled, pulling me up off little Ricky, who was shielding his face with his hands.

"Nah, let me get at him, Plus," I hollered, trying to make my way out of his firm grasp.

Plus pulled me away from the loud crowd that was now laughing and pointing at little Ricky. He was struggling to get up off of the ground, and from what I could see, he had a bloody nose. *Serves him right,* I thought.

"P, your pop's gonna have a shit fit if he finds you out here fighting again," Plus said, shoving me so hard in the back that I tripped forward a little.

"I know, but I couldn't let that nigga punk me. We made a bet for three dollars and now he don't wanna pay up," I said, adjusting the drawstrings of the navy blue basketball shorts I had on.

"I'll give you the three dollars, Perri, damn."

"Keep your money, Plus. You already know it's about the principle. I'm gonna beat his ass every time I see him until he coughs up my three dollars," I snapped, picking my book bag and basketball up off the ground. Plus simply shook his head at me in response.

I was 12, and my best friend, Plus, was 13. He was much calmer and more even-tempered than me. Although his name was actually Ahmad, everybody around the way called him Plus for "A plus." He always made straight A's in school and could figure out any math problem or riddle you threw at him. We all considered him the smartest boy in the hood.

While Plus could hang out all night in the streets with me, he never even had to crack open a book to make straight A's. I, on the other hand, had to study hard and do my homework each and every night just to make decent grades. Though Plus was somewhat of a nerd, everybody was cool with him because he was a beast on the basketball court and also in the game of *Madden*.

All of our lives we lived in row houses two doors down from one another in the Millwood Community housing projects. We were the closest any two friends could be. In fact, you rarely saw one of us without the other. Every day we walked to school together, ate lunch together, and played ball together only to get up and do the shit all over again the very next day. Most nights we even ate dinner together.

His mother and my father, Phillip, were also close. Ever since my mother died from breast cancer six years ago, Plus's mother stepped up and helped my dad out a lot with things like feeding me dinner, taking me school shopping, and just helping me stay out of trouble in general. While I lived in the house with my father and older brother, Tez, Plus lived with his mother and little sister, Aria.

As we navigated the filthy streets of our neighborhood, Plus and I passed the basketball back and forth to one another. The sounds of bike wheels spinning, dogs barking, and children playing all floated around the scene. It wasn't uncommon to see trash, crack pipes, and needles littering our streets. We lived in a drug-infested neighborhood with dopefiends and dope boys on damn near every other corner. As a matter of fact, Plus lost his Pops to drugs around the same time my mother passed, so we both vowed to always steer clear of that lifestyle.

"Chile, what happened to your lip?" Ms. Tonya asked when we entered the kitchen.

"Fighting again, Ma. What else?" Plus sarcastically responded, making his way into their freezer to toss me a bag of frozen peas.

I placed the cold bag on my swollen lip and took a seat down at the kitchen table. For some reason, I always picked the one chair that didn't have a tear in the vinyl covering. As I sat there watching Ms. Tonya cook at the stove, my lip started throbbing. It was a warm pulsation that was starting to turn into pain. I didn't even realize that little Ricky had gotten a good hit in on me until now. The adrenalin that was once coursing throughout my body was slowly coming down, and not only was my lip hurting, but my knuckles were also starting to get sore.

"You eating dinner over here tonight?" Ms. Tonya asked.

"Yeah. Pops ain't getting off 'til late again tonight," I replied.

My father was a warehouse security guard and worked most nights during the week. Although his job kept us from spending a lot of time together and only paid minimum wage, it did keep a roof over our heads, food in our mouths, and clothes on our backs. Whatever Pops and my brother Tez couldn't provide though, somehow Ms. Tonya and Plus found a way to. I considered them to be my family. Not by flesh and blood, but based on how our lives always intertwined and supported one another's.

"Well, let's go get this homework done," Plus stood up and said.

"Ughh!" I sighed, slowly getting up. My feet were almost dragging along the floor beneath me as I followed him.

Plus and I sat up in his room studying and doing homework for the next hour or so before Ms. Tonya finally called us back downstairs for dinner. She cooked fried chicken, green beans, and mashed potatoes. We ate fried chicken at least four times throughout the week, and although Plus grew tired of it, I never complained, because Ms. Tonya was an excellent cook. There were many nights I remembered only having ramen noodles to coat my stomach, so any full-course meals put in front of me were definitely going to get eaten.

"Momma, are you ready to do my hair?" little Aria asked with a hairbrush in one of her hands and a jar of that blue bergamot hair grease in the other.

At only 8 years old, Aria was a beautiful little girl with milk chocolate–colored skin and a head full of curly black hair, so black that no hints of brown could even be seen. Unfortunately, the neighborhood drunk, Ronnie, was her father. He only found his way home to Ms. Tonya's house a few nights out of the week, but when he did, he was always drunk and looking for trouble.

"After we eat, I will do your hair, Aria. Not right now," Ms. Tonya said.

"And can you do Perri's hair too please?" Aria asked seriously.

Plus bent over laughing like that was the funniest thing he'd ever heard. Even Ms. Tonya let out a light chuckle behind him.

"You gonna let me do something to that head of yours, Perri?" Ms. Tonya looked over at me and asked.

"Nah, I'm straight," I told her.

"No, you not. Running around here looking like a Troll Doll with your hair all over your head," Plus said.

The next thing we heard was a quick knock on the front door followed by my brother Tez walking in.

"What's going on, family?" he shouted out before entering the kitchen.

At just 16 years old, my brother Tez was already six feet tall and had a deep caramel complexion. He had the same amber eyes and long, curly brown hair as me, which he kept neatly braided down his back. Just recently, Tez had started in the drug game. He was one of the newest corner boys in the Millwood Community projects, and he didn't think any of us knew about it. If my father ever found out, he would probably kick Tez out of the house, so for that reason alone, I kept my mouth shut.

"Hey, baby," Ms. Tonya said. Tez was her godson, so they naturally had a special bond.

"Something sure smells good," he said, dapping Plus up. He then playfully swept his hand back and forth over the bushy mass on top of my head before taking a seat next to me at the kitchen table.

"Yeah, we're tryin'a get her to let Momma do something with her hair," Aria's grown butt said with her hand on her hip.

That's right. I'm a girl!

"That's why these little boys thinking you one of them now. Walking 'round here looking all rough like a li'l nigga," Tez said.

"Shut up, Tez," I said, rolling my eyes.

Plus laughed, but I didn't see anything funny. I really didn't care if people made fun of me, not even Tez. However, when Plus would laugh at me, it would hurt my feelings for some reason. I wasn't ashamed to admit that I was a tomboy. While most girls my age were playing double Dutch and making up cheers, I was hooping, fighting and playing video games. To make matters worse, I only wore boy clothes. Basketball shorts and white T-shirts were my favorite things to wear. I simply wasn't cut out to be a girly girl.

Although I had a light caramel complexion, amber eyes, and full pink pouty lips, that's where the beauty ended for me. I had a head full of long, thick, bushy hair that I never combed. Usually I kept it in a big, nappy puffball on the top of my head, but every now and then, when Plus would make fun of me bad enough, I would allow Ms. Tonya to cornrow it for me. And when she did, I swear it would hang so low I could feel it graze just the top of my butt. My eyebrows were also extremely thick and bushy, looking as if they were going to connect into a unibrow any day now, like one furry caterpillar just sitting above the eyes. Lastly there was the issue with my skin. Ever since I turned 12 this past November, my face had been riddled with acne. Bumps on top of bumps filled with pus and ready to be squeezed. I was far from this pretty little princess everyone wanted me to be, which was why I always hung out with the boys where I felt most comfortable.

"Yeah, Perri, you're gonna have to stop running around here like a little boy. Your period is gonna start soon," Ms. Tonya said before taking a sip of her red Kool-Aid.

"Ugh! Yuck, Ma," Plus said, frowning up his face in disgust. Tez just laughed though.

I was sure my face turned bright red because I felt so flushed from embarrassment. Mortified, I put my head down while Ms. Tonya continued to talk about my impending menstrual cycle at the dinner table. I couldn't believe she was doing all that, especially with Plus around. My appetite was now gone, so I simply pushed the food back and forth across my plate with my fork, hoping that no one would notice.

"What's wrong, P?" Plus asked, looking at me. Like always, he could tell when something was wrong with me. Just one easy glance was all it took for him to figure me out. He was the only one who could solve the mysteries running around in my head or any emotions I was trying to hide.

"Nothing," I replied lowly.

"I think you pro'ly just embarrassed her," Plus said to Ms. Tonya.

"Oh, I'm sorry, baby. You know we're all family here, and it's just a part of life," she tried to explain.

Later that night, around nine, I decided to let Ms. Tonya cornrow my hair. She always said that Tez and I looked like twins with our hair like that. As I sat on the floor Indian-style between her legs, Tez played a game of *Madden* on the PlayStation. Plus was still in the kitchen studying for his earth science test, while little Aria was now fast asleep in bed.

"All righty, you're all done," she said, tapping me on the shoulder with a long orange rattail comb.

"Thanks, Ms. Tonya."

Slowly I stood up from the floor and stretched out my arms before walking into the kitchen to dap Plus up and say my final goodbye for the night. Moments later, Tez and I made our way out of the door, immediately feeling the sticky summer's air mask our faces. The dark blue sky without a single star in sight floated above us while the one lone streetlight on the corner flickered about.

After making it just two doors down, we finally entered our home that was habitually dark and quiet this time of night. Cutting on the lights, I immediately took in the sight of Momma's brown plaid sofa, worn and frayed from over the years yet sturdy enough to last the test of time. I walked into the kitchen, putting the plate of food Ms. Tonya had wrapped up for my father in the microwave before going to my room. Our father usually made it home by eleven each night, and he always knew to look in the microwave for his dinner.

After a few hours passed, my sleep was suddenly interrupted by the sounds of loud fussing and fighting coming through the thin walls and windows within my room. My room was on the first floor of our row house, while Daddy and Tez's bedrooms were upstairs. Moments later, I heard a familiar knock at my window, just a light tapping sound that probably wouldn't even be heard to the untrained ear, but I'd heard it many nights before.

Widening my eyes, I glanced over at the digital clock on my nightstand that read 1:43 a.m. before throwing my covers back and going over to my window. Standing there on the other side with a large red handprint across his face was Plus. His expression was filled with so much anger as his chest heaved up and down. His shoulders were hunched with his arms straight down at his sides, both holding angry fists that were balled ever so tight. Yet there was something in his eyes. Something that reflected sadness.

"He's at it again, huh?" I asked knowingly after raising the window to let him in.

He shook his head and climbed inside. Tossing one of my many pillows and a throw blanket to the floor, I watched as Plus took the shoes off his feet. This was our normal routine. Whenever Mr. Ronnie would come home drunk in the middle of the night, he would bother Plus. Literally wake him right up out of his sleep and find something to fight with him about. It could be something as minor as the trash not being taken out or Plus leaving the PlayStation on in the living room. Either way, he would put his hands on Plus each and every time. Sometimes it would be a hard whack to the face while other times it might be a blow to his back or chest. Mr. Ronnie never messed with Aria or Ms. Tonya, though, only Plus. The only thing that we could ever conclude was that Mr. Ronnie resented him for being another man's child.

"You good?" I asked, sinking down into my bed and pulling the covers up to my chin.

"Yeah, I'm straight," he whispered. "Oh, and Perri?" he said, raising his voice just a little.

"Yeah?"

"I'm sorry for laughing at your hair earlier."

I let out a light snort of laughter. "It's all good, Plus. What's 220 times 64?" I asked, closing my eyes.

"14,080," he whispered.

"355 times 72," I whispered again, this time feeling myself starting to fall into a sleep.

He let out a yawn then said, "25,560. Now go to bed, Perri."

"A'ight, good night."

"Good night, P."

Chapter 2

Perri

"She wanna be a boy so bad," Nadia muttered as she walked past me.

It was lunch period at school, and as usual, we were hanging out in the hallway before going inside the cafeteria to eat. I was standing there with my crew, which consisted of Plus, TK, and Jamal. We were all in the seventh grade and attended Amherst Middle School.

"Heyy, Plus," Sadie sang with a little wave as she walked past, following Nadia and Shanae.

"Whaddup," he replied coolly with a nod of his head.

"Sadie's ass done gotten fatter, yo," Jamal muttered. This was the only part I hated about hanging out with all boys.

"Damn sure has," Plus said, grinning and rubbing his hands together.

"Aye yo, Nadia, come let me holla at you for a minute," TK said. This was their usual game of interference they ran with the girls, because TK definitely wasn't interested in Nadia.

Nadia was the ugliest girl I had ever seen. She was a pimply faced, dark-skinned girl with short, nappy hair. The nasty brown gel she used to slick back her coarse hair would always flake up in her scalp and around the edges of her face. Her nails were chewed down to the meat of her fingers, and the clothes she wore were always dirty and dingy. Yet, somehow, somehow, her swamp-donkey behind constantly found a reason to pick on me.

TK, on the other hand, was almost six feet tall at 13 years old. He was biracial with his mother being white and his father being black. His fine, curly hair was a very light shade of brown, almost blond, and his skin was fair. Although you could tell from his facial features that he was a black boy, his eyes were the color of the Caribbean Sea. All of the girls in the Millwood housing projects thought that he was good-looking and he could have his pick of just about any one of them. I'd been friends with TK long enough to know that Nadia definitely wasn't his type.

Then there was Jamal. Jamal was the short, skinny, little dark-skinned boy of our crew. He had a dark set of beady eyes and a small gap between his two front teeth. Sometimes he would spit a little when he talked from the lisp he had. He actually stayed in the neighborhood just outside the projects in a nice two-story brick home. You'd never know it, though, as much as he hung out with us in the hood. His mother was an elementary school teacher, and his father worked for the city's sanitation department.

As Nadia, Sadie, and Shanae switched back over toward us, I couldn't help but to roll my eyes. The girls looked me over from head to toe with a disgusted look on their faces. Their noses were scrunched and flared with their lips curled up as if I stank. They proceeded to whisper back and forth into each other's ears before laughing out loud. I knew they were probably talking about the fact that I was dressed like a boy. Typical. It was the last week of school, and it was warm outside, so I wore black basketball shorts and a plain white T-shirt. On my feet were some faded black Chucks that Tez bought for me just last year. My hair was still braided back in frizzy cornrows that were now two weeks old.

"You gonna walk me to my next class, Plus?" Sadie asked, batting her eyes.

Smirking, I looked at him and waited for his response. I'd admit that Sadie was a pretty, light-skinned girl with long sandy brown hair. All of the boys in our school drooled over her like a hot piece of pot roast straight out of the oven. However, she was a part of what I called the mean girls crew, so I didn't care too much for her. In my opinion, birds of a feather always flocked together, so she and Nadia were one and the same in my eyes.

"Maybe," he responded coolly, leaning back with his foot propped up against the wall, arms folded across his chest and chin chucked up high like he had some point to prove.

For Plus to be such a geek, my best friend had swag all day. I'd also admit that he was easy on the eyes. His skin was the color of milk chocolate just like his little sister Aria's, and they also shared that same curly black hair. He wore it in a low, curly blow out with the edges neatly faded and lined up to a crisp. In a sense, he was pretty to me because his eyelashes were really long and he had this little black beauty mark underneath his left eye.

"What, you and your boy gotta walk to class together?" she asked sarcastically, looking at me with her hand on her hip.

Cocking my fist back, I instantly jumped in her face, causing her to flinch.

However, when she realized I wasn't going to hit her, she kept talking. "Boys aren't supposed to hit girls, Perri," she teased.

I shook my head and turned to walk away, heading toward the cafeteria by myself. There was no way I was going to stay there and let her humiliate me like that.

Sadie thought she was being cute by calling me a boy, but I didn't see anything funny. If I wasn't being called a boy, then I was being called gay. It made me so furious at times because both depictions couldn't be further from the truth. I knew what I looked like, so I didn't need anyone reminding me of that. If I dressed any differently, I feared that the boys would no longer want to hang with me. And I didn't get along with girls, so I was always caught between a rock and a hard place. I could have easily punched Sadie in the mouth for talking slick, but it was the last week of school, and I swear I didn't need any trouble with my daddy.

The next thing I felt was Plus's heavy arm around my shoulder. I looked over at him, and he just smirked, showing that slight curl of his lips that occurred when he was trying to hide his smile. "Don't pay that ugly girl no mind, P," he said. I knew he was only calling Sadie ugly to make me feel better, and sure enough, it did.

"I'm not paying her no mind." I shrugged.

He twisted his lips to the side, instantly knowing that I was telling a bald-faced lie.

When we entered the cafeteria, all of the food lines were really long. The entire space was jam-packed, and all of the noise from people laughing and talking was so loud that I could hardly hear myself think. Since we were both really hungry, Plus and I decided to go to the shortest line, which was serving hot dogs, French fries, and chocolate milk. When we walked up to the cash register with our lunch trays in hand, an old white lady with silver hair stood before us. She had a hairnet on her head and a large, hairy mole above her upper lip that jiggled a little when she talked.

"What's your account number, suga?" she asked in a raspy smoker's voice.

"4562," Plus replied.

"All right, and yours?" she asked me after allowing Plus to walk through.

"4831," I told her.

"Sorry, but your account has a balance of negative two dollars," she said.

"Well, can I just get lunch this one time?" I whispered shamefully.

"There will be no more free lunches given this last week of school. I'm sorry. Next!" she hollered out, picking up my lunch tray and putting it behind the counter.

I walked out of the line empty-handed and totally embarrassed, making my way back into the cafeteria in search of Plus. He was sitting at a nearby table with TK and Jamal, who were both eating large slices of cheese pizza. As I walked over toward them, my head hung slightly low from embarrassment. I forgot to tell my dad that I needed lunch money on my account this week. While Plus qualified for free lunch because Ms. Tonya didn't work, I still had to pay a reduced lunch fee.

"Where's your food at?" Plus asked, looking confused.

"I forgot to tell my dad that I needed some money on my account."

"Here, eat some of mine," he offered, pushing his Styrofoam platter toward me.

Listening to the growl of my stomach, I realized that I was even hungrier than I was ashamed. I quickly took him up on his offer, eating half of his hot dog and a few of his French fries. TK and Jamal, on the other hand, just scarfed down their pizza right in front of me without a care in the world. They didn't even ask if I wanted anything to eat, but then again, they probably figured Plus had me. Plus allowed me to drink some of his chocolate milk, and I also ate one of his butter crunch cookies, something he never shared with anyone. That's just how we were though, always looking out for one another. We were the epitome of best friends.

When lunch was finally over, we all headed out of the cafeteria to hang in the hall some more before it was time for class. That's when we ran back into Sadie, Nadia, and Shanae. Sadie was blowing her pink gum into bubbles while twirling her fingers through her hair. Her body twisted side to side almost in a timid manner while she stared at Plus. I could tell that she really liked him. Then there was Nadia, who stood to the right of her, chewing on her nonexistent nails, occasionally spitting them out onto the floor. To Sadie's left was Shanae, who was looking down, cleaning her glasses with the tail of her shirt. She was an average-looking brown-skinned girl with chin-length hair. I knew she was also a smart girl because she and Plus shared a lot of the same classes.

"How was lunch, ladies?" TK asked with his eyes fixed on Sadie.

"It was good. I thought you said you were gonna sit with me though," Nadia said in between gnawing on those nails.

"Nah. If you don't fuck wit' all of us," he said, gesturing with his hand, "then you don't fuck wit' none of us." He strolled past the girls with his chest poked out as I smiled.

A devilish grin was painted on my face as I sarcastically gave a seductive wink to Sadie.

I rolled my eyes at them one last time before continuing with my crew. I had known TK and Jamal since kindergarten and Plus even longer than that. Since the age of 5, the four of us had been inseparable. They were an extension of my family, and it was a good feeling knowing that these guys would always have my back.

Chapter 3

Plus

It was officially the first day of summer, and school had been out for almost two weeks. Perri, Jamal, TK, and I were on the basketball court playing a little game of two on two. I always made sure to put Perri on my team because she could ball better than most boys our age in the hood. Although TK and Jamal tried, they sucked when it came to playing basketball.

"Yo, pass the rock," Perri said, rushing past Jamal.

I faked right then went left before passing her the ball. She did a quick chest pass right back to me before I did a layup and put the ball right in the hoop. That's how we always worked: as one.

"You traveled, nigga," TK whined.

"Man, shut up. Ain't nobody travel," I said, pushing him in the chest.

We all walked over to the bleachers on the side of the basketball court to take a quick rest and grab a drink of water. That's when I noticed a wet red stain on Perri's gray basketball shorts. I guessed she didn't feel it, because she was sitting on the bleachers with her legs gapped wide open, carefree and unconcerned. I just sighed because I already knew what it was.

"Come on, Perri, we gotta go," I said.

"Why? I thought we were gonna play another round."

"Nah. I forgot we gotta get back home. My mother needs our help today," I lied. Perri looked at me with a confused look etched on her face, but she didn't question it.

After dapping up TK and Jamal, we headed through the projects making our way back home. That's when we saw Tez on the corner wiggling his index finger at the cars that drove by. This was to indicate to any buyers that he was selling. His long braids hung down low beneath the navy blue Yankees cap he wore. A gold herringbone necklace sparkled around his neck, and a simple black pager was attached to his waist. Tez was definitely getting money these days.

Then we saw a skinny black woman with stained, holey clothes approaching him. As she limped closer to him, I noticed her swollen cracked feet, which were stuffed in a pair of dirty bedroom slippers. While a few pink sponge rollers dangled from half of her hair, the other half was in a messy ponytail. Her eyes were sunken in, and her lips were severely dry like she hadn't had a drop of water in years.

"I just need a ten of that red," she said weakly while scratching at her arm. She was clawing at it as if she were trying to break the skin.

I watched as Tez went into his pocket to pull out a small red vial, which I knew to be crack-rock cocaine. Growing up in the hood, it was one of those things that you just knew when you saw it. When she weakly handed him her money, Tez quickly noticed that she had some change in her hands. He twisted his mouth to the side and shook his head.

"Get the fuck on wit' that change, Lottie. I already done told your ass once before," I could hear him say as we grew near.

"Please, Tez. Just this one time. I need this hit bad," she pleaded, now scratching at her neck.

"A'ight, damn!" he fussed, taking her money and passing her the little red vial.

Seeing us pass him by, he gave a simple head nod in our direction. It was just a slight dip of the head where anyone looking from afar wouldn't even have noticed. He didn't speak to us when he was working on the corner. Tez always wanted me and Perri to keep it moving so we wouldn't get caught up in any trouble. I nodded my head back in return and kept walking with Perri toward my house.

"What does Ms. Tonya need our help with?" Perri asked.

"Nothing. I just lied. I think you came on your period."

"What?" Perri asked, looking down at herself. Her caramel-colored face quickly turned red when she realized that there was a small bloodstain on the back of her shorts.

With just one glance at her, I could tell that she was mortified. Quickly I took off the T-shirt I was wearing and handed it to her. I told her to just tuck it in the rear of her shorts and let it hang down the back. When we finally got to my house, I went into the kitchen first and then marched up the stairs to find my mother, but she wasn't there.

"Ma!" I yelled out, running back down the stairs.

"She isn't here, Plus. What am I going to do?" Perri asked with tears in her eyes.

Pausing, I stopped and stared at her almost as if she were a stranger. Realization had hit that this was the first time I had seen Perri cry since her mother died. When one lone tear slipped down to the top of her cheek, I knew I had to figure out what to do to help her.

"Wait right here," I said, leaving her in the living room downstairs.

I went back up to my mother's room and began searching in her bottom dresser drawer. That's where I thought I saw those things she always used when her period came on. In the drawer, I found lots of maxi pads, tampons, panty liners, and even a few pregnancy tests. I grabbed Perri a pack of my mother's maxi pads then hurried back down the steps.

"Here, put this on," I said. Delicately pinching just the edge of the pink plastic wrapper as if it were dirty or diseased, I handed it over to her.

"What do I do with these?" she asked with a confused look fixed on her face while holding up the pack.

"I don't know. Are there instructions on the back?" I asked, shrugging my shoulders.

Perri turned over the package and read. Moments later, she left for her house so that she could shower and change her clothes.

I stayed at home and played *Madden* on the PlayStation for the next couple of hours to take my mind off of her. I had never seen blood between a girl's legs like that before, so in a way, it frightened me. I just hoped that Perri was okay.

"Hey, Ahmad baby," my mother said, walking through the door with shopping bags in her hand.

"Hey, Ma. You need help?" I asked with my eyes on the screen, still playing the game.

"No, me and Aria got it."

"Oh, uh, Perri got her period today, and I had to give her some of your things."

"What? Where is she?" she asked, somewhat in a panic.

"She went home a couple of hours ago to get cleaned up. I didn't know what else to do so I gave her a pack of those pad thingies you have in the drawer upstairs."

"That's fine, Ahmad," she said, bending down to kiss the top of my head. "That's just fine."

After taking her bags upstairs, she came back down and told me that she'd be right back. I knew that she probably went to go over and check on Perri. My mother was over there for about two hours or so before she finally returned home that evening. Mr. Phillip was working the late shift again that night, and she probably didn't want to leave Perri home alone given the circumstance.

"Ahmad, you still up?" she asked when she came through the front door.

"How's Perri?" was the first thing I asked, turning around.

"That's all you care about, huh?" She smirked.

I just shrugged my shoulders in response.

"Perri's fine. I talked with her about becoming a woman and how to make sure she stays clean down there every month during this time. I don't want her walking around here smelling like a two-week-old tuna-fish sandwich, ya know?"

"All right, Ma, I've heard enough," I said, covering up my ears. A simple "she's fine" would have sufficed, but my mother was extra like that. I shook my head and got up to cut off the game before making my way upstairs. It was a little past eleven, and I was getting tired.

Later that night, around two in the morning, I was abruptly awakened from my sleep when I heard fussing along with the clanging sounds of pots and pans from within the kitchen. I knew it was nobody but Ronnie's drunk ass down there causing trouble. I swore I couldn't stand that nigga. The last time he put his hands on me, I vowed that it would be his last. I wasn't sure if I'd have to fight his big ass or kill him dead, but either way he was no longer going to use me as his punching bag. That was my word.

Before he could even come into my room and start a fight with me, I immediately got up, slid on my sweatpants, and slipped out the front door. I trekked over to Perri's house as usual and knocked on her window. She peeked through the blinds before lifting up the window to let me in.

"Is it Ronnie again?" she asked, wiping the sleep from her eyes.

"Yeah, you know it."

"Here," she said, tossing me a pillow and the blanket I always used.

"How are you feeling? I mean, since earlier," I asked, getting my pillow adjusted beneath my head on the floor.

"My stomach has been hurting a little bit, but other than that I'm fine," she said.

"Cool," was all I could think to say. An awkward silence fell over the dark room before she spoke again.

"Do you look at me differently now?" she asked just above a whisper.

I thought about it for a minute because I wanted to give her an honest answer. "Nah, you still my homie. You still my best friend for life, P," I confirmed with a smile. Even in the dark, I could see Perri smiling back at me.

"Plus?"

"Yeah," I replied with my eyes already closed.

"A boy has as many sisters as brothers, but each sister has only half as many sisters as brothers. How many brothers and sisters are in the family?" she asked.

"A hell of a lot more than we have, Perri," I answered with a light chuckle. I didn't know why she always did this. I guessed this was her way of keeping me on my toes.

"Really, Plus? I thought you knew everything," she whined.

"I'm tired, P," I groaned, wiping my hand down my face.

"All right. Good night," she said, almost sounding disappointed.

"Good night. Oh, and Perri?"

"Huh?"

"It's like seven of 'em. Four brothers and three sisters."

"See, I knew you couldn't resist."

"Night," I whispered.

"Good night."

Chapter 4

Plus

Three Years Later: 2001

It was the middle of January, and we were now 15 years old in our sophomore year of high school. Although Perri and I remained close, between basketball practice and school we were finding less and less time to kick it with one another. I had just made the varsity basketball team, and already college recruiters were coming to see me. Perri, on the other hand, was still playing on JV. She was by far the best player on the team and was a definite shoo-in for the varsity team next season. Although Perri was doing well in basketball, she continued to somewhat struggle with her schoolwork, getting mostly B's and C's. It was crazy, though, because if she brought home just one A on her report card, we would all celebrate like she was the smartest girl in the world.

After I made the varsity team a couple of months prior, more and more girls began talking to me and showing me interest. There was this one particular girl named Tasha I had been talking to on the phone regularly. She was a pretty, dark-skinned girl with a dimple in her chin. Nothing over the top, just a soft little crater, smaller than the size of a pea. She had this long, straight black hair that fell to the middle of her back. And for some reason, it always had this natural, almost brilliant shine to it, like a white girl's hair. She actually stayed over in the same neighborhood as Jamal, but Perri couldn't stand her.

"So you finally going to hit Tasha or what?" TK asked as we got dressed in the locker room after practice.

Don't ask me by what means, but somehow TK's sorry ass actually made the varsity basketball team. He was our power forward while I was the point guard. "I'on know, man," I replied with a shrug.

I wasn't ashamed to admit that at 15 years old I was still a virgin. While all my boys made fun of me for it, the girls all seemed to be more attracted to me because of it. Some of the girls at school had even made a bet to see who would be my first, but I wasn't having sex until I was good and ready. The same way women were supposed to value their bodies, I valued mine, and I wanted my first time to mean something. Despite the fact that Tasha was cool and all, I wasn't quite sure if she would actually be the one.

"You the only nigga in the hood I know who's proud to still be a damn virgin," TK said, shaking his head.

"I'm not waiting for marriage or no shit like that. I just ain't found the right one yet. Besides, I can't be giving my dick to just anyone," I joked, grabbing myself for emphasis.

"What is it? You scared or something?"

"Nah, not really," I said hesitantly, scratching my ear.

"Not really?" TK hollered, throwing his arms in the air. "Yeah, nigga, you scared," he said, laughing and shaking his head.

After basketball practice was over, I began my long walk home from school in the cold. With the boys' varsity practice ending an hour after the girls' JV practice, Perri and I no longer walked home from school together. As

I trekked through Millwood, I saw Tez sitting in his car, talking to one of the local dope boys through his window. He drove an all-black 2001 Acura with eighteen-inch chrome rims and black-tinted windows. Tint was so dark, I knew it had to be illegal. Tez had come a long way from the corner boy he was three years ago. Mr. Phillip finally put him out last year when their house got raided, but since then, Tez had gotten his own luxury apartment and was doing his thing.

"Whaddup," I hollered out with a head nod. Tez just nodded his head in response. He still didn't speak to us when he was working.

When I walked into the house and entered the kitchen, Perri was sitting at the table doing her homework while my mother was at the stove cooking. After throwing my book bag to the floor and removing my coat, I looked over at Perri and laughed a little to myself. Other than her skin clearing up and her not getting into fights anymore, she hadn't changed much over the past three years. She still wore her hair in either a bushy ponytail or cornrows that hung down the length of her back. Her eyebrows were still wild and thick, and she still loved wearing her basketball shorts and sweatpants.

"Hey, baby," my mother greeted me.

"Hey, Ma," I said, kissing her on the cheek, feeling the warmth of her skin merge with the coolness of my own.

I then leaned down to kiss Perri on the forehead. It was nothing but a soft peck of my lips, which I had gotten accustomed to doing over the years. She was special to me, and the affection between us came naturally as we matured.

"What are you studying?" I asked, taking a seat across from her at the table.

"I got a geometry test tomorrow," she said with her eyes still glued to the book in front of her. She pulled the pencil out from behind her ear.

"You got it, or you need some help?"

"Nah, I got it," she said.

"Oh, Ahmad, that fast-ass little girl keeps calling here for you. I told her several times that you don't get home from practice until about six, but she keeps calling. I'm gonna cuss her li'l ass out the next time, so you better talk to her," my mother fussed.

I didn't have a cell phone yet because I couldn't afford one, so everybody still called the house for me. "Okay, I'll tell her, Ma."

"You still talking to Tasha?" Perri asked, looking me in the eyes for the first time since I'd entered the house. Her face was scrunched up to the point where I could clearly see the disappointment.

"Yeah, I am. I mean, I've been talking to Shanice and Vonnie a little too, but I already know she's talking 'bout Tasha," I explained.

Perri let out a deep sigh and rolled her amber eyes. I always openly talked to Perri about the girls I was dealing with, but lately, for some reason, she seemed to be aggravated by it. I wasn't sure what that was all about so I decided to change the subject.

"So, Ma, did you think about what I asked you the other night?"

"What? About having a house party for your sixteenth birthday?" she knowingly threw over her shoulder and asked.

"Yesss, Ma," I griped, feeling a childish whine about to rise from my throat.

"I don't know about having all them wild-ass kids up in my house, Ahmad."

"It's only going to be like twelve of us, and you already know most of them," I pleaded.

There was an awkward silence in the room as she pondered my request. I knew that I was asking for a lot given that my mother was pretty strict. The other problem was that I had already started inviting people to my party and the guest list was well beyond twelve people. So far there were about twenty-two people coming, but in the hood, you always had to double that number.

"I guess, Ahmad," she finally said.

"Yess!" I said with excitement. Perri just smirked and shook her head.

My mother then turned around and held up a wooden spoon before she spoke. "Uh-uh, before you get excited, let me set the ground rules."

"I'm listening," I said, kicking off my shoes.

"There will be no drinking. No smoking. And the party needs to be over by twelve."

"Twelve! Really, Ma?" I whined this time.

"Yes, and you have to clean up after they leave. Oh, and me and Ronnie will be chaperoning."

Yes, Ronnie's drunk ass was still hanging around. He was more of a nuisance than anything else, but I knew my mother only kept him around because of Aria. He still caused a lot of commotion in our household. The only difference now was that he wasn't putting his hands on me. At over six feet tall and 165 pounds of pure muscle, I no longer tolerated Ronnie's abuse.

"I'm about to be sixteen, Ma. What I look like with a chaperone?" I asked, sucking my teeth.

"Well, that's the only way you are throwing a party in my house. My house, my rules!" she said, finally plopping my sloppy joe down on the table in front of me.

"Well, what about getting a DJ?" I asked, pushing my luck.

"We have a radio and a record player over there." She pointed toward the living room. "You don't need a DJ, Ahmad."

"Yooo!" Perri let out with a chuckle as she held her fist up to her mouth. Seeing the corners of her lips turn up into a slight smile prepared me for the clowning she was getting ready to do. She leaned forward and lowered her voice. "Yo, she said a record player, B." Perri shook her head and let out another light laugh.

"Whatever," I mumbled under my breath.

As the four of us, including Aria, all sat around the kitchen table eating our sloppy joes for dinner, the house phone began to ring. My mother instantly cut her eyes at me, and Perri let out another deep sigh as if it was bothering her. I quickly got up and rushed over to answer it. At the same time, Aria, who was now 11 years old, got up from the table and ran for the phone too. I grabbed the back of her shirt and pulled her backward so that I could get to the phone first.

"Ahh! You make me sick, Plus," she squealed.

"Hello," I answered, blowing my little sister an air kiss, causing her to frown.

"Hey, Plus. Whatcha doing?" Tasha asked on the other end of the phone, her voice sounding all perky and preppy like the captain of the cheerleading squad.

"Oh, hey. Whaddup?"

"And, Ahmad, tell that little girl to stop calling here before six o'clock!" my mother yelled out in the background. My momma had no problems embarrassing the shit out of me.

"Aye, Tash, hold on, a'ight?" I said before laying the phone down on the kitchen counter. "Perri, hang up the phone for me when I get upstairs."

"Really, Plus? We're still eating dinner," she said, rolling her eyes and getting up from the table with an attitude.

"Yo, stop tripping. I'll be back down in a minute," I told her.

Dramatically, she huffed into the phone as she picked it up and rolled her pretty eyes once more. I didn't know what her sudden attitude with me was all about, but I figured it was probably a woman's thing. Yeah, she was my best friend and all, but at the end of the day, she was still an emotional-ass female like the rest. I knew eventually I would have to make the time to talk about what was bothering her, but right now I was trying to see what was up with Tasha's pretty ass.

Chapter 5

Perri

It was finally the night of Plus's sixteenth birthday party, and he was so excited. The two of us were up in his bedroom while he was deciding on what to wear. Tez had bought him a few pair of LRG shirts and jeans with a fresh new pair of wheat Tims for his birthday. I, myself, was slowly trying to get out of wearing sweatpants and basketball shorts all the time. Wearing a pair of dark blue boot-cut jeans and a red Gap T-shirt, I looked down at the fresh pair of red and blue Jays on my feet. Ms. Tonya had also braided my hair for me, which was now so long it swept the middle of my butt.

In nothing but a white wife beater and navy blue boxers, Plus paced back and forth, looking at the outfits sprawled across his bed. "What shall I wear, what shall I wear?" he sang, rubbing his hands together. He was always so goofy like that whenever it was just the two of us.

I didn't know why, but as I sat in the chair in the corner of his room, my eyes started to roam his athletic body. It wasn't the first time I had been up to his room, and truthfully speaking, it wasn't even the first time I had seen him in his boxers. This was, however, the very first time my body was responding to the sight of his smooth, muscular brown arms and brawny chest that poked out from underneath his shirt. Then there was the obvious bulge in the boxers he wore. I began feeling a light, fluttery feeling in the pit of my stomach and this warm, tingly sensation way down in between my thighs.

"Why you sitting over there looking all goofy?" Plus asked, eyes squinted with a weird grin on his face.

I didn't know what the hell I was feeling or why I was even feeling that way. The last thing I wanted was for Plus to think I was acting creepy, so I had to get out of there and fast.

"Ahh, nothing. I'm going back downstairs," I stammered before quickly darting out of his room.

Junior M.A.F.I.A.'s "Player's Anthem" was blaring from the speakers of Ms. Tonya's boom-box radio as I made my way down the steps. The smell of lavender Fabuloso combined with the hot wings she ordered smacked me hard in the face. They were Plus's favorite, so Ms. Tonya made sure to have them at his party. In fact, she had all of his favorites, which included crab chips, Twizzlers, pineapple upside-down cake, and strawberry soda.

The house was sparkling and cleaner than I had seen it in a very long time. In the living room, the coffee tables were removed to create additional space, and the carpeted floors were vacuumed to perfection. Each decorative pillow was purposely placed in its rightful corner of the couch, while several scented candles flickered throughout the room. There were also six additional folding chairs that lined one of the walls. Plus didn't think there were enough seats to accommodate everyone, so his mother borrowed the extra chairs from our community rec center. I had to admit that Ms. Tonya went all out for Plus's sixteenth birthday.

"Have you seen his cake yet?" Ms. Tonya eagerly asked when I stepped into the kitchen.

"Nah, lemme see it."

She had ordered him a birthday cake from Walmart that had a basketball and a royal blue jersey with his number 23 on it. Lying on the table beside it was a number 16 wax candle and a small box of matches. Inwardly, I chuckled because Ms. Tonya still treated Plus like he was 5 years old. If it were up to her, I was sure we'd all be gathered around the cake singing "Happy Birthday" and watching him blow out his candle by the end of the night. That was her baby, though, and couldn't nobody tell her any different. Times like that made me really miss my own mother, so I didn't poke fun.

"Whatcha think?" she asked proudly with a smile stretched across her face.

"It's nice, Ms. Tonya. I think Plus will love it," I lied. Plus would think it was babyish, but there was no way I was going to hurt Ms. Tonya's feelings. Simultaneously, the phone on the kitchen wall began to ring, and Tez walked through the door.

"Hello," she answered, then cut her eyes at me. "Yes, this is she," she said into the phone. I watched as her face twisted up with confusion and frustration.

"He did what?" she quizzed in a shocked tone of voice right before her eyes closed. She allowed a big puff of air to escape her mouth.

"What's going on?" Tez asked, grabbing a handful of chips.

"I don't know," I whispered, still eavesdropping on Ms. Tonya's conversation.

"How much is bail?" Ms. Tonya then asked the caller.

"Bail?" Tez and I mouthed to one another.

"I'll be down there as soon as I can. Thank you," she said, ending the call and all but slamming the phone back down on the hook.

"What's wrong, Godma?" my brother asked her.

"Ronnie! That's what's wrong. His ass has gotten arrested again. Drunken and disorderly for Christ's sake! I just can't catch a damn break," she fussed, massaging her eyebrows with the tips of her fingers. Her other hand firmly gripped her hip.

"So, whatchu gon' do?" Tez asked.

"I'm about to go meet the bail bondsman, but I need you to stay here and chaperone these kids. Can you do that for me?"

"Yeah, I gotchu, Godma. Where Aria at?"

"She's spending the night over at Ms. Bessie's house. You don't need to worry about her."

"Oh, okay. Well, we'll be fine here. Go handle your business."

"Thank you, baby. And look, don't tell Ahmad," she said in a hushed tone of voice, looking back and forth between me and Tez. We both nodded our heads in agreement. Then she gave Tez a kiss on the cheek before grabbing her purse and heading out the front door. We all knew that Plus would have his ass on his back the whole night if he found out Ronnie was the reason for his mother not being at his sixteenth birthday party.

"The birthday boy is in the building," Plus announced, walking down the stairs with his arms spread wide as if he were making some sort of grand entrance. He was wearing a black LRG T-shirt and black LRG jeans with wheat-colored Tims. Courtesy of Tez, he also wore a gold Cuban link chain around his neck. I hated how good my best friend looked, yet I couldn't seem to take my eyes off of him when he walked into the kitchen.

"Ain't nobody even here yet, nigga," I told him, rolling my eyes. I was in the kitchen setting up where Ms. Tonya left off.

"Where my momma at?"

"She had to run out, but she said she'd be back a little later. She told Tez to chaperone."

"Word?" He looked over at Tez for confirmation. A wide smile then extended across his face before they dapped each other up, already making some sort of silent agreement between the two of them.

It was finally around ten o'clock that night when people actually started arriving in droves. I should have known better than to think that Plus was going to only invite twelve people to his sixteenth birthday party. There had to be at least sixty people, if not more, in that little row house. Ms. Tonya's entire living room, kitchen, front yard, and backyard were all filled with kids from the neighborhood and also from school.

In the dead middle of January, we had the windows raised in the kitchen and in the living room so that it wouldn't be so hot and steamy from all of the bodies packed inside. Tez also said that with the windows up, the music could be heard outside so people could party out there, too. As Jodeci's "Freek'n You" boomed in the background, I sat on the steps, watching people turn Ms. Tonya's living room into a dance floor. TK and Jamal had a pretty heavy-set girl sandwiched between them while they freaked her at the same time. The smell of Kush permeated the small space while red cups were being held up high in the air. I swore every last one of Ms. Tonya's rules had been broken that night.

My eyes then landed on Plus, who was in one of the far corners of the dimly lit room. He had his back up against the wall while Tasha shook her ass and ground her body all over him. I could see her mouthing the words to the song as she seductively danced. "'Every freek'n night and every freek'n day, I wanna freek you baby in every freek'n way.'" I couldn't stand her fast ass.

She then turned around to face him and wrapped her arms around his neck. As her body pressed against his, I watched one of his hands leisurely slide down her backside. Her hair was wild and puffy from sweating, so he gently pushed it out of her face. I could see his eyes slowly taking in all of her features as if he were silently telling her how beautiful she was. Within a matter of seconds, he gradually went in and planted a long, opened-mouth kiss on her lips. I didn't know what came over me, but in that moment, my stomach grew queasy, and I could feel the chunks slowly rising into my throat. I jumped up and ran to the nearest bathroom, allowing the vomit to spew right into the toilet.

Moments later as I was still hovering, there was a knock on the bathroom door.

"Open up," Tez hollered from the other side.

"I'll be out in a minute," I told him, wiping my mouth with the back of my hand. I didn't know if it was from throwing up, but uncontrollable tears started streaming down my face. I couldn't even begin to explain my behavior if I tried.

"Open up!" Tez hollered out again. I quickly wiped my face with some toilet tissue and rinsed my mouth out with some water from the sink before opening up the door.

"What's wrong?" my brother asked.

"Nothing, I just threw up. I think it was the wings," I said.

"Nah, it wasn't the wings, P. But you good?"

"Yeah, I'm straight," I said, trying to convince myself of that more than anything.

Later that night, or morning I should say, around one thirty, everyone was finally starting to clear out. Ms. Tonya still hadn't returned. I knew that Plus was forever grateful that she hadn't because he had the time of his life. While he and Tasha were saying their final good-byes in the living room, I was cleaning up the kitchen. Surprisingly, the house didn't get too messed up. Other than the red cups scattered everywhere and some trash on the floor, there really wasn't that much to clean.

As I walked into the living room to cut the radio down, I heard Plus say, "A'ight, call me and let me know you made it home safe."

"Are you sure your momma won't mind if I call the house this late?" she asked.

"Yeah, she gon' mind. He'll see you at school, Tasha," I said bluntly, rolling my eyes. *Oops, did I just say that out loud?*

"Y'all tryin'a play me," Plus said with a chuckle. "But, yeah, she's right, Tash. I'll just see you at school on Monday. Be safe."

"Night, Plus," Tasha said with a small wave.

"Night, shorty."

Once she left, I walked into the kitchen and began tying up the last bag of trash. Tez made TK and Jamal clean up the front yard and backyard before they left, and now it was just the three of us. After putting the rest of the food away, I wiped down the kitchen counters with Fabuloso and swept up the kitchen floor. Glancing around the room one final time, I made sure that everything was just as Ms. Tonya would have wanted it. I then bent down to grab the bag of trash so that I could take it outside.

"Did you have a good time tonight?" Plus asked from behind me.

"I should be asking you that," I said, looking at him over my shoulder.

"Yeah, I had a real good time." By just the slow sound of his voice, I could tell he was buzzing from the little bit of beer he drank.

Tez then walked into the kitchen from the back door and grabbed the bag of trash from my hands. "Y'all gon' smoke a little sum' with me tonight or what?" he asked with a grin.

"Nah," I quickly replied. Neither Plus nor I had ever smoked weed before, and when we were younger, we vowed that we never would.

"Come on, P. I only turn sixteen once," Plus said to my surprise.

Plus was always the levelheaded one of the two of us, but something about that dynamic was slowly shifting, and I could feel it. He was the smartest and kindest boy I knew, so I trusted him. I'd follow him to just about anywhere on this earth, and for that reason, I nodded my head and agreed to smoke weed for the very first time. Hesitantly, I followed him and Tez out onto the back patio, immediately feeling the cold winter's air. Looking up at the sky, I saw a lone star twinkling in the center of what was the prettiest shade of dark blue.

The three of us sat down on the stoop before Tez pulled a rolled blunt right out of his jacket pocket. "A'ight, so just put it between your lips and slowly suck it in, but don't wet my shit up. No spit," Tez explained before demonstrating.

I studied as he placed the lit blunt between his lips, only taking a few small puffs. He then pulled it from his mouth, letting a small stream of smoke escape before looking down at the burning tip. He hit the blunt a few more times, inhaling the smoke before passing it over. Plus took a deep breath before taking the blunt from Tez's fingers. He positioned it between his lips, just as Tez had shown us moments before, and took two big puffs. All of a sudden, Plus began coughing dramatically and beating hard on his chest.

"Nigga, I said suck it in slow, not take a big-ass puff and hold that shit in," Tez fussed, taking the blunt away. With his lips pursed, Tez cocked his head to the side before shaking his head as if he were disappointed.

I just patted Plus on the back even though I knew it wasn't going to help relieve anything.

Once Plus had gotten himself together, Tez looked over at me, indicating that it was finally my turn. Plus just looked at me and smiled. Nervously, I took the blunt from his hand and delicately placed it between my lips. Little by little I dragged on it, inhaling just as Tez instructed, before taking it out, allowing the smoke to emit through my lips.

"Damn. That's what I'm talking 'bout, baby sis," Tez said with a smile. His amber eyes glowed back at me in the night as he gave me a look of pride.

"The one thing that yo' ass is better than me at," Plus muttered with a smirk, shaking his head.

"Don't hate, nigga, congratulate," I teased before taking another pull on the blunt. And just like that, I was hooked.

"Yo, pass that shit, sis," Tez said.

Once the joint was done, Tez left and told us to go inside and lock up. It was about two thirty in the morning, and we were sitting in the living room listening to Xscape's "Who Can I Run To" play softly in the background. We were so high out of our minds that I couldn't stop giggling even when I tried. I'd glance over at Plus every so often and would catch him staring off into space, eyes drooping, mouth ajar, and head falling forward ever so slowly, which would cause me to giggle some more.

"Plus?"

"Huh?"

"So, you finally gonna do it, huh?"

"Do what?" he asked with a puzzled expression on his face.

"You gon' do the nasty with Tasha, aren't you?"

"I'on know 'bout all that. Why? You mad?" he asked, looking over at me with a lazy grin.

I sucked my teeth. "Nah, I ain't mad. You could do better though," I said seriously. I looked over at Plus again, and we stared into each other's eyes. Even though my heart started to race and my high was slowly beginning to fade, I swear I couldn't look away.

"Who do you think is a better choice, P?" he asked in almost a hushed tone of voice.

"I'on know," I whispered, still gazing into his eyes.

I could feel the gap that was once between us gradually starting to close. I felt the warmth of his body as he slowly shifted toward me. He gently reached for one of my braids and stroked its length between his fingers. The uncomfortable feeling of butterflies in the pit of my stomach had returned, as well as the emergent moisture between my legs. As his face grew closer to mine, our breathing intensified, and instinctively I closed my eyes. In that moment, I wanted nothing more than to feel his soft lips on mine, kissing me the exact same way I saw him kiss Tasha earlier.

Then suddenly I felt the tip of his nose rub against mine. Slowly I peeled my eyes opened one at a time before I saw him staring back at me. He gently grabbed the back of my head and planted a soft, wet kiss to my brow. All I could do was smile to mask the disappointment I felt. I wanted him to kiss me differently. Passionately and lovingly. It was in that very instance I realized the strong feelings I had developed for my best friend. I was indeed in love with Plus.

Chapter 6

Plus

Two Years Later: 2003

It was the last week of April and the night of our senior prom. Over the past two years, Tasha had officially become my girl, and tonight was the night it was all supposed to finally go down. After much consideration on the matter, I had ultimately decided to lose my virginity at the ripe age of 18. While I wasn't in love with Tasha, I did actually care for her, and I wasn't ashamed to admit that my raging hormones were at an all-time high. There was only so much that getting head could do for a nigga my age. With Tasha practically begging for the dick every other day and then all of my boys clowning me, I had finally caved.

The clock on my nightstand read 6:45 p.m. when I looked myself over in the long mirror hanging on the back of my door. I was dressed in an all-black tuxedo that I had rented from Men's Warehouse. It wasn't Armani or no shit like that, but I looked good in it. Damn good. I had my curly hair cut low, sporting waves, and in my ears were small diamond studs that Tez copped for me. As I stroked my chin and modeled in the full-length mirror, admiring myself, there was a sudden knock on the other side of the door.

"Yo," I hollered.

"Nigga, open up the door and stop staring at yourself in the mirror," Perri said.

I couldn't do shit but laugh and shake my head because she knew me like the back of her hand.

When I opened up the door, I saw that she was wearing a sour look on her face. She didn't even want to go to our senior prom, but my mother and Mr. Phillip made her. To make matters worse, she was going with Tez. He said that she was only allowed to go to prom with me or him, and since I already had a date, he was her only option.

I quickly grabbed her up in my arms for a tight squeeze, smelling the fresh soap on her skin before pecking her forehead, but she only rolled her amber eyes in response. When I released her from my hold, I looked her over from head to toe and slightly chuckled. Perri wore her hair up high in a pin-curled bun with two spiral curls dangling from each side of her face. Her eyebrows were still thick and bushy, but my mother tried to put makeup on her, which made her look even funnier to me. She wore a red long-sleeved lace dress that snugged her athletic frame like armor. It might have actually looked nice on her had she walked a little more elegantly in it.

"Fuck you, Plus," she spat before taking a seat on my bed. She had her red heels in her hand, carelessly dangling from the straps.

"What's wrong witchu, P?"

"I just don't want to go," she whined.

"Look, it's just one night and we all rolling together. You already know TK got some liquor and Tez gon' let us get faded with him, so it's gon' be a fun night. Chill out, P. A'ight?" I said.

"I guess." She shrugged. "And what about your girl? You know she's not about to share you with your friends," she pouted, putting on her shoes.

"Nah, I got sum' for her a little later on tonight. Trust me, she'll be cool," I said, grinning and rubbing my hands together.

"So you're finally going through with it, huh?" she asked while adjusting the large bun on the top of her head.

"Yeah, I think it's about that time."

She got up from the bed and stumbled toward me in her heels, showcasing her inexperience walking in them. When she finally reached me, she came in close and delicately put her hand on my shoulder. I looked down into her beautiful eyes and smiled before I felt the tender kiss she placed to my cheek.

"Good luck, Plus," she whispered.

"Thanks, P, but I ain't gon' need it," I was quick to respond with a smirk.

"I swear you's one cocky-ass nigga," she retorted, shaking her head.

I just chuckled because she was telling the truth. With my good looks, outstanding grades in school, and game in the paint, couldn't nobody tell me shit.

"You ready?" she asked, smoothing down her dress and looking herself over in the mirror one final time before we left the room

"I was born ready, P," I said before looping my arm through hers and heading out of my bedroom door.

As we walked down the staircase connected to one another, my mother, Mr. Phillip, Aria, Tez, and Tasha all waited below. We smiled for most of the pictures they took of us. Then P and I did our thing by throwing up our deuces, making stank faces for the camera. The final picture we took before making it down to the very last step was one of me kissing Perri on the cheek. I didn't know if it was from the kiss itself or the oohs and aahs we received from our family, but I caught Perri blushing. Her cheeks grew bright red right before she timidly looked away from me.

"Don't be kissing all on my date like that, son," Tez joked.

"Just showing my homegirl some love on our big night." I shrugged with a laugh. That's when my eyes met Tasha's. She appeared to be the most beautiful I had ever seen her, in a pale blue satin gown that exposed the smooth chocolate skin of her neck and shoulders. Her black hair was straightened with a part down the middle, and her makeup was soft and pink.

"You look gorgeous, shorty," I said, making my way over to her.

"Thank you, Plus. You don't look so bad yourself," she remarked. I leaned in and kissed her full lips before pecking away at her neck and shoulders, loving her sweet lavender scent.

"Okay, you two, that's enough," my mother scolded.

My mother never did warm up to Tasha. She only tolerated her because of me, but time and time again she would warn me. Although Tasha never claimed to be a virgin, my mother said she was a little too eager to give up the pussy. She feared that Tasha saw me as a goldmine being that I was a basketball superstar. I had a full ride to Georgetown and a clear path to the NBA. I trusted my mother, so her warnings didn't fall on deaf ears. I took heed of her every word.

After TK and Jamal arrived with their dates, we made our way outside. Jamal went with his girlfriend, Shivon, and TK went with a girl named Nikki he had been feeling for the longest. In typical hood fashion, all of our neighbors gathered in our yard to take pictures and talk among themselves. Everyone, myself included, was impressed when the stretch limo Tez rented for the night finally pulled up. We took one last group photo in front of the limo before saying our final goodbyes.

"Let's take shots before we get there," TK said, pulling a small brown bottle of E&J out of his tuxedo jacket as we rode to prom.

"Man, y'all knuckleheads wild as shit," Tez said, shaking his head.

"So what that mean? You don't want none?" TK asked with a smirk.

"Hell yeah, but I got my own shit," Tez said with a laugh before removing the small bottle of Hennessey from his jacket.

Using the glasses in the back of the limo, we all began taking shots of liquor, downing them two and three at a time like it was water from a well. Before we even arrived at the convention center that night for prom, we were all a little more than tipsy.

When we walked in the large ballroom, several couples were already on the floor slow dancing to Michael Jackson's "You Are Not Alone." There were lit candles and red rose petals scattered on top of every single table, giving the room a romantic feel. I could smell a mix of sweet perfume and birthday cake as we walked through, attempting to find a table up front. Even though it was my and Perri's high school prom, Tez got more recognition than we did. The girls all stared at him like he was a celebrity, and he dapped up at least twenty people, if not more, before we finally took our seats.

We only sat down for a few minutes before Tasha wanted to slow dance. "Plus, I wanna dance," she whined.

I sighed and rubbed my hand down my face before nodding my head. I really didn't want to dance, not yet anyway, but I wanted to make her happy, so I got up to dance.

As we were getting up, I heard Tez ask Perri, "You wanna dance too?"

"No, fool," she said, rolling her eyes.

I chuckled before pulling Tasha's chair out for her. Perri looked up at me from where she sat, and I could see sadness in her eyes. This was one of the happiest times in our lives, so I wasn't sure what she was sad about. Before Tasha and I walked over to the dance floor, I leaned down and whispered in Perri's ear. "Is everything a'ight, P?"

"Yes. Now please stop worrying about me and go have fun, Ahmad," she said.

I placed a simple kiss to her forehead before she shooed me away with her hands. Perri never called me Ahmad, so I knew something was bothering her. But before I could say another word to her, Tasha grabbed me by the hand and pulled me out onto the dance floor. When we made it through to the center of the crowd, she placed my hands around her teeny waist and threw her arms around my neck. She gently laid her head against my chest and swayed her hips to the sounds of Faith Evans's "Soon As I Get Home." It was Tasha's favorite song.

Although Tasha felt good in my arms and I was enjoying the dance, my eyes stayed on Perri. I hated that she wasn't enjoying herself at our prom, and I hated even more that I didn't know why. Suddenly, I could feel Tasha glaring up at me, her eyes cutting so hard into my skin like a damn cigarette burn.

"If you were just gonna stare at her all night, then why did you even bother coming here with me?" she asked with a frown, showcasing the little dimple in her chin.

"What are you talking about now, Tasha?" I retorted, already knowing exactly what she was referring to.

"I'm talking about the fact that you've been catering to Perri's ass all damn night, and now that I have you all to myself on the dance floor, you're still staring at her from across the room." Taking her hands from around my neck, she placed them on her hips.

"You already know that's my best friend, Tasha. Ain't no need to be jealous."

"Yeah, you keep telling yourself that," she said before walking off with an attitude.

About an hour or so had passed, and Tasha still hadn't said two words to me since our dance. Childishly, she made small talk with only Nikki and Shivon. I ignored her simple-minded behavior and tried my best to still enjoy the night. I even got up to dance a few times without her.

All of a sudden, the music began to quiet, and I could see Principal Ryan making his way up onto the stage. "It is finally time to announce this year's prom queen and king. Drum roll please," he said. We all began tapping on the tables, trying to give him the sound effects of a drum roll, while he opened up the sealed envelope in his hand.

"This year's queen is Sadie Williams," he said. The crowd all cheered as Sadie made her way onto the stage. To this day, she was a sight for sore eyes with smooth, pale skin and the same long sandy brown hair, only now she had a womanly figure. These days, however, she was dating my boy Big Tony, the school's star linebacker.

After placing the crown on her head, it was time for Principal Ryan to announce the king. The loud applause and whistles from the crowd grew the anticipation in the room. "And now for this year's prom king." He paused as our drum rolls softly sounded off in the background. "Ahmad Taylor!" he proudly announced.

I looked over at Perri, and she was all smiles. She began to cheer loudly with her fist pumping in the air, imitating Arsenio Hall's Dog Pound. Then she began to obnoxiously whistle through her fingers like a nigga. I chuckled to myself because even though she was slowly beginning to outgrow it, she was still a tomboy at heart. After getting up from my chair, I began walking toward the stage with my head held high. Looking back, I gave her a wink. She shook her head and smiled at me.

After Sadie and I danced as king and queen of the prom to Luther Vandross's "Always and Forever," Principal Ryan asked that everyone get on the dance floor for the final song of the night. I looked over at Tasha, and she gave me a half smile before getting up and making her way toward me. Immediately we embraced, silently forgiving one another for our childish behavior that night. As she wrapped her arms around my neck, I looked down into her big brown eyes and placed a simple kiss on her lips.

"I'm sorry, Plus," she said.

"Me too, shorty."

Chapter 7

Perri

"Let's make a toast," Tez slurred as we rode back in the limo. He was already drunk, but apparently he wasn't finished. He pulled out a shiny gold bottle of Cristal with a few champagne flutes in his hand. After filling them up to the brim one by one, he passed them around.

I wasn't in the mood to toast or drink any champagne. I just wanted to go home and get into bed.

"I'll go first," he said, holding up his glass for us to follow his lead.

Annoyed, I held up my glass with one hand, taking the bobby pins out of my hair with the other. I was so over this night that I couldn't wait to take my hair down and wipe all the makeup off my face. My plans were to take a shower and crawl up under my covers as soon as I hit the door.

"Tonight, I want to toast my baby sister," he slurred, tilting his glass toward me. "Yo, she's the realest chick out here. Been down with all y'all niggas since the sandbox," he said, looking around the limo. TK, Jamal, and Ahmad all nodded and raised their glasses in agreement.

Then he looked at me and lowered his voice a little. "I know this wasn't your dream prom night, P, but I was glad to be by your side. Even if the feeling wasn't mutual," he chuckled before taking a swig of his champagne. I loved my brother, but I hated when he got drunk and emotional like that.

"Then I want to toast to my li'l nigga. My brother from another mother. 'A' Plus," he slurred again, tilting his glass.

"I ain't never had a brother," he said, cutting his eyes over at me. "Unless you count Perri's mannish ass," he joked. Of course, everyone in the limo besides me erupted in laughter.

"Shut up, Tez," I fussed, elbowing him in the side. At this point, he was working on my last nerve.

"Nah, but for real. I've always considered this li'l nigga right here my brother. You can ask any nigga on the street, and they'll tell you that Plus is Tez's little brother, the only nigga out here I trust with my family. So, cheers to that nigga right there," he said, tilting his glass in Plus's direction. "And that ass he's finally getting ready to get tonight," he said, spilling a little of his champagne on me. While all the guys in the limo fell out laughing and raised their glasses to toast Plus's first piece of ass, I rolled my eyes. Tasha just smirked.

When we finally pulled up to the hotel, it was around one in the morning. TK and Nikki slid out of the limo first, followed by Jamal and Shivon. Plus then dapped up Tez before his eyes finally landed on me. He reached over and gave me a tight hug before placing a kiss to my forehead. I didn't know why, but I closed my eyes tight and held on to him as if it would be my very last time.

"Good luck," I whispered.

"Already done told you, girl, I'on need no luck," he said with a wink.

As soon as he exited the car to meet up with Tasha, I broke down crying. I didn't even care that Tez was sitting right there next to me. The only thing going through my mind was that my best friend, who I was madly in love with, was getting ready to make love for the very first time to another woman. I sobbed loudly into the palms of my hands until I felt Tez's comforting arm around my shoulder.

"Why haven't you told him, Perri?" he asked with a sober voice.

"Because he doesn't look at me that way. He looks at me like a sister. I'm his fucking homie, remember? The last thing I want is to ruin what we have, so I just suffer. Silently," I cried.

"I don't even know what to do, yo," he said, shaking his head. "I can't take seeing you like this." He ran his hands down his face, unsure of exactly how to console me.

"I'll be all right, Tez. I just needed to get this out," I explained, wiping my face with the handkerchief he handed me.

"Well, I know it's not a permanent solution, but it'll make you feel better for now," he said with a smirk.

I already knew he was talking about smoking weed, and at that point, I was all for it. I needed something to take my mind off of Plus, so I sniffed back my tears and nodded my head. Reaching down into the pocket of his jacket, Tez pulled out the weed before passing everything over to me. I was better at rolling a blunt than he was, so whenever we blazed together, I always rolled.

"You know Tasha don't mean shit to him, right?" he leaned forward in his seat and asked. Sucking in my cheeks and clenching the inward flesh between my teeth, I simply shook my head, unable to even respond. "She's just something to do right now, but that shit ain't gon' last, P. Are you ever going to tell him how you feel?"

"I don't know, Tez. Shit, in my mind I've had that conversation with him at least a thousand times. From the time I was 15 years old up until tonight. It never goes right though. I'm scared it will only make things awkward between us, and I can't lose him, Tez," I said, shaking my head. "I'd rather have just a part of him than risk losing him completely," I admitted, feeling more tears starting to rise.

Tez finally passed the blunt back to me. "I feel you, but you never know, P." He shrugged his shoulders then repeated, "Tasha's ass don't mean shit to him."

I puffed on the blunt a few more times and allowed the smoke to slowly creep out of my mouth before I spoke. "It's not just about Tasha. Now don't get me wrong, I still don't like the bitch, but it's not about her. If it weren't her, it would be some other chick on his arm who looked just like her. Damn sure wouldn't be me and my boyish looking self."

"You're beautiful, P. Trust me. I get bad-looking shorties all the time, yo. And in the back of my mind I still be like, 'She ain't got shit on P though.' Yeah, you a little rough around the edges and shit, but there ain't a bitch out here I've seen prettier than you. I'm not trying to sound perverted or no shit like that, because you are my baby sister, but as a nigga, I'm telling you. You have that good-ass hair like your big brother, plus those pretty-ass eyes like me. Man, that shit drives them bitches wild, yo," he gloated, stroking the hair on his chin.

"And you're cool as fuck, P. You can ball, watch football, and you play video games. Shit, I don't know too many niggas out here who wouldn't want a girl like you. To keep it one hunnid, I ain't wifing a bitch up until I meet one who's on your level."

I laughed at his dramatics.

He cocked his head to the side. "What? You think I'm joking about that shit, but that's my word." He chuckled with a wink.

"Don't be comparing me to your bitches, Tez," I sassed, passing him back the blunt.

A small chuckle escaped his lips. "I would compare them to Momma if she were here," he said lowly before letting out a sigh. "But since she ain't, you the next best thing. You're the most beautiful girl I know."

Hearing Tez compliment me like that actually made me feel a little bit better. However, I wasn't quite sure if he was saying it because he truly felt that way or because he just wanted to take the pain of my broken heart away.

When we finally got back to the house, I wasn't ready to go in just yet so we sat out on the front stoop talking. Tez wrapped me up in his suit jacket to keep me warm from the cool night's air. He then shared memories of our mother from a time that I was too young to remember. He told me that the love she had for our father was unparalleled. Even to this day, he said he had never seen two people more in love than them. He painted a vivid picture of our mother standing by the front door and peeking out of the window.

Every night she would stand there, he said, waiting for our father to get home from work. Nights when Tez was supposed to be sound asleep in bed, he said that he would be at the top of our stairs witnessing her stand on the tips of her toes just to greet him with a kiss. He then said Momma would immediately go warm up Daddy's plate for him. Then they'd sit at the kitchen table, quietly telling each other about their whole day while my father ate his food. That was their nightly routine. there was nothing overly romantic about their love, but it was pure and true. It was something that I craved.

"I don't think I'll ever have what they had," I muttered.

"Yo, I guess that makes two of us then," he said, standing up to stretch. It was now going on three o'clock in the morning.

"Good night, P," Tez said, giving me a hug.

"Night," I said just as my eyes landed on the yellow taxicab pulling up in front of the house.

Plus got out of the cab and started walking over toward us. His bow tie was undone along with the top three buttons of his dress shirt.

"How was it?" Tez asked with a wide smile. Although Tez knew my feelings on the matter, he still was a man and considered Plus to be his little brother.

"Man," Plus responded with a suck of his teeth, shaking his head with his hand on the back of his neck.

"Nigga, please don't tell me you couldn't do it," Tez said.

"Pshhh," Plus sighed.

"Wowww!" was all Tez could say, shaking his head while getting into his Acura. I secretly smiled as we watched Tez pull off into the night.

"What you still doing up?" Plus asked.

"Me and Tez was just talking about old times and shit. Getting faded."

Plus then reached down to softly touch some of the curls that were dangling in my face. "Yo, what happened to your hair?" he asked.

"I had to take out all those damn bobby pins your momma put in my hair. You know I'm not used to no shit like that," I said, making him chuckle. "Well, I'm heading in for the night," I told him before turning toward my door.

"I think I'm gon' crash with you," he said.

When we got to my bedroom, I immediately grabbed my nightshirt and shorts from the drawer. Then I went into the bathroom to get showered and changed. When I got back to my room wearing the extra-large white T-shirt and black basketball shorts, I was met by the sight of Plus. He stood there in the center of my room shirtless, attempting to take off his pants. I tried hard not to stare, but I couldn't help it. The perfect muscles in his arms and chest were practically begging for my attention. He had not one tattoo on his body. His skin was so flawless and smooth, like melted fudge. Instinctively, I licked my lips, taking in the view of his rock-hard abs and the protruding bulge from within his black boxer briefs.

"Damn, you eye raping a nigga and shit," he joked, taking me out of my trance.

"Nigga, shut up!" I fussed, rolling my eyes. I was embarrassed that he caught me gawking at him. After making my way over to my bed, I got under the covers and threw his blanket and pillow to the floor.

"Yo, I can't do that floor shit tonight. Slide over," he said, pushing my body out of the way. He cut my lamp off and pulled up the covers. We both lay side by side, staring up at the ceiling in the darkness. The only source of light in my room was the streetlight seeping in through the cracks of the blinds. The only sounds were neighboring dogs sporadically barking in the distance.

A few minutes of silence had passed before he finally muttered, "I just couldn't do it, yo."

"Well, I'm sure there will be more opportunities for you and Tasha," I said with sarcasm.

"That's just it. I don't want to lose my virginity to Tasha. I know I sound like a bitch right now but . . ." I could hear him release a soft snort before he said, "I want it to be special. I just want that shit to be right, ya feel me?"

Inwardly I laughed, listening to Plus talk about how he wanted his first time to be special. He sounded like a straight-up female, but I could feel where he was coming from because I felt the exact same way. "The right person will come along, Plus. Just be patient," I whispered before rolling over on my side.

Facing the wall with my back toward him, I closed my eyes just before he said, "Man, I don't want to go to Georgetown still a virgin and shit."

"You don't have to. Plenty of girls throw themselves at you every day, Plus," I yawned.

After a few more minutes of silence, I could feel myself starting to drift off to sleep. All of a sudden, Plus's strong hand slid across my waist, skimming just across the top of my shirt, only to stop and rest on my side. As he snuggled his body up against me, I could feel that warm bulge pressing on the center of my butt. Instantly, I started feeling that tingling sensation and moisture between my legs. My breathing started to pick up speed, and the muscles in my body locked up so tight from the nervousness I felt. He then sat up a little and combed back the curls of my hair with his fingers, exposing the side of my face.

"Perri, I know we don't look at each other like that, and honestly, I'm not even trying to take it there with you, but . . ." He paused.

"But what?" I whispered, still facing the wall.

"You are the only person special enough for me to share this moment with," he said.

Swallowing hard, I tried to find the right words to say, but in that moment my voice was literally caught beneath the lump in my throat.

When I didn't say anything in response, he finally asked, "Will you let me take your virginity, Perri?"

Chapter 8

Plus

When she didn't respond, I slid down into the bed underneath the covers and pulled her close to me. She didn't pull away, so I let my hand slowly travel up her T-shirt until it found her breasts. Although Perri could be boyish at times, her body was everything but. Her breasts had grown to the size of large apples, and her ass was nice and round. Her skin was soft and clean, smelling just like fresh Irish Spring soap.

As I gently caressed her skin, I ground my manhood against her with our clothes still on. I was hard as a rock and needed a release bad. Moving her wild hair off of her face again, I swirled my tongue across the flesh of her neck, and although it was soft like a whisper, I could already hear her begin to moan. I knew some people looked at us like siblings, but I actually never thought of Perri as my sister. I merely considered her to be my best friend.

"Perri," I whispered, placing kisses to her neck.

"Yes," she hissed. It was obvious that she was enjoying the feel of me kissing on her.

"Do you want to?"

When I felt her nod, I turned her body over so that she was facing me. I looked directly into her amber eyes because I needed to make sure she was okay. The lust I saw in them told me that she wanted it just as bad as I did, so I gently grabbed her face and sucked on her bottom lip. Right off, I could tell that Perri had never kissed a boy before because she didn't exactly know what to do with her mouth or her hands. Taking the lead, I placed her hands to the sides of my face and continued to suck on her lips. I took it a step further and rolled her over onto her back so that I could lie in between her thighs. Then I slipped my tongue into her mouth and kissed her deeply. The thought of doing something like this with Perri, I imagined would feel awkward, but instead, I actually felt at ease.

I lifted the T-shirt up over her head to take her breast into my mouth, teasing her nipple with just the tip of my tongue. My dick was so hard that all I could think about was being inside of her. I pulled down her basketball shorts along with her panties and carelessly tossed them onto the floor before looking her body over, fully naked and exposed.

"Damn, P, you ain't shave?" I asked her. Perri had a lot of hair down there, and although it was pretty hair, it was still a distraction.

"Nigga, for what?" she snapped.

I wasn't trying to ruin the moment for us, so I lowered my voice and said, "You need to shave that shit down some."

She nodded her head then aggressively pulled me in for another deep kiss. I guessed I wasn't the only one who needed a release. While still kissing her, I lowered my boxer briefs until they were right beneath my knees before sliding the head of my dick up and down her slippery center. Perri was so wet and slippery that I naturally began to insert myself inside of her.

"Ooh, Plus, it hurts," she whined.

"Just relax, P. Relax and breathe," I told her like I really knew what the hell I was doing.

Gradually, I began making my way in and out of her, a half inch at a time, until she finally could take me all in. Her whimpers of pain slowly began to turn into pleasure-filled moans. I swear hearing the natural sexy sounds she made was like music to my ears. Her tight, wet walls and the sight of her titties slightly bouncing up and down had me excited as shit. With each stroke I took, I began gaining more and more confidence. That was up until I came inside of her unexpectedly!

"Aaargh! Fuckkk!" I groaned, collapsing on top of her, feeling both of our bodies connected, panting in unison. I lay there on top of her in silence for a few seconds before I heard her laughing.

"What are you laughing for?"

"In all seriousness, I swear I never knew what the fuck girls be talking about when they say, 'He's a minute man, a one-minute brother, a preemie,'" she joked.

"Fuck you, P," I said. Shit, I couldn't help that my body responded to hers like that.

"Well, you already did that. Now get up off me, nigga," she said, still laughing.

Most niggas would be in their feelings the way Perri was clowning my ass, but that's just the way we were with one another. We kept it real at all times. After she was done with the jokes, we lay there quietly facing one another, not knowing exactly what words to exchange.

"This stays between you and me, right?" I asked.

"Yes, Ahmad," she said before rolling over.

I waited for a few minutes to see if she would say anything else, maybe a math problem or even a riddle. Instead, there was nothing except the light sounds of her snoring. I sat up in the bed and placed a soft kiss to her forehead, admiring her quiet beauty. Then I lay back and closed my eyes, preparing to have the best sleep I'd ever had in all of my 18 years of life.

Over the next several weeks, I bought a large box of condoms and had finally slept with Tasha. I allowed her to believe that she was my first, and sure enough, she walked around school as though she had truly won the prize. Vonnie and Tracy also got a chance to sample the dick. Already addicted to the feeling of sex, I was determined to perfect my stroke game. Being a one-woman man was definitely out of the question.

On the last day of school before graduation, I stood out in the hallway with TK, Jamal, and Perri. We had skipped our last period of the day just to clown around and shit. The teachers were lenient since it was the last day of school and also because we were graduating seniors. Over the past week, TK and Jamal went around school snapping pictures of girls. TK would hold a conversation with them while Jamal would sneakily go behind them with the camera, snapping a picture up under their skirts. It was hot outside, and it seemed like all the girls were wearing either shorts, dresses, or skirts to school.

"Damn, look at Tracy's fat ass," TK said, looking down at one of the pictures.

"Hol' up. How you know that's Tracy?" Jamal asked with a confused look on his face.

Looking over at the picture, I immediately started smiling. "Yeah, that's definitely Tracy's fat ass," I said. In every picture he had, all you could see was the meat of their ass cheeks and the panties they wore, but I couldn't forget the way Tracy's body looked if I tried.

"Told you that was Tracy," TK said, snatching the picture back away from Jamal.

Totally unengaged, Perri was posted up against the locker throwing her basketball in the air. She was rocking a pair of black basketball shorts and a Nike T-shirt with some black-and-white Air Max on her feet. Her hair was in a bushy ball that sat right on the top of her head. Just looking at her I could tell that she wasn't trying to hear none of the foolishness we were talking about.

Then Tasha walked up with Shivon. Tasha was looking beautiful as usual in a dark denim skirt and a pink peasant blouse that exposed her brown shoulders. She even wore tan wedge heels that complemented her smooth dark-chocolate legs. Her long black hair hung down, sweeping the middle of her back like a horse's mane.

"Hey, y'all. What's this?" she asked, trying to take one of the pictures out of my hand.

"Nothing," I said, putting them behind my back and puckering up my lips for a kiss.

She pecked my lips, but I was always greedy. I slipped my tongue into her mouth and began a full make-out session right there in the hallway. Sliding my free hand down, I grabbed a handful of her ass underneath her skirt. Just the sight and touch of her soft skin had me ready to fuck. Our sloppy kiss was abruptly interrupted when the final bell of the day rang.

"Are you going home with me?" she asked seductively.

I looked over at my boys and Perri to see if they had any plans, but when they didn't say anything, I nodded my head. After returning the pictures to TK, she grabbed my hand, and we began to walk away.

"Don't hurt him, Tash," TK hollered out with a laugh.

"I might have to. Ever since I broke him in his ass been getting cocky," she joked.

That's when I heard a small, sarcastic snort of a laugh coming from behind me. Already knowing it was Perri, I looked back and gave her a cold look so she'd know to shut the fuck up. If Tasha only knew the truth about Perri being a nigga's first, she would try to slap the fire out of me, especially since I knowingly allowed her to go around the school bragging and shit. Looking back at Perri one more time, I watched as she rolled her eyes and gave me her middle finger before walking off in the opposite direction.

Chapter 9

Perri

An hour after our high school graduation, I sat with my father and Aria at a table in Ms. Tonya's tiny backyard. Although Ms. Tonya threw both of us a graduation party, Tez and my father were the only family I had to actually attend. My father was an only child, so I didn't have any family on his side. Plus, on the other hand, had all of his aunts, uncles, and cousins there to support him. My mother did have one sister and one brother. However, it seemed that ever since she passed away, I'd seen that side of the family less and less until the relationships were finally nonexistent. That was okay though because all of Plus's aunts, uncles, and cousins considered me to be real family. Besides, just having Ms. Tonya, Plus, and Aria, my family was already complete.

"I'm so proud of you, Perri. I know your mother is smiling down on you today," my father said to me.

"Thanks, Daddy."

"I'm serious, Perri. You will be the first in our family to go on to college. You don't know what that means to me," he said with tears in his eyes.

"Dad, stop," I said because he was making me cry and I hated that mushy stuff.

"You don't know what it feels like to be a man raising a little girl all on your own. Then you go graduate from high school and get accepted into not one but two

colleges. And on a basketball scholarship. Lord knows
you've always struggled in school. So you damn right I'm
emotional," he said, beaming with pride.

I shook my head because everything he said was true.
Knowing my mother would have been more than proud
of me today, I also knew that she would have been
proud of my father. It had to be hard raising a little girl
and boy on your own while working ten- to twelve-hour
shifts every night.

"Why you not eating nothing, Perri?" Ms. Tonya came
up and interrupted, holding a tray of raw chicken in her
hands.

"My stomach has been bothering me a little today. I'll
try to eat something a little later though," I said.

"Oh, okay. I hope you feel better, baby."

Ms. Tonya walked off and made her way over to Tez,
who was manning the grill. The smell of barbecue filled
the hot summer's air while Biggie's "Mo Money Mo
Problems" played on the boom-box radio. As the yard
continued to fill with family and friends, I saw Plus
coming out of the back door of the house with TK and
Jamal trailing behind him in the yard. With each day
that passed, I swear Plus looked better and better to me.
Wearing Nautica from head to toe, he had on a navy blue
collared shirt, khaki cargo shorts, and navy blue boat
shoes with no socks on his feet. The lone diamond in his
ear, the Cuban link chain around his neck, and his curly
tapered fade made him look very preppy. I sat back and
admired his good looks.

Once he made his way over to me, he leaned down and
placed a kiss to my forehead like he always did, but this
time I closed my eyes and inhaled his scent. He wore
Curve, which was one of my favorite things to smell on
him. I then stood to dap TK and Jamal up. They were
dressed nicely as well but nothing like my best friend.

"I like your hair like this, P," Plus said, softly stroking the fish-scale braid Ms. Tonya had put my hair in.

"Thanks," I replied.

"Look at Perri, finally becoming a woman and shit," TK joked. Not only was my hair in one single braid down my back, but I wore a white tennis skirt with a matching white collared shirt. I even wore small bamboo earrings and a gold anklet, complementing the all-white shell-toe Adidas I wore. Although I really wanted nothing more than to slip on a pair of comfortable basketball shorts and a T-shirt, I was trying. I was glad I did, too, because it seemed to have gotten me a little bit more attention from Plus.

"Shut up, TK," I said, punching him in the arm.

"You look really nice today, P," Plus complimented me, all the while stroking my braid.

"Yeah, you do," TK admitted, making me smile.

Plus and the guys had all pulled up chairs to sit next to me. We were all just talking shit and laughing for a few before I looked at the back door to see Tasha and Shivon walking out to the backyard. When Plus stood up to go greet her, I immediately rolled my eyes, letting out an unintentional sigh of annoyance.

"Damn, you really don't like shorty, do you?" TK asked with a smirk.

"Nah, I really don't, but hey, if Plus likes it, I love it," I stated with my eyes fixed on Plus and Tasha.

Just the sight of them kissing and touching all over one another had my stomach somersaulting. Of course, she looked beautiful in a bright yellow sundress that was flawless against her dark brown skin. Silently I watched them with envy. He trekked through the yard, affectionately holding her hand while introducing her to the family. My family. They looked like the perfect couple.

That's when my stomach really started to bubble, and I could feel the chunks of vomit slowly rising from the pit of my stomach. Getting up from my seat, I immediately covered my mouth, but I couldn't hold it in. I threw up all over my new white outfit and my all-white Adidas. Instantly, my face grew hot and flushed from embarrassment. When I looked up, I saw that Tasha had a look of disgust written all over her face as she looked me over from head to toe. Her nose was turned all the way up as if she could smell the stink of my breath. I ran as fast as I could in the house and found myself inside the bathroom. As I was kneeling over the toilet, throwing up everything left inside of me, there was a sudden knock on the door.

"Are you okay, baby?" Ms. Tonya asked from the other side of the door.

"Yeah, I'm all right," I said, but as soon as those words left my mouth, another heap of vomit flew from my throat and plopped right down into the toilet.

Ms. Tonya immediately opened up the bathroom door and gently rubbed my back. "Well, I know your ass ain't pregnant 'cause you still a virgin," Ms. Tonya said.

When I didn't respond, Ms. Tonya lifted my hunched body up straight and looked me dead in the eyes. "Well? You are still a virgin, right?" she quizzed with a concerned look on her face. I just held my head down because I really didn't want to lie to Ms. Tonya.

"Lord Jesus, whyyy?" she asked, dramatically looking up toward the ceiling. Then she took a long, deep breath before lifting my chin to look at her.

"I knew you looked a little different these past few weeks, but you ain't never around no guys so . . ." I could tell that her words were cut short by the thoughts rapidly running through her mind. When her eyes grew wide and she covered her mouth with her hand, I just knew she had figured it out.

"Was it with TK?" she asked. I simply shook my head to respond.

"Well, Jamal is dating Shivon," she said more to herself than to me. She tapped her index finger against her chin, thinking, mulling over the different combinations in her mind. Suddenly, her eyes bulged as if a light bulb had gone off inside her head.

"Oh, shit," she muttered, staring at me. When our eyes spoke, I knew for a fact that she had figured it out.

"Come with me," she said, flushing the toilet and guiding me out of the bathroom.

I followed Ms. Tonya up to her bedroom, where she pulled out fresh, clean clothes for me. She also opened a drawer that was full of pads, tampons, and a few pregnancy tests.

"Here. Go clean yourself up first, then open this up and pee on it," she instructed, handing over the pregnancy test box with a trembling hand.

"Ms. Tonya, it was only the one time. I seriously doubt I'm pregnant," I told her.

"Did you two use a condom?" she asked.

I shook my head in shame.

"Then do as I say, child," she fussed.

Doing exactly what she said, I went into the hall bathroom to pee on the stick. In all honesty, I really didn't believe I was pregnant, because my jealousy was known for making my stomach churn. There was a small window in the bathroom that overlooked the backyard. I saw Plus with Tasha sitting in his lap, laughing without a care in the world. It hurt me, not just because he was with Tasha, but because he didn't even bother to come check on me. I was supposed to be his best friend.

After a couple more minutes, there was a soft knock on the bathroom door. I sighed because I knew it was Ms. Tonya and it was now time to look at the results. Looking down at the test before opening up the door, I shrugged because I didn't know exactly what I was supposed to be looking for.

"What does it say?" Ms. Tonya asked, making her way into the bathroom.

"I don't know. Here," I told her, handing her over the stick.

She looked a little disgusted, and I guessed I couldn't blame her because I did just pee on it, but she still took it from me like a good mother would.

"Don't be offended that I'm asking you this, but"—she swallowed—"is Plus the only one you've ever been with?" she asked lowly, still looking down at the stick.

"Yes, ma'am. We lost our virginity to one another on prom night," I answered.

"Well, it looks like I'm going to be a grandmother sooner than I thought," she said with a slight smile on her face.

"I'm gonna get an abortion, Ms. Tonya. I got a scholarship to George Mason to play ball, and Plus is going to Georgetown," I told her.

"Plans change, Perri," she said.

"Not for Plus they can't. I pray every night that one day he'll make it to the NBA. That's his dream. I don't want this to interfere with that," I said. Tears were suddenly running down my face.

She shushed me and wiped my face with her hands. "No, we're not killing my grandchild, but you will have to sacrifice, Perri," she said.

"What about Plus?"

"Well, you were right about Plus's future, Perri. He has a special gift that can be beneficial to all of us. He will go to Georgetown and one day make it to the NBA. If not, Plus is smart enough to land a six-figure job after he graduates. I have no doubt in my mind about that."

"And what about me?" I pointed to my chest. "My plans to go to college? It's not fair!"

She sighed and lifted my chin with her finger. "Life isn't fair, Perri. Especially not to young girls in this situation. Trust me, I know. We're the ones who make all the sacrifices, baby. First with our bodies, then our sleep, then with our time, and before it's all over and done with, we've ended up sacrificing ourselves. It's a part of being a woman and a mother. Unfortunately, it's the consequence you'll have to bear for having unprotected sex."

"But it's not fair, yo," I mumbled, sniffing back tears. "What's he sacrificing?"

"Well, would you prefer that Ahmad give up his scholarship too? That both of you stay home to raise this baby? Because he has the ability to change all of our lives for the better. We both know that."

Without giving me a chance to respond, she kissed my cheek and wiped a few more of my tears away. When we finally returned to the backyard, Plus was still sitting there with Tasha in his lap, stroking her long, pretty hair just as he had done mine merely moments before. I felt so conflicted.

"Ahmad! Phillip!" Ms. Tonya called out to Plus and my father, waving them over. It was as if Tez knew something was up, because he started walking our way as well. I wished Ms. Tonya had given me some additional time to digest all of this, but I guessed it was now or never. I just hoped that I wouldn't be seen as a disappointment in my father's eyes and that Plus would eventually forgive me for telling our little secret.

Chapter 10

Plus

I lifted Tasha up off of my lap and walked toward the house. Seeing Perri standing there behind my mother, it looked like she had been crying. Then again, I knew she wasn't feeling well. I was actually on my way to go check on her after she threw up, but my mother stopped me and told me that she had it. At first I hesitated, but after looking back at Tasha and seeing the pissed expression on her face, I went against my better judgment and sat back down with her. I didn't feel like hearing her nag about me always catering to Perri.

"What's up, Ma? Something wrong?" I asked.

"What's wrong?" Tez asked, walking up to Perri.

She shook her head before burying her face into her brother's chest. I hated seeing Perri upset, so I immediately went around my mother and pulled Perri from Tez into my own embrace.

"Somebody fucking wit' you?" I asked, peering down at her. She shook her head.

"Come on, y'all. We all need to go inside the house and talk for a minute," my mother said.

"Ms. Tonya, can it wait until after the party is over?" Perri asked lowly.

"No. I don't do that fake shit, Perri. You know me better than that. We have to get this out now," she said.

We went inside the house and into the living room after my mother locked the back door behind us. As soon as we all sat down on the couch, Perri started weeping again, and it was starting to scare the shit out of me. My stomach instantly knotted up, and the palms of my hands grew sweaty from anxiety. I looked over and saw Mr. Phillip rubbing Perri on her back, waiting for whatever it was my mother needed to discuss.

"What's going on, Tonya? Why is Perri so upset?" Mr. Phillip asked.

"Perri, do you want to tell everyone or do you want me to?" my mother looked over and asked Perri. With her hands still covering her wet face, Perri shook her head.

My mother then grabbed my hand and gave it a gentle squeeze before clearing her throat. "Y'all, Perri is pregnant," my mother revealed.

"No! Perri, no. Please tell me this is not true," Mr. Phillip said, looking at Perri with disappointment. Perri didn't say anything. She just continued to cover her face and cry.

"Who's the father?" Tez immediately stood up and asked, all before cracking his knuckles and pounding his fist into the palm of his hand.

That's when Perri looked over at me with apologetic eyes. I knew without a shadow of a doubt that the baby was mine, because Perri had only slept with me. Shit, when she wasn't with me and the crew, she was in the house by herself, so I knew she didn't have time to get pregnant by another nigga. I also knew Perri didn't get down like that.

Without so much as a word, I stood up and punched a hole in the wall before storming out the door. Was I mad at Perri? No, but was I mad at the situation? Hell yes. In just a few more months, I'd be off to Georgetown to start my college and basketball careers. The last thing I needed was a baby tying me down at this stage in my life. "Ahmad, wait!" I heard my mother call out to me, but I just kept right on walking.

I walked for hours just thinking until darkness had completely taken the sky. Before I knew it, I was right back where I started: at my house with a sore hand and a heavy heart. The loud music that was once bumping in the backyard was now replaced by silence. Only the sound of crickets in the night could be heard. And although the many cars lined up and down the block earlier were now gone, the faint smell of Tez's barbeque still lingered in the air. I had finally calmed myself down to the point where I could actually have a conversation with Perri, but it was a little after ten o'clock, so I was sure she had gone back home. In fact, from the outside, it looked like all of the lights were out in my house as well as hers.

I opened up the front door to my crib and walked into darkness. When I cut the living room light on, I was surprised to see that Perri had been sitting there in the dark all by herself.

"Where's my mother at?" I asked.

"She and Aria are over at my house," she said. From the redness and puffiness around her eyes, I could tell that she probably cried the entire time I was gone.

Sitting down on the couch beside her, I let out a deep breath before running my hand down my face. "I'm sorry, P. I fucked up."

"I'm sorry too, Plus. I know I told you that it would stay between us, but I didn't think I would end up pregnant when I made that promise," she explained. I shook my head and shushed her to let her know I understood where she was coming from. Truthfully, I really didn't care that she told about us having sex. I was just worried about how having a baby right now would ruin my future.

"So, what are we gon' do?" I asked.

"Well, I told your mom that I would get an abortion, but she said that wasn't an option."

Letting my head fall back on the couch, I felt myself getting upset over the fact that an abortion wasn't an option. But then I reminded myself that I was having a baby with Perri. That fact alone gave me hope that at the end of the day everything was going to work out to be okay.

"So then how are we gonna work it out? I know it sounds selfish, P, but I don't want to give up Georgetown," I told her.

"And I don't want to give up George Mason!" she shot back with her eyes wide.

I sighed.

After a few seconds of silence passed between us, she said, "Look, yo, I would never ask you to give up Georgetown or any of your dreams for that matter. I've decided that I'm just going to stay home and go to community college." She shrugged. "Your mom said that she would help me with the baby, so I could probably get a part-time job. But," she said, looking me square in the eye, "if I do this, you had better go all the way."

I nodded, fully understanding her words.

"And no matter what, don't you ever forget about me," she said.

"I got you," I told her, feeling somewhat relieved. I reached over and grabbed her face before gently kissing her lips. "I love you, P. You're my best friend, so a nigga could never forget about you. I promise I'm gonna do everything in my power to be a good dad, and as soon as I'm able to support y'all, you know I got you."

She reached out and hugged me tightly around the neck. I could tell I had given her all the reassurance she needed, because just like that, her body melted into mine. Mentally, I was still a little torn because I truly did want to be a good father and be there every step of the way for my child. Yet, on the other hand, I also wanted to live out my dreams. I didn't have money or the means to take Perri with me to Georgetown, so for now, this would just have to be the plan.

"Oh, and you need to tell Tasha's annoying ass, too. She asked me what was going on after you left, and I told her that she needed to speak to you," she said.

I sighed, already dreading the "I told you so" conversation I would have to have with Tasha. My mother thought that I just liked having a beautiful woman on my arm to brag about and that was the only reason I kept Tasha's pretty ass around. However, that was only half-true. I had actually started to care for her, and honestly, I wasn't ready to give up our relationship. If she would accept me and my child, then I'd probably still rock with her throughout my college career, but as for now, the ball was in her court.

Chapter 11

Perri

It was the second week in September, and I was now eighteen weeks pregnant. At ten o'clock in the morning, I found myself sitting in the back of my American history class, waiting for Professor Farrell to begin his lecture. Taking this boring class early on a Friday morning, combined with the side effects of being pregnant, had me yawning every other second. I was beyond tired, but I was even more determined to graduate from this community college and someday go on to a university like I'd originally planned.

"Good morning, class. Settle down and let's begin," Professor Farrell finally said. He was an older white man with white hair and wrinkly, pale skin. He walked real slow and talked even slower. However, those were the only things slow about him, because the man definitely knew his history.

"Can I borrow your notes from the last class?" the pretty girl sitting next to me whispered. Her skin was a warm cocoa brown while her naturally curly hair was light, like the color of cinnamon. Her facial features were small and delicate, which only added to her beauty. She had on a fitted Pink jogging suit with pink and gray Air Max on her feet. I actually liked her style. It was feminine but not over-the-top.

"Sure," I said, flipping through my binder to find her the pages of my notes.

"I'm Nika by the way," she said, extending her hand for me to shake.

"Perri," I replied, shaking her hand.

After class was over, I headed down the hall toward the exit.

"Perri, wait up!" I heard Nika call out from behind me.

"What's up?" I turned around and asked.

"Do you have time for a bite to eat or do you have another class?"

I raised my eyebrows, feeling a bit confused. Girls never talked to me, so the first thing that ran through my mind was, *she must think I'm gay.* Although I was pregnant, you really couldn't tell, especially with the extra-baggy clothes I always wore. I had on a gray Champion hoodie with gray sweatpants. Rocking wheat-colored Tims with the tongue flapping, I ran my hand down my hair, which was neatly braided down my back into two cornrows.

"I got time to eat," I told her.

We headed over to the small cafeteria that was in the dead center of campus. The place was completely packed, and every line was long. I scanned the seating area, and sure enough, there was only one table left with two seats by the window.

"You can go grab us that table, and I'll get our food. What do you want to eat?" I asked, pulling my sweatpants up higher around my waist.

"Just a slice of pepperoni pizza and a Coke," she said.

"A'ight, I got you."

As I made my way through the crowd and got in line to get us two slices of pizza, I saw Tasha standing in the fried chicken line. Unfortunately, she went to the same community college as me, and although I would occasionally run into her on campus, she never parted her mouth to speak. Usually, she'd roll her eyes at me, and if she was with one of her friends, she'd whisper in their ear while looking at me. Then they'd both just burst out laughing. You know, typical high school shit. This day would be no different. I watched and shook my head as she laughed with the pretty Hispanic girl standing next to her before making my way back over to our table.

"Here you go," I told Nika, setting her tray down in front of her.

"Thanks. How much?"

"Don't worry about it. So how are you liking the class?" I asked because I didn't know what else to say.

"Girl, I hate that class. Mr. Farrell's ass puts a bitch to sleep," she said.

"Yeah, he puts me to sleep too," I laughed.

"I've been trying to meet some new people and figure out what's fun to do around here. I actually moved down here about a month ago from Connecticut to live with my grandmother, and now I'm enrolled in school."

"Oh, I probably can't help you out with the fun part. I'm actually four months pregnant, and when I wasn't pregnant, all I did was play ball and video games," I told her.

"Damn, so you don't even know where the cute guys be at," she joked.

"Nah. I got knocked up by my best friend," I said, shrugging my shoulders.

"Your first love, huh?"

"Something like that," I replied, not really wanting to get into all the details.

"That's sweet. So where does everyone go shopping at around here?"

"Well, I shop at Dicks, Hibbett, and Foot Locker, but you're probably looking for the big mall over on the east side."

"No offense but you are way too pretty to be dressing like a boy, especially being pregnant. You are straight, right?" she genuinely asked, causing me to laugh a little.

"Yes, I only like boys," I confirmed with a smile before taking a bite of my pizza.

"Oh, well, it seems like everyone's a lesbian these days, so I had to ask."

I nodded my head before I felt the cell phone in my book bag vibrate beside me. I quickly pulled it out to answer it. "Hold on, Nika, I gotta get this," I said, putting the phone up to my ear. "Hello."

"Perri? Perri, Tez has been shot. You need to get over to University of Maryland hospital now!" my father said with panic lacing his voice.

The phone immediately fell from my trembling hand, crashing down onto the floor.

"Perri, are you okay?" Nika asked.

I was completely speechless. The only thing I could think of in that moment was losing my big brother. Although he was three years older than me, we were extremely close. Tez was my heart, and I knew that if I lost him, it would destroy me forever.

"Perri, what's wrong?" Nika asked, taking me out of my thoughts. I hadn't even realized that I was crying until I felt a tear drop down onto my hand.

"It's my brother. He's been shot. I gotta get over to University of Maryland hospital now," I cried.

"I can drive you. Come on, let's go," she said before kneeling down and picking up my cell phone for me.

We rushed over to the hospital, which was about a fifteen-minute drive from campus. On the ride over, I called Plus and told him what had happened. Plus had been at Georgetown for the past six weeks. Although he lived less than an hour away, he didn't have a car, so I knew he wouldn't be able to come home. Nonetheless, the sound of love and concern in his voice was enough to temporarily calm my fears.

When we walked into the waiting room, I saw Ms. Tonya and my father in a corner by themselves. My father sat with his head hung slightly between his legs while Ms. Tonya rubbed his back. When she looked up at me, I instantly started crying and ran into her embrace. With just one look in her eyes, I could tell that she had been crying, and immediately I began thinking the worst. My father then stood up and wrapped his arms around me, letting me know that they were still waiting to hear about Tez's condition. After introducing them to Nika, we all took a seat and patiently waited.

After another twenty minutes or so had passed, two guys I recognized as my brother's partners came into the room. My brother didn't really have friends, and the guys he did associate with he kept far away from me and Plus. Following the two guys was a tall brown-skinned girl with curly black hair that fell past the middle of her back. She had dark, slanted eyes like an Asian and full, pretty lips that were painted a soft shade of pink. Her figure was a perfect size eight, and her walk was goddess-like.

"Perri, right?" one of the guys asked.

"Yeah," I responded, cutting my eyes up at him from where I sat.

"How's Tez doing?" he asked.

"We're still waiting to hear from the doctor," Ms. Tonya cut in.

The beautiful girl walked up to me and extended her hand. "Hi, I am Tez's girlfriend, Myesha," she said softly. Although she was stunningly beautiful, I could look in her face and tell that she was sad and had been crying.

"Girlfriend?" I asked in disbelief. Tez had never mentioned having a girlfriend.

"Yes. We've only been dating for a few months now, but he talks about you guys all the time," she said, looking between my father, Ms. Tonya, and me.

She and the guys all sat down beside us and waited another hour or so before the doctor finally walked out to see us. He had a tired look on his face that was hard for me to read. "Family of Montez Daniels?" he said.

"That's us, Doc," my father stood up and said.

"Yes. Montez arrived with three gunshot wounds, all of which entered and passed through his body. One went through his right shoulder, one through his thigh, and the last one went through his abdomen. He lost a lot of blood, which was our main concern, but he is now stable. He is heavily sedated so that his body can heal, but we do expect him to make a full recovery. You can go back to visit with him two at a time, but again, he will most likely not be responsive."

Everyone immediately let out several sighs of relief.

"Phillip, you and Perri go in first," Ms. Tonya said.

When we walked in the room, all I could hear was the beeping of several machines. Tubes and wires were all connected to my brother's fragile body as he lay there in a deep slumber. Quietly, I walked over and gently held his hand while my father went on the opposite side of the bed.

"I told you this life was gonna catch up to you, son," my father whispered to Tez. He stroked the top of his head and placed a fatherly kiss on his brow.

"Stay strong, brother. I'm praying for you," I told him. His eyes fluttered a little, but they never opened. I swear, in that moment, I would have given anything to see his beautiful amber eyes again.

After spending a few more minutes with Tez, we made our way back out to the waiting room. That's when my eyes landed on him. Plus was sitting there with Ms. Tonya and Tez's girlfriend, Myesha.

"Plus, what are you doing here?" I asked, walking over to where he sat.

He stood up from his seat and began making his way over to me. "I had to come check on my brother and make sure you were all right," he said lowly before giving me a hug and a kiss on my forehead.

While he was rubbing my belly, I glanced over at Nika, who was sitting next to a guy I had never seen before. He was tall and dark skinned with gold fronts and shoulder-length dreads. He was handsome but not as fine as Plus. When she saw me looking at the two of them, she smiled and nodded her head toward Plus, giving me a little wink.

Chapter 12

Plus

As soon as I got the call from Perri saying that Tez had
been shot, I had my roommate, Jorell, drive me back
home. Jorell was a freshman like me who also played
ball. He came all the way from Prichard, Alabama, to go
to school at Georgetown on a basketball scholarship. I
had only known him for the past six weeks, but so far, he
seemed pretty cool.

After going back to visit with Tez, I walked into the
waiting room to see Jorell macking on some pretty-ass
brown-skinned girl. The nigga was laying it on real thick,
too, spitting game like the shit was going out of style.
Within forty minutes of us being in the hospital, he was
already smoothing shorty's curls back with his hand and
making her laugh like he'd known her for years. This is
how this nigga always was though. Whenever we were
on campus together, he spoke to damn near every girl
we'd pass. We hadn't even been in school a good two
months, and I couldn't even count the number of times
I'd come back to the room only to find a bandana tied to
the doorknob, indicating that he was fucking.

"Yo, Jorell, you going back to school or you staying with
me?" I asked, interrupting their flow.

"Yuh, I'ma chill wit' you for the weekend, breh," he said
with his thick Southern accent.

"A'ight, well, we about to be out. A nigga's tired as fuck right now," I said. I got the call from Perri about twenty minutes after basketball practice ended and then jumped on the road shortly after that. It was only going on seven o'clock, but I could barely hold my eyes open.

Finally, we all made our way down to the hospital parking lot. I could see that the ground was wet. I knew it had just rained because I could still smell it in the air, plus all of the cars were covered in raindrops. Tez's girlfriend Myesha ended up staying behind. She was determined to stay by Tez's side the entire time, and for that, I liked her already. I always looked up to Tez like a big brother because he had the money, the cars, and the clothes. Now he had one of the baddest chicks I had ever seen standing by his side.

"We'll see y'all at home," my mother called out before getting in the car with Mr. Phillip.

"You riding with us, P?" I asked with a yawn.

"Yeah, I'm riding with y'all. Nika, thank you so much for driving me here today and staying this whole time. You really didn't have to do that," Perri said.

"Girl, it was no problem at all. I just did what any decent person would do," Nika said.

"Well, I've got your number now, so I'll call you tomorrow," Perri told her.

"Yeah, we'll call you tomorrow," Jorell cut in with a smirk. I just looked back at him and shook my head. Here it was that my brother was all shot up in a hospital bed and this nigga was over here trying to get pussy.

"All right then, I'll talk to you tomorrow," Nika said with a giggle before getting into her car.

Once Nika pulled off, we all got into Jorell's 1988 apple red Chevy Impala. He had twenty-inch chrome spinner wheels on it and two Atlanta Falcon flags waving on the back. After cranking up the engine, the car dropped then lifted right back up with a jerk from the hydraulics.

"Yo, this is some country-ass shit right here," Perri said in reference to his ride.

"Mane, yo' baby momma got a slick-ass mouth, breh," Jorell said with a grin that exposed the gold grills in his mouth.

"Baby momma?" she remarked with a scowl on her face.

"Man, chill, P. What you want him to call you?"

"How about what your ass has been calling me for the past eighteen years?" she snapped.

"Jorell, this is my best friend, Perri. Perri, this is my roommate and teammate, Jorell," I sarcastically introduced them again. I had already introduced them to one another back at the hospital.

When we pulled up to the house, I saw Ronnie's drunk ass sleeping on the front porch. I hadn't seen him since a month before I left to go to college. I figured that while I was away, he would try to slither his way back into the house. In all these years, my feelings toward Ronnie still hadn't changed. I couldn't stand that fuck nigga.

After I let Jorell inside, I told him that I'd be right back after walking Perri down to her house. It was barely nightfall, and the crackheads were already standing out on the corners in our neighborhood. Police sirens and the murmured cries of babies were sounding off in the distance. I didn't miss that shit for nothing. If it weren't for my family, I doubted I'd ever come back.

"So how you been feeling? I mean, other than this shit with Tez?" I asked Perri as we walked.

"A little tired but no more morning sickness, so I can deal with it."

"You been taking your prenatal vitamins?"

"Yes, baby daddy," she sang with a smile, sounding all girly and shit.

I laughed. "Oh, so I can't call you baby momma, but you can call me baby daddy?" I asked.

"Yep. Pregnant woman rules," she boasted.

"Oh, so now you're a woman?" I joked.

"Unless your ass is gay, hell yeah I'm a woman!"

"You're right about that, baby momma," I said, noticing her beauty. The streetlight had just cut on, and the way it reflected off her amber eyes made me feel some type of way. I'd never really thought about it, but my baby momma was actually really pretty. Secretly, I hoped our baby had her same beautiful eyes.

After a few seconds of silence passed between us, we finally reached her doorstep. Mr. Phillip and my mother were already home, because I could see his car parked out front, and the porch light was on. I stepped in close to Perri and let my hands gently glide up underneath her hoodie. Tenderly I rubbed on her smooth, hardened belly while looking her over again, taking in her boyish attire.

"You do realize that if it's a girl, you're going to have to change a little. Teach my li'l momma how to be a woman and shit," I said, still rubbing on her belly.

"I know," she said softly, looking into my eyes.

I leaned in close to give her a kiss good night and instantly noticed that she closed her eyes, bowing her forehead out for me. However, to my own surprise, I actually didn't want to kiss Perri on the forehead. Instead, I wanted to feel her pouty pink lips against mine. Hooking my index finger up under her chin, I lifted her face and planted a simple kiss on her mouth. As I began deepening our kiss, I noticed that her eyes had opened wide. Although our mouths were intertwined with our tongues lightly dancing, she kept her eyes trained on me. When I finally broke our kiss, I grabbed her by the waist and placed one final peck on her lips. My body was responding to hers like never before. I looked down and noticed that my mans was even hard, making a tent in my pants. Evidently, Perri saw it too.

"What was that, Plus?" she asked, confused.

"I can't kiss my li'l one yet, but I can pass the message through you," I said with a devious little smirk.

"Yeah, whatever, nigga," she said, pointing at my dick. "That damn sure wasn't no message for the baby."

I couldn't do shit but laugh, because she was right. A nigga was horny as shit.

"Luh you, P," I told her before kissing her lips again. This time she closed her eyes and so did I. As soon as I reached down and grabbed a handful of her fat ass, she moaned into my mouth. The pregnancy had filled her body out nicely, and in that moment, I couldn't help but to show my appreciation. Never in a million years did I think I would be standing here kissing on Perri the way that I was, but I had to admit I was enjoying every minute of it. Perhaps it was seeing her pregnant with my seed, or the mere fact that I just missed being around my best friend.

"I'ma stay with you tonight, a'ight?" I told her, breaking our kiss.

"What about Jorell?" she whispered.

"That nigga will be all right."

As we crept through the dark, quiet house on our way to her bedroom, I fondled her body. I was rubbing all over her pussy through the sweatpants she had on, and I pinched away at her swollen nipples. The pregnancy must have been making Perri horny too, because as soon as we got to her bedroom and shut the door, she attacked my mouth. Our tongues were damn near wrestling with one another as she tried unzipping my jeans. While she was undressing me, I was struggling to get her sweatpants down and her panties off. We wanted each other bad and were being so aggressive about it that anyone looking from a distance would have thought we were damn near fighting. As soon as her clothes were completely off, I gently slipped a finger inside of her wet pussy.

"Damn, shorty, you already wet for me," I said lowly, sliding my finger in and out of her.

"I've been horny as shit lately," she whispered into the crook of my neck, eagerly grinding on my finger.

"I'ma take care of that tonight, baby momma. Don't you worry," I said before laying her back on the bed.

I tried taking it really slow, making a trail of kisses from her earlobe all the way down to her breasts.

"Stop playing with me, yo, and just put that shit in already," she fussed. I chuckled because her ass was horny for real.

In one swift motion, I entered her and closed my eyes. "Mmmm," she moaned. She was so tight and wet around me that I felt like I would nut at any moment. As if she read my mind, she leaned up and whispered, "Don't cum fast this time, Plus, okay?"

"A'ight, I got you, P," I told her, but honestly, I didn't know if I could keep that promise. I prayed that I would last, because she just felt too damn good.

Mentally, I got myself together real quick and pushed her legs up around my shoulders. Immediately, I started going to work grinding in and out of her. Her eyes were closed tight, and her mouth hung slightly ajar, so I knew I was hitting that shit right. My stroke game had come a long way since the night Perri and I had lost our virginity to one another. I had bitches at my school practically begging for the dick, and then there was still Tasha, who just couldn't get enough of me. My confidence level was through the roof. Feeling myself, I started rolling my hips just so I could hear the sound of her wet pussy on me.

"Ohhh, shittt!" she moaned out in pleasure. There was something about hearing Perri all sexy-like that made me feel weak. I had to start thinking about baseball, basketball, my statistics class, anything that would allow me to last a little bit longer.

"Damn, P, you got that wet-wet," I hissed, feeling my nut rise again. Perhaps it was the pregnancy that had her pussy feeling so bomb, but whatever it was, it topped any I had ever had.

"Mmmm, can you fuck me from the back?" she whispered.

She caught me completely off guard. I jerked my neck back and looked at her. "Yo, you been watching porn, P? Fuck you know about getting hit from the back?" I quizzed, still working myself in and out of her.

"Can you? Pleaseeee," she all but whined.

"Turn over," I told her, pulling out. She got on all fours, and I started handling my business. I had a nice grip on her long braids, which instantly made her back arch. Her juicy ass was jiggling every time as I pounded inside of her from behind. I bit down on my bottom lip at the mere sight.

"Ahhhh, I'm about to pee," she wailed.

"Nah, you about to cum. Cum for me, P," I told her, slapping her softly on the ass.

"Ahhh, fuckkkk," she wailed again.

"Cum on this muthafucka, P," I told her again, firmly gripping her ass and thrusting deeper inside of her.

"Unngghhh!" she moaned out, finally cumming all over me. Seconds later, I was releasing my load right behind her.

"Your pops gon' fuck us up with all that noise you was making," I panted with a chuckle, still trying to catch my breath.

"I couldn't help it," she whispered, letting out a light laugh.

After we both collapsed down onto the bed, I spooned her from behind and rubbed on her belly some more.

"So what you think? A nigga's skills done improved, right?" I knowingly asked with a smirk.

"Yeah, you have. Shit, that was my first orgasm. Thank you," she said lowly.

"You know I got you," I told her, feeling myself drift off to sleep.

"Am I the only one you don't use condoms with?"

"Of course," I told her without hesitation. That was true for the most part, but I had slipped up with Tasha a time or two. That was it though.

"Plus?"

"Yeah, P."

"What's 255 times 67?"

"Shit, uh . . . 17,085," I said with a yawn.

"I love you, Plus," she whispered.

"Luh you too, P," I said before going to sleep.

The very next day after going to go visit Tez at the hospital for a few hours and learning that he would make a full recovery, Perri, Jorell, and I decided to chill. We were all at my crib, playing a game of *Madden,* while my mother and Aria were out grocery shopping.

"Call your homegirl over, shawty, so we can chill," Jorell told Perri.

"Nigga, you call her. I thought you got her number last night," Perri said in between whipping my ass on the game.

"Breh, I don't see how you gon' put up wit' shawty's difficult ass for the next eighteen years," he said to me, shaking his head.

"Eighteen years? Nigga, don't play! His ass is stuck with me for life. Fuck you think this is?" Perri snapped, rolling her pretty eyes.

"Yo, what I tell you about that shit, P? You gon have to calm all that shit down before my baby comes."

"In other words, talk like a fucking lady," Jorell's instigating ass said.

Perri stood up from her seat on the floor and mushed him in the face. "Fine. I'll talk like a lady, but his mother-fucking ass better watch himself. I fight niggas, too," she said, throwing the controller to the floor before walking off to call Nika.

"Yo' baby momma is a straight-up nigga, mane," Jorell whispered. "She would be pretty if she knew how to act, but nah, her attitude is a straight-up nightmare. I don't know how you gon' do it, breh. I really don't," he murmured, shaking his head. It was funny hearing him talk so low because Jorell's ass was really scared of Perri.

"Shut the fuck up, Jorell!" she yelled from the kitchen. I couldn't do shit but laugh.

Chapter 13

Perri

2004

It was a cold day in January when I found myself studying at Ms. Tonya's kitchen table. I was now eight and a half months pregnant, and we still didn't know what we were having. We tried twice to find out the sex, but both times my baby's tiny legs were closed tight. At that point, Plus and I just agreed to find out when I gave birth.

I hadn't seen Plus in almost a month from when he last came home for Christmas break. While he was at home, I learned that he and Tasha were still a thing. My heart broke a little bit more knowing that the man I secretly loved was loving another woman, but there was nothing I could really say or do. I had hoped that after we made love that last time a few months back, he would see me in a different light, but he never spoke on it and was still on that same "friend" bullshit.

To make matters worse, Plus and Tasha spent most of Christmas break together, so I didn't even get a chance to kick it with him like I really wanted to. We played one game of *Madden,* and he went to a doctor's appointment with me. Other than that, he was stuck up Tasha's ass the entire time. For Christmas, however, he did give me a beautiful silver bracelet with BFF engraved on one of the charms. While I thought the gesture was really sweet, I wanted Plus to see me as more than his BFF. I wanted him to see me as his only lover, his only girl.

"What are you studying, Perri?" Ms. Tonya asked as she stirred mashed potatoes on the stove.

"Biology. It's kicking my ass, too," I said.

"Call Ahmad and see if he can study with you over the phone," she suggested.

"Nah. Between basketball and Tasha's birdbrain ass, he doesn't have time for me," I sulked.

"It will get better when he comes home for the summer, Perri."

When I didn't respond, she said, "Well, you know he's gon' finally play in his first game tonight."

I knew she was only trying to lift my mood, because just like Tez, Ms. Tonya probably knew that I was deeply in love with her son. "Yeah, I'm excited for him. I told him I'd watch."

"Yeah, Tez and your daddy are coming over here at eight to watch it," she said. Tez had been spending a lot more time with us since he had been shot. He had made a full recovery, and I was truly grateful for that.

"Oww!" I said.

"What's wrong?" Ms. Tonya turned around from the stove and asked.

"Nothing. Just these damn Braxton Hicks again."

She turned on the faucet and pulled a glass down from the cabinet. "Well, here, drink some water and then go lie down. You need to put your feet up for a little while," she said, handing me a glass of water.

"Oww! Fuckkk!" I yelled out in pain.

"Are you all right? You're scaring me. And you're gonna have to stop all that damn cussing when the baby comes, too, Perri," she scolded me.

"Yeah, I'm straight," I said, standing up to grab the water from her. As soon as the glass touched my hand, I felt a huge contraction hit my lower abdomen, causing the glass of water to crash down onto the floor.

"Ahhh shittt!" I yelled, grabbing my stomach.

"Shit! It must be time," Ms. Tonya said in a panic.

She helped me into the living room to lie down on the couch before going back into the kitchen to cut off the stove and clean up the mess I had made. Then I heard her say, "Let me call Ahmad now."

"No! Don't call him!" I yelled out to her.

"What the hell you mean don't call him?" she asked, walking back into the living room with a confused look on her face.

"He's finally getting some play time at Georgetown. I don't wanna mess that up for him," I said, still wincing in pain.

"Well, he doesn't want to miss the birth of his firstborn child either, Perri. I'm calling him now!" she repeated.

"Please, Ms. Tonya. Please don't call him," I begged.

Ms. Tonya looked at me and thought about it for a few seconds before she finally said, "Fine. Fine! Let me at least call your daddy."

As my father drove frantically to the hospital with me in the back seat and Ms. Tonya sitting up front, I cried like there was no tomorrow. My contractions were three minutes apart, and I felt like the baby was literally ripping its way up out of me. I had never experienced such horrible pain in all my life, and believe me, over the years I'd definitely had my fair share of bumps, bruises, and broken bones. That was just the price of being a tomboy.

Shortly after my father wheeled me inside the hospital, I found myself set up in a labor and delivery room, hooked up to an IV and a fetal monitor. Once my water broke, I quickly discovered that I was already eight centimeters dilated. In that moment, I wanted nothing more than to have an epidural because I knew it would help numb the pain, but the doctor told me it was too late. So I had no other choice but to have a natural birth.

"Push, Perri. Pushhh!" Ms. Tonya shouted as she held my hand.

"Ahhhh!" I screamed, bearing down to push. I was under so much physical stress that my face was nearly covered in sweat and tears.

"All right, Perri, the baby's head is now crowning. Just a couple more pushes, and you'll have your baby in your arms," Dr. Rosenthal coached. Not that I didn't want to meet my baby, but in the moment, I was just relieved to hear that I only had a few more pushes before the pain would all end.

"Ahhhh, shitttt!" I screamed, giving another push. My entire body was trembling so badly from the pain that I could literally hear my teeth chattering.

"Oh, my God, Perri, I can see the baby's whole head," Ms. Tonya squealed with a light squeeze to my hand.

"One more big push is all we need, Perri," Dr. Rosenthal said.

I took a deep breath to regain what little strength I had left and prepared myself to bear down one more time. "Muthafuckaaaa!" I screamed out, giving that final push with all my might.

That's when I heard her cry for the very first time. It's like something inside of me instantly awakened. All of the pain and tears from just moments before suddenly vanished. Even inwardly I felt different. I was no longer Perri, the tomboy from around the way. Instead, I was now a woman and the mother of a beautiful baby girl.

Looking over as Ms. Tonya cut her umbilical cord, I couldn't do shit but cry. Yes, I cried because I was happy to finally have my baby girl, but I also cried because Plus wasn't there. Not long after I found out I was pregnant, I dreamed day and night of what this day would be like. I envisioned Plus by my side, holding my hand every step of the way.

"Congratulations, Perri. You have a beautiful baby girl," Dr. Rosenthal said, placing her tiny body in my arms.

"I'm going out to the waiting room to get your father and then call Ahmad and Tez," Ms. Tonya said excitedly before walking out of the door.

I looked down and instantly fell in love with my baby. She had a head full of black curly hair like her father, and from looking at her ears, I could already tell that she was going to have his complexion, too. She even had a small beauty mark under her left eye like Plus did. The only thing she had of mine were her amber eyes and full, pouty lips. I couldn't wait for Plus to see what the two of us had created.

Chapter 14

Plus

"Plus! Plus! Plus!" my team cheered, hoisting me high up in the air. We were celebrating another victory, but it was now my time to shine.

As an incoming freshman, I had been riding the pine for the whole first half of the season. However, coach told me that tonight I would finally get some playing time. Although I only got two minutes in the second half, I did a lot in that short amount of time. We were down 62-70 with only two minutes left on the clock. Within the first few seconds, I stepped out on the court and did a sweet layup, followed by a three-point shot. Nothing but net. With only eight seconds remaining, Jorell forcefully passed me the rock. I was a cocky nigga, so I went for another three just to tie the game. Even when number 26 from Villanova fouled me, I still heard the swoosh from the shot I'd made. The final shot of the night was made by me at the free-throw line, delivering a 71-70 final score.

When we made it back to the locker room, I checked my cell phone and noticed that I had two missed calls from my mother and one from Tez. I immediately checked my voicemail messages.

"Ahmad, we're up at the hospital because Perri had the baby," I heard her say excitedly.

The next message was from Tez. "Yo, son, congrats on your little one. Hit me back so I'll know when you on your way," he said.

I immediately called my mother, and she told me that Perri gave birth to our beautiful baby girl almost four hours ago. Instantly, I grew pissed because no one called to tell me that Perri was even in labor. I wanted to be there for her, and even more so, I wanted to see my child being born. Immediately, I went into urgency mode because I knew I needed to get there and fast.

"Yo, Jorell!" I hollered across the locker room. He looked at me, raising his eyebrows and chin in response. "Man, I need a ride home. P just had the baby," I told him.

"Word? Congrats," my other teammate Derrick said.

Jorell walked over and dapped me up before congratulating me as well. "Just let me shower and change, and then we can be bounce," he said. In just a little over six months, Jorell had proven to be a loyal and reliable-ass nigga. Along with TK and Jamal, I now considered him to be my boy.

After we both showered and dressed, we got into his Impala and headed straight for the hospital. The whole ride there I was silent, just watching the highway signs go by. I couldn't believe that just a week shy of my nineteenth birthday, I had actually become someone's father.

When we finally pulled up in the hospital's parking lot that night, I felt a sense of nervousness instantly wash over me. I immediately shook it off and headed for room 318 like my mother said. As I walked into the room, I noticed it was completely full. Not only was our family there gathered around Perri, but my niggas TK and Jamal were there too. Even Nika and Myesha were posted up in the back of the room. Apparently, I was the last one to arrive, and it made me feel some type of way. But when I looked at the tiny being sleeping in Perri's arms, I forgot all about being the last one to get there and made my way farther inside.

"Hey, baby momma, what you got there?" I said, walking up to her bedside. Everyone was congratulating me, but my eyes were solely focused on Perri and my baby.

Perri's teary eyes lit up with love and joy as soon as she saw me. I brushed her wild, bushy hair back and kissed her forehead before looking down at my daughter for the very first time. No lie, she was the most beautiful thing I had ever seen. I chuckled a little looking over her features because she was the spitting image of me.

"She looks just like you, doesn't she?" Perri said, reading my thoughts. I nodded in response.

"You wanna hold her?" she softly asked.

"Yeah, let me hold my li'l momma after I wash my hands," I said, making my way to the sink in the room.

As I held her carefully in my arms, my mother made everyone leave the room. She said Perri and I needed to have our bonding time. Having this baby with Perri made me realize that we would forever be connected, and that shit just made me smile. I couldn't ask for a better person to be joined to for the rest of my life. Yeah, I had my boys, but Perri was my best friend. She was irreplaceable.

"What's her name?" I looked over at Perri and asked.

"I didn't name her yet. I wanted to wait for you," she said softly.

I took one more look down at my sleeping angel and instantly knew what her name would be. "Her name is Camille," I confirmed with a smile.

Perri gasped before looking up at me with tears pooled in her eyes again. "You wanna . . . name her after my mother?" she asked. Her amber eyes were wide as she held a look of surprise.

"Of course. What else would I name her?" I rhetorically asked.

She covered her mouth for a few seconds and slowly shook her head. "Thank you, Plus. That really means a lot to me."

***

Later that evening, I lay back on the recliner with my daughter sleeping peacefully on my chest. Just as I was about to close my eyes, there was a soft knock on the door. Before Perri or I could even say come in, the door opened, and Tasha appeared. I had called her when I was on my way to the hospital.

She was dressed down in a pair of boot-cut jeans, black boots, and a red sweater. Her long black hair casually swung in a high ponytail, while her pretty face was makeup free. When our eyes met, she only gave me a half smile. Things between us were still rocky. She was so upset about me sleeping with Perri and getting her pregnant that she didn't speak to me for four whole months. No matter how much I tried to assure her that Perri and I weren't like that, she would somehow bring the situation back up all over again. Then we would go back and not talk for weeks at a time. Since Christmas, she and I had been kicking it pretty heavy this go-round, so I was hopeful about our relationship.

"Congratulations, Plus," she said lowly, walking over to me. She never even acknowledged Perri's presence, and that's the shit I couldn't stand.

"Shorty, you ain't even gon' speak to my baby's mom?" I asked, wearing a pissed look on my face. She knew I didn't play that shit, especially when it came to Perri, whether I cheated on her ass or not.

"My bad. Congratulations, Perri," Tasha quickly responded in a low tone without even looking Perri in the eyes. I just shook my head because shorty was a trip.

Tasha then looked down at baby Camille, who had begun to squirm on top of me. Turning her over, I propped her up in my arms so that Tasha could have a better look. Specifically, I wanted Tasha to see her beautiful light eyes. I kept talking to baby Camille, playing with her tiny hands and feet in hopes that she would open them, but my little angel just flat-out refused.

"Her name is Camille," I told her, still looking down at my daughter with a smile.

"She's beautiful, Plus. She looks just like you," Tasha commented.

That's when I heard Perri let out a deep sigh. I guessed she took Tasha's comment as some type of shade, but I let it ride because I wasn't really for the drama. When I looked over at Perri, she was glaring hard at me with the meanest mug on her face. I'd known her all my life, so I knew I needed to hurry up and get Tasha the fuck out of there before Perri went off.

"But yeah, this my li'l momma," I said, trying to bring Tasha's visit to a close. "I'm gon' be staying here with P until they get discharged so . . ." I told her, letting my voice trail off. I was hoping that she could take a hint, but of course, she pulled up a chair and sat her ass right down beside me.

"Can I hold her?" she asked me sweetly.

Before I could even answer, Perri cut in and snapped, "No, Tasha, you cannot!"

Tasha scrunched her face up in response and was already snaking her neck, so I knew she was getting ready to pop off at the mouth. But before she could even come back with something slick, I decided to dead the whole situation. The last thing I needed was for my baby to be around all that cussing and fussing bullshit when she hadn't even been in the world a full twenty-four hours.

"Yo, Tash, I'm just gon' holla at you tomorrow, a'ight?" I quickly stood up and said.

I passed Perri the baby and started walking toward the door. When I looked back at Tasha, her ass was still sitting down with her arms folded across her chest. With my lips twisted, I slightly jerked my head back and questioned her with my eyes.

"Fuck is you doing?" I barked because she knew what time it was.

"You always put this bitch before me, and I'm tired of that shit, Plus," she fussed, getting up from her chair and stomping over toward the door.

"Bitch?" Perri questioned with a scowl.

I just held my hand up to stop her, letting her know I'd handle it.

"Yeah, that's what I said, bitch," Tasha said again, rolling her eyes. Then she focused her eyes directly on me and reached down into the pocket of her jeans. "G'on 'head and play family now, nigga, but you gonna be doing this same shit with me in about nine more months." After pulling her hand out of her pocket, she roughly placed a positive pregnancy test in my hand before turning on her heels and storming out the door.

Chapter 15

Perri

Sitting on Nika's bed after class, I blankly stared at the wall, allowing my mind to drift. It had been almost three months since Camille was born, and although I still hadn't found a job, I was going to school. With the money Tez gave me and the little bit Plus sent to Camille from his college refund check, we were doing just fine anyway.

Nika was going on and on, talking my head off about something, but I hadn't heard a word she said because my mind was contemplating the invitation Ms. Tonya extended to me. She wanted me and Tez to ride up to Georgetown with her and Aria this weekend. It was Plus's final game of the season, and since he'd gotten a bunch of free tickets, they were going to go show their support. Plus also told Ms. Tonya that he wanted to see the baby since he hadn't been home in almost a month. Truthfully, that was the only reason I was even considering going in the first place.

After Camille was born, my relationship with Plus started to take a dive. When I first heard that Tasha was pregnant, I literally felt my heart breaking to the point where I couldn't even breathe. Not only was Plus sharing something so precious with her, but he lied to me about always using protection. Crushed and ashamed of just how stupid I could be, I stayed to myself and cried myself to sleep for almost a whole week after that.

"What are you over there thinking about?" Nika asked, taking me from my thoughts.

"Nothing, just thinking," I said, not really wanting to talk.

"Thinking about that fine-ass baby daddy of yours, huh?" she asked knowingly through the mirror with a smirk on her face. She was sitting down at her vanity, putting her curly hair up into a ponytail.

I let out a small snort of laughter and shrugged my shoulders. Over the past few months, Nika and I had been joined at the hip. While Plus, TK, and Jamal were all either off at college or doing their own thing, Nika had quickly become their replacement. I never thought I'd like hanging around females, but she was actually cool. She helped me out with Camille and even gave me rides whenever I needed them. She listened diligently as I told her the whole story of Plus and me. And while she'd offer advice every now and then, she wasn't pushy. She was simply a good friend.

"Ms. Tonya asked for me and Tez to ride up to Georgetown this weekend with her to see Plus. It's the last game of the season, and you already know he wants to see Camille," I said. Just to say her name aloud had me thinking about my little munchkin and how cute she was. It seemed as though she was getting fatter by the hour and looking more like her father with each day that passed.

"So you going?" she asked with a sneaky smirk on her face.

Twisting my lips to the side, I shrugged my shoulders again. "I'on know. Probably not."

"I think you should, and as a matter of fact, I'm going with you," she said, standing up from her vanity chair.

"I don't know, Nika. I'm really not ready to deal with Plus's baby-making ass just yet."

"Hmm?" she quizzed with her finger up to her chin.

"Hmm what?" I asked with my eyebrow raised.

"Okay, now keep an open mind pleassee," she started saying before coming to sit next to me on the bed. "What if you let me do a little something to your hair?" she continued, grabbing the end of one of my braids. "Maybe even a little makeover. I can wax your eyebrows, and you're about my size so—"

"No offense, Nika," I said, putting one hand up to stop her, "but I'm not changing myself for no nigga." I shook my head and licked my lips, preparing to further explain. "I mean, don't get me wrong. I love Plus and always will, but if he doesn't like me for me, ain't shit a makeover can do to help that."

"Yeah, you're right, but have you ever told Plus the way you truly feel about him?"

"No, but I shouldn't have to get a makeover just to get him to notice me in that way."

"I wouldn't be so sure about that, Perri. I mean, he is a man, but hey, I won't push the issue. Hell, I think you're bomb just the way you are anyway, so if he can't see that, then fuck 'im."

"Yeah, fuck 'im!" I said with a smile. "I like that." Nika and I both fell out laughing.

After chilling with Nika for about another hour or so, she dropped me off at Ms. Tonya's house. When I walked in, Camille was sitting in the baby swing, fast asleep. Some old-school R&B played softly in the background while the smell of fried chicken being cooked lingered in the air. I quickly dropped my book bag to the floor before leaning down and placing a gentle kiss on the top of Camille's head. She stirred a little but remained asleep. When I walked into the kitchen, Ms. Tonya was standing at the stove, cooking, with her housecoat on and pink rollers in her hair.

"Hey, baby, how was class?" she asked, looking back at me.

"It was okay," I replied, taking my favorite seat at the table. "How was my baby? She didn't give you any trouble today, did she?"

Ms. Tonya pursed her lips. "Now you know Camille don't give me any trouble. That baby is an angel."

"Ummhmm. You just spoil her is what it is."

"So, have you given any thought to what I asked you?" Ms. Tonya asked.

"About what?" I asked dryly, already knowing exactly what she was referring to.

She sucked her teeth and cut her eyes back at me from where she stood in front of the stove. With a wooden spoon in her hand, she let out a heavy sigh and turned around. "Look, I know that son of mine has some player ways, and I don't agree with them at all. And I also know that you're angry about Tasha being pregnant, and rightfully so," she said, putting her other hand in the air. "But you two are bonded for life, Perri. Not only because of the history you share, but because of that precious little angel in there," she explained, pointing toward the living room with her spoon. "Whatever it takes, you two need to move past this shit and make it right, okay?"

I took in everything that Ms. Tonya had said and simply nodded my head. She was right. I had to put my feelings aside for once and think solely about Camille. Just because her father was an asshole who got the one girl in the world I couldn't stand pregnant, it didn't mean she had to suffer. She deserved two parents who not only loved her but who could also get along.

"Fine. I'll go," I huffed. "But only if Nika can go too."

"I don't have no problems with Nika going. I need to check with Tez to make sure he's still going too."

"Yeah, he told me yesterday that he and Myesha were going up there."

"Oh, good. I'm getting excited now." Ms. Tonya smiled, setting a plate of fried chicken, dirty rice, and green beans on the table in front of me.

It seemed as though the week had flown by, and Friday morning was now here. As Nika and I packed Ms. Tonya's car, getting all of our luggage and Camille's car seat inside, I could hear the loud bass of an oncoming car. With my head still dipped down inside the trunk, I looked back over my shoulder only to see Tez riding up in a green Honda Accord. Driving his black Acura right behind him was Myesha.

"Y'all ready or what?" Tez hollered out, honking the horn just to be annoying. His arm was hanging out of the window, and a shiny Rolex was sparkling on his wrist. I walked over toward him and stuck my head in the car, immediately taking in the tan leather seats and the sweet scent of vanilla mixed with a hint of weed.

"Whose car is that?" I asked, getting excited. I didn't have a car, so secretly I was hoping that my brother had bought it for me.

"I copped this shit for Plus. Nigga needs to be able to get home from school if something were to happen to y'all. Nah mean?"

He licked his lips, and with one hand on the steering wheel, he leaned all the way back in his seat. I just sucked my teeth and rolled my eyes before walking away. Don't get me wrong, I understood where he was coming from about Plus needing a way to get back home, but shit, I needed a car too. Here I was in school with a baby and also trying to find a job. Sure, Nika and Ms. Tonya were a big help, but it wasn't their job to assist me. Tez was my blood family, not Plus's.

As Aria hopped in the front seat of Ms. Tonya's car and Nika jumped in the back, I walked inside the house to grab

Camille. Dressed in a tiny Georgetown jersey that had the number 23 and "My Daddy" displayed on the back, she squirmed in a little rocker seat that sat on the floor. After grabbing up the diaper bag, I quickly scooped her up in my arms and placed a tender kiss to her chubby cheek. She smiled and cooed at just the sight of me. Moments later, Ms. Tonya, Camille, and I all headed out of the door and got into the car.

It was a short ride up to Georgetown, being less than an hour drive. Our first stop was to the Washington Plaza hotel over on Thomas. Tez had booked us three separate rooms, and I couldn't be more pleased. Sure, I had stayed in a nice hotel a time or two in my lifetime, but none of them compared to this. My mouth slightly dropped when we entered the lobby, seeing the beautiful marble floors gleam from the bright light cascading down from the crystal chandeliers. Bellhops stood around in fine three-piece suits, all just waiting to serve us while the white people walking by just waved and smiled. Tez had truly outdone himself.

As soon as Nika and I entered our room, she belly flopped down on the first bed seen with both her arms and legs spread out wide. The two queen-sized beds in the room were neatly made with a thick white down comforter, and several fluffy white pillows were stacked up against the headboard. To say that the room was inviting would have been an understatement. In fact, the beds were practically begging to be slept in, and when I walked over to the window, skimming my fingertips gently across the sheer white fabric of the curtains, I could have sworn I felt silk.

"Damn, yo. Tez hooked us up," I said, peering out the window.

"Yes, he did! Girl, if your brother weren't already taken, I swear I'd holla," Nika said, making me scrunch my nose up at her. I knew girls found my brother attractive but I damn sure didn't want to hear about it.

"Whatever," I said, opening up my suitcase to take out my outfit for the game. I planned on wearing a plain white tee with a Georgetown jersey on top of it. Light blue jeans and navy blue New Balance sneakers on my feet would complete my look. As I laid out everything on the bed, I noticed a frown etched on Nika's face.

"That's what you're wearing?" she asked with her nose turned up.

"Yeah, why? We're just going to a basketball game."

"I know but . . ." she said with her voice trailing off.

"Well, what are you wearing?"

Nika held up a small Georgetown T-shirt and some tight-fitting boot-cut jeans. It was nice, but to me, it wasn't any different than me wearing my jersey. Yes, my shirt and jeans were a little baggier than the cute, feminine outfit she had to wear, but all in all, there wasn't much difference in my opinion.

"Cool," was all I said before heading to the bathroom to take my shower.

About an hour later, we all got in the cars and headed over to the game. The coliseum was packed with raging Georgetown and Villanova fans alike. Our first stop was to the concession stand because Ms. Tonya just had to get her some popcorn, and after that, we all headed for the stairwell. With Camille strapped to my chest, we finally made our way up to the club seats Plus had reserved. The first person my eyes landed on, sitting right in our row, was Tasha. I wanted to kill Plus in that moment, because at this point, the nigga was really playing with my feelings.

"Hey, Tasha. How you doin', baby?" Ms. Tonya asked, leaning down to give her a half hug. Ms. Tonya didn't care for Tasha too much, but she respected the fact that she was Plus's girl. Besides, now she was also going to be the mother of one of her grandchildren.

"Hey, Ms. Tonya. When did y'all get here?" Tasha asked, letting her eyes roam over to me and the rest of the crew.

I took my seat and sat four chairs down from where Tasha was sitting. With Nika and Aria on my left and Myesha and Tez to my right, I simply ignored her. As things started to progress on the basketball court, I found myself not paying attention to the game. Between bouncing Camille on my knee and listening to Nika talk my ear off, I found myself consumed with thoughts of Plus actually having a baby by someone else.

When the final buzzer sounded, Georgetown had won 90-74. Plus himself had scored a total of 32 points, so I knew he was happy as shit. After making our way back downstairs, we stood waiting outside of the locker room where he told us all to meet him. As I glanced over at Tasha, I had to admit that she was beautiful in every sense of the word. Even just after the wintertime, her dark brown skin glowed like it had been kissed by the damn sun. She had on a cute little Georgetown T-shirt that fit snug across her breasts, while her long black hair just poured over her shoulders like running water. My hair, on the other hand, was braided back into two long, frizzy braids that Ms. Tonya had put in four days ago.

"What up, fam," Plus hollered, finally coming out of the locker room.

Ms. Tonya and Aria were the first to go up and give him a tight hug. Then Tez quickly went over and dapped him up. When his eyes finally landed on me and Camille, he grinned so wide I swear I could see damn near all the teeth in his mouth. I guessed Ms. Tonya didn't tell him that we were coming so he'd be completely surprised. He walked right over to us and gave me a hug first before pulling Camille out of my hold. She was so happy to see her daddy that she was bouncing and flailing all around in his arms. Although I was pissed at Plus, I couldn't help but smile seeing the two of them together.

"There goes Daddy's sweet girl," he said, kissing her on the cheek. "And look at your jersey. My baby's looking fly, y'all." He then cut his eyes over at me and gave me a half smile as if he knew I was the one to dress her. "I know you ain't fucking wit' me like that right now, but I really do appreciate you coming, P."

I shrugged my shoulders as if it were no big deal. "Yeah, I just wanted you to get a chance to see Camille," I said nonchalantly. Plus knew me like the back of his hand, so he was fully aware that I was still mad.

He simply nodded his head in return before making his way over to Tasha. Inwardly, I cringed when he leaned down to gently peck her on the lips. Holding Camille in just one of his arms, he took his right hand and placed it to Tasha's flat pregnant belly. I felt my eyes begin to water at the mere sight. Just months ago, he was doing that same shit with me, and now I was having to watch the two of them with my baby in his arms. They were looking like the perfect fucking family while I felt alone and completely out of place. To avoid anyone seeing me upset, I quickly turned away and played it off by looking down at my phone. Nika knew what was up though, because I could feel her hand gently stroking my back from behind in an attempt to comfort me.

"Aye, man, y'all going out tonight with us to celebrate?" another one of Plus's teammates passed by and asked. He was a big, tall, light-skinned guy who was easy on the eyes. He was definitely a pretty nigga, but somehow he gave off this bad-boy vibe. A few tattoos were scattered across the smooth caramel flesh of his muscular arms, and in his left eyebrow were two perfectly sliced nicks.

"Umm, nah, man. Probably not," Plus answered with uncertainty in his voice.

Ms. Tonya cut right in. "No, y'all go on out, and I'll watch the baby back at the hotel. Y'all are too young to be cooped up with me on a Saturday night," she said.

"Yess," I could hear Nika murmur in excitement.

"All right then. We'll probably see you out there," he said, dapping his teammate up.

After spending a little bit more time with Camille, Plus and Tasha left to go their separate way while the rest of us headed back to the hotel. As soon as Nika and I entered the room, I sat down on the edge of the bed, thinking about Plus and all the things that had transpired between us over the years: the ups, the downs, and everything in between.

"What you over there thinking about, girl?" Nika asked, looking through her suitcase for something to wear.

I scratched the top of my head and smirked. "You still wanna do a makeover?" When I saw the devilish grin spread wide across my friend's face, I said a silent prayer in hopes that I was making the right move.

Chapter 16

Plus

I really hated that Perri was mad at me. As soon as I saw her standing over there with Camille in her arms, I wanted to run over and give her a forehead kiss like I always did. This was the longest she had ever stayed mad at me, and I was missing my best friend something terrible. I realized that it was me who fucked up by getting Tasha pregnant in the first place, and now I was suffering the consequences.

As for Tasha and me, we were still together, trying to make this shit work. When she walked into the hospital that night after my daughter was born, I was just getting ready to say fuck it and end it with her. At the first sight of Camille's beautiful little face, I knew my full attention had to be on her and basketball, so a relationship with Tasha was quickly going to become the least of my worries. But when she dropped that bomb on me about being pregnant, I swear a nigga just didn't have the heart to break up with her.

Sitting down in the dimly lit club, I watched as Tasha swayed her hips to the beat. She had her hands up high in the air above her head, waving them to Petey Pablo's "Freek-A-Leek." Being that she was pregnant and all, I told her that she should probably just chill back in my dorm room for the night and get some rest, but she wasn't trying to hear none of that shit. Instead, she threw a fucking hissy fit and insisted on coming. Looking at her now, you wouldn't even know she was pregnant the way she was bending over to touch her toes and shit.

"Come on, shorty, cut that shit out," I said, tapping her on the thigh. All my teammates knew Tasha was pregnant, so she was embarrassing the shit out of me right now. Turning around, she scrunched up her pretty little face and rolled her eyes. She pulled down the tiny blue dress she wore that was slowly rising up on her thighs and took her seat down beside me. She instantly folded her arms across her chest.

I looked out to the crowded dance floor to see Jorell making his way toward us with a white towel draped around his neck. Even though the club was dim, I could still see his gold teeth shining from the flirtatious smile he gave while passing all the ladies by. I swear, watching him in the club with Master P's "Mr. Ice Cream Man" playing in the background was like looking at a low-budget rap video from down South. After switching the toothpick over to the other corner of his mouth, he leaned down to dap me up.

"What's going on, mane?" he asked, taking a seat down next me.

"Ain't shit. I saw you doing your thing out there," I told him, referring to the way he was just grinding up on some shorties in the center of the floor.

"Yuh, I be freakin' 'em, mane," he said with a light chuckle.

Two of my other teammates, Derrick and Vince, also walked over and sat down with us. Vince was the shortest player on the team, standing at only five foot eight inches tall. He was dark skinned and wore a high-top fade. Derrick, on the other hand, was taller than me by an inch or so and had a light caramel complexion. He was our power forward, and just like me, everyone assumed he'd be next to make it to the NBA.

"What's up, man?" Derrick said, leaning over to dap me up.

"Ain't shit. Just here kicking it with Tasha and waiting for the rest of my peoples to come through," I told him.

"What, your homeboys from back home?" Derrick asked, twisting his Yankees cap to the back.

"Nah, my brother, his girl, and my baby momma," I told him.

He leaned up in his chair and cut his eyes over at Tasha, who was dancing in her seat, not paying either one of us any attention. Raising his right eyebrow, he asked, "Your other baby momma coming here tonight too?"

I let out a light chuckle. "Yeah, she's my daughter's mother, but honestly it's not like that between us. She's my best friend. Like one of the guys. You'll see."

Derrick just shook his head, not believing a word I'd said. I was used to seeing that reaction. No matter how hard I tried to explain my relationship with Perri, no one ever believed that we were just friends. Even TK and Jamal started questioning us after she got pregnant. True, I didn't look at Perri like a sister, or else I wouldn't have had sex with her, but I wasn't lying when I said she was my best friend.

"Yeah, man, she's just like one of the guys. I mean, she ain't bad looking or nothing, but she fa damn sho act just like a nigga," Jorell cut in and said with a shake of his head. I let out a small snort of laughter before he continued. "I'm fa real, breh. You sure your baby momma ain't gay?"

As I playfully punched him in the arm for making that dumb-ass remark, Tasha leaned up and just had to put her two cents in. "That's the same shit I said, Jorell. Ain't no way in hell her manly ass ain't gay," she said matter-of-factly with her lips pursed to the side. My boys all fell out in laughter at Perri's expense while I just shook my head.

"Man, Tasha, stop assuming shit," I told her.

"I'm serious, Plus. You need to watch her and that little girl she's been kicking it with too," she said with a simple-ass smirk on her face.

Again, I shook my head at Tasha's stupidity. *If only she could hear the way Perri moans and screams my name when I'm fucking the shit out of her,* I thought. I mean, don't get me wrong. Physically, Perri wasn't my style, nor was she the kind of girly girl I wanted to have on my arm, but I knew for a fact that she wasn't gay.

All of a sudden, I could hear a lot of gasps and mumbles coming from off the dance floor over the music. When I looked out into the crowd, I noticed that a lot of guys had stopped dancing and were all looking toward the door as if a celebrity was entering the building. Narrowing my eyes, I tried to see what all the commotion was about. My mouth practically hit the floor when Perri and Nika appeared.

In all my life I had never seen Perri look more beautiful than she did that night. Her long brown hair was straightened into silk, cascading all the way down to her ass. She wore a little bit of light makeup on her face, and even her eyebrows looked different. Arched, I believe is what it's called. The tight red dress she had on clung to her curvy, wide hips and full-sized breasts, showing off the unforeseen figure of a video vixen. And on her feet were a pair of low gold heels that she could barely walk in.

"Damn," Derrick muttered lowly, eyeing Perri from afar.

As Perri tried making her way through the thick crowd, I saw a bunch of dudes grabbing at her and trying to spit game. She didn't pay them any mind though. Instead, she balled her face up, and even from a distance I could see that she was cussing niggas out. When she glanced up to where I was, we locked eyes for a brief moment, and she gave me a half smile similar to the one she had given me earlier after the game.

Just as I thought she was about to head our way, Nika quickly pulled her in the center of the dance floor. Without even thinking, I stood up from my seat so I could watch the two of them in action. Perri wasn't the most feminine girl in the world, so I was curious to see how she was going to move. Shyly she stood frozen in place while Nika danced in front of her, grabbing ahold of her hips. After a few seconds of Nika swaying her body from side to side, Perri began to dance on her own. It wasn't anything sexy or over-the-top, just a little two-step, but at least she was on beat.

"See, I told you them bitches was gay," Tasha said.

Honestly, I was so mesmerized by Perri that I had completely forgotten Tasha's ass was even still sitting there. I looked down at her where she sat next me and sucked my teeth at her comment. I knew she was probably just jealous, so it wasn't worth even saying anything. When I looked back at the dance floor where Perri and Nika were previously dancing, they were no longer there. Immediately, I let my eyes roam all around the club in search of the two of them, but they were nowhere in sight.

"Who you looking for, mane?" Jorell asked.

"Let me guess. Shorty in the red dress with all that long, pretty-ass hair," Derrick said knowingly with a slick grin on his face.

"Man," I said, waving him off with a suck of my teeth. "That's just my baby momma I was telling you about."

"Damn! That's your baby momma?" he asked with wide eyes. "Nigga, I was expecting her to look like a dude, the way y'all was talking. Shorty bad as fuck. I can see those pretty-ass eyes she got from all the way over here," he said, shaking his head.

As soon as Derrick let those words fly from his mouth, Nika and Perri appeared, walking straight toward us. It seemed almost as if they were walking in slow motion because I could see each of my boys' heads turn one at a time. Their eyes lit up with lust as they followed the girls' every move. Even Nika looked pretty in her tight mustard yellow dress that exposed the tops of her smooth brown shoulders. Her cinnamon-colored curls were put up loosely in a ponytail, displaying her gold hoop earrings and long, pretty neck.

Hearing a loud sigh of annoyance coming from behind me, I opened my arms up wide to give Perri a hug. After giving her a tight squeeze, I looked back to see Tasha rolling her eyes. I just shook my head before making my way back down into my seat. While Nika went to go sit next to Jorell, Derrick and Vince both slid over a seat, making room for Perri so that she could sit next to me.

"Damn, P. What the fuck did you do to yourself?" I leaned over and whispered in her ear, taking in the light scent of her sweet-smelling perfume.

She smiled and shook her head. "Nigga, wouldn't you like to know." After a teasing grin stretched across her face, she crossed one smooth-shaven leg over the other.

"You look . . ." Pausing, I licked my lips, allowing my eyes to slowly travel her body from head to toe. There were absolutely no words to describe how beautiful and sexy she looked in that moment.

"I look what?" she quizzed with her eyebrows scrunched together.

"Damn," I muttered, biting down on my bottom lip because that was all I could even think to say or do at the time. Perri quickly turned her head away in response, trying to hide her blushing smile.

As I sat there all but drooling over my best friend and the mother of my firstborn child, Tasha came and abruptly sat on my lap. To say she caught me completely off guard would be an understatement. Jerking my neck back, I glared hard at her with my eyes silently asking what the fuck she was doing. Just as I was about to cuss her ass out for interrupting the vibe I had going on with Perri, I remembered that she too was pregnant with my child and that technically she was my girl. After running my hand down my waves, I let out a deep sigh and softened the hard look on my face.

I leaned up to talk directly in her ear over the loud music. "What's up, Tash?"

"Baby, I'm feeling nauseous, and I don't feel well. You 'bout ready?" she whined.

"Tasha, we just got here," I said, already feeling myself growing pissed.

"I know, but I can't help it. I think I just need to lie down."

"That's why I told you to stay yo' ass back at the room, Tasha!" I yelled, causing her to jump a little.

As I was sitting there going back and forth with Tasha's silly ass, I could hear Perri and Derrick start a little conversation all of their own. I knew by the way Derrick had been looking at Perri and talking about how good she looked that he was most likely feeling her. But the fact still remained that she was my baby momma. So in my eyes, she was off-limits.

"Yo, you out?" Jorell asked when I dapped him up.

"Yeah. Tasha ain't feeling good," I said, twisting my lips to the side.

"Damn, mane, y'all just got here," he said disappointedly, putting his arm around Nika. "Well, I hope she feel better."

"Y'all rolling with us? Where Tez and Myesha at?" I asked, looking first at Nika then back to Perri for a response.

"They stayed back at the hotel. Ms. Tonya just let me drive her car," Perri explained. "We just got here, so we're gonna chill for a little while. I'll call you when we make it in though."

Even though I wanted her and Nika to leave with me and Tasha, I didn't say shit. For me to cut her and Nika's fun short just for Tasha would be fucked up, so I simply nodded my head in response. After giving Perri a simple kiss on the forehead and dapping up all my niggas, I made my way out of the club, pissed, with Tasha trailing behind me.

Chapter 17

Perri

Never in all my years of living had I gotten this much attention from the opposite sex. I mean, as soon as Nika and I hit the club, guys were fondling us and catcalling like men who'd been imprisoned for the last ten years. Just when I thought sweatpants and basketball shorts were the way to go, Nika put me in this hot little red dress that had me starting to be a believer. For the first time in my life, I felt beautiful.

Judging by the way Plus and all his friends gawked when we walked up, I knew I must have looked good. Even Tasha's ass was jealous, which was why she got Plus to leave early. When they both stood up announcing that they were heading home, I was actually thinking about leaving too. But seeing as how I was all wrapped up with this Derrick guy and the attention he was giving me, I decided to hang out for a bit.

I'd seen him talking to Plus earlier after the game, and I'd be the first to admit that he was easy on the eyes. He had a tall, muscular physique like Dwayne Wade but with a pretty, caramel complexion and dark brown eyes. Underneath the Yankees cap he wore turned to the back, I could see the fresh edge up of hair. And although he had this low-cut beard growing slightly across the line of his jaw, he actually had the face of a baby. Deep dimples pierced the sides of his face each and every time he smiled while just a few light freckles were sprinkled above his cheeks. His teeth were so white and perfect, I couldn't help but to stare. Before now, Plus had been the only guy I was ever attracted to, but there was something about this Derrick guy that I found myself instantly drawn to.

"So what's going on, ma?" he asked, licking his full dark pink lips.

Feeling a little bit nervous, I squirmed in my chair. Sure, I hung out with guys all the time, but this was different. The way he had his arm thrown over the back of my chair and leaned into me whenever he spoke, allowing me to feel the warmth of his breath across my skin, was just intense. Tucking a piece of wispy hair behind my ear like I'd seen the girly girls do a million times before, I cleared my throat. "Nothing. What's up with you?"

"You looking all scared and shit. I'm not gon' hurt you, ma. You want me to get you a drink?" he asked, gently placing his hand on the top of my knee.

I knew I shouldn't have been feeling this way, but my pussy started to throb from that gesture alone. Every time he licked his lips and spoke in that deep, rugged voice of his, it seemed as if my internal temperature would rise a single degree, if not more. The tattoos decorating both of his arms and the gold chain around his neck gave off this bad-boy vibe that I found to be damn near magnetizing. I could hear my father's voice in my head now telling me to stay away from them "yo boys."

"No. I'm good. Thank you though," I said, turning my head away to gain my composure.

"So what's up with you and that nigga Plus? Y'all got a baby together?" he came right out and asked.

"Yeah, something like that."

"But he's with the other girl, right? What's her name?" he asked with a snap of his fingers, trying to remember. "Tasha?"

Just hearing it out loud that Tasha was indeed Plus's girl had me feeling angry all over again. Initially I came out to the club all dolled up just to let Plus know what he was missing out on, but the fact that Derrick was showing me so much attention and Plus had already left with Tasha's birdbrain ass had me feeling some type of way.

"Yeah, he's with Tasha," I said softly, coming to the realization of the actual words I spoke.

Derrick stood up from his seat and reached his hand out for me to grab. Cutting my eyes over in Nika and Jorell's direction, I hoped to get some signal of approval. But they were both wrapped up in what seemed to be a pretty hot and steamy make-out session. Timidly, I took his hand and stood up next to him. Placing his hand gently on the small of my back, he led me back down to the dance floor. I grew so nervous that I was beginning to sweat a little, all because I knew I couldn't dance to save my life. The way these chicks in here were throwing their asses from left to right, there was no way I could compete, and I honestly didn't know how he'd feel about that.

"Gahdamn, nigga! That's you?" some lame in the crowd asked Derrick while pointing at me. In between a bunch of other chauvinistic comments, we continued to walk through the crowd. Derrick ignored them all though, pulling me into a private corner right there on the dance floor. Wedging his back up against the wall, he placed me directly in front of him so that my back was pressed up against his muscular chest. As J-Kwon's "Tipsy" blared throughout the club, he firmly grabbed me by the waist. His strong hands just gripped at my sides like he was ready to fuck right then and there. My breath instantly grew shallow, feeling his hard manhood pressed up against my ass.

"Shake something fa me, ma," he leaned down and whispered in my ear, two-stepping to the beat behind me. Although I was nervous, I knew I needed to move. Rhythmless, I began dancing in the complete opposite direction as him. Offbeat and damn near stepping on his toes, I continued to sway. However, to my surprise, he spun me around to face him and pulled me in close.

"Don't worry, sweetheart. I got you," he whispered. His warm breath slightly tickled at my ear, creating a single pulse between my thighs just before he wrapped his arms around my waist.

As if on cue, the music slowed down. Derrick held me so close that I had no choice but to rest my head on his brawny chest. Closing my eyes, I took in the soft, clean scent of his cologne as he sang the lyrics directly in my ear. While our bodies rocked side to side, he all but purred.

I smiled hearing that this nigga could actually sing. I mean, he was hitting every high note, run, and falsetto. Damn, everything about this nigga was perfect, from the top of his head to the bottom of his size-twelve feet. We stayed cuddled up in that corner, pressed together like two pages in a book, dancing for the rest of the night.

When the club finally closed down a little after two, we walked outside and waited for Nika and Jorell in the parking lot. It was a little chilly, so as we stood next to Ms. Tonya's car, he enclosed me in his arms.

"What up, D?" A tall, lanky guy stopped and dapped Derrick up. "No disrespect, but your lady is beautiful, man," he said, slowly looking me over.

"'Preciate it, son," Derrick told him with a nod of his head right before we both watched the guy continue on his way.

"Your lady, huh?" I questioned, looking up into Derrick's eyes.

Shifting his eyes up toward the dark sky, he gave me a sneaky smirk. He glanced back down at me then licked his lips. "On my muva, if it's the last thing on this earth I do, I'm gon' make you my lady, ma."

"Just like that? After knowing me for all of, what, four hours?" I said in disbelief.

"Have you ever heard of love at first sight?"

I laughed because this nigga was really running game.

"Why you laughing, yo?" he asked and then chuckled himself. "I'm serious right now," he said with a grin so wide, each of his dimples suddenly appeared. Allowing my eyes to slowly roam over his entire face and all of its handsome features, I smiled. Then a thought occurred.

"I'm leaving to go back home tomorrow," I damn near whined with a little frown.

"Where is home?"

"PG County," I said.

"Huh?"

"About thirty, forty minutes away," I explained. I looked up into his eyes again, silently hoping that it wouldn't be too far away. With my arms still wrapped tightly around his waist and my breasts securely pressed up against his abs, I waited for what felt like a lifetime for his response.

He stared down at me almost as if he was trying to figure out what was going through my mind. Taking his bottom lip between his teeth, he shook his head and gave that same small smirk. "Ain't no problem, ma. I got a whip," he finally said, leaning back on the car and widening his stance.

Silently, I prayed that he couldn't see just how desperate I was to see him again.

"I'm from the Boogie Down myself," he said, twisting his Yankees cap to the front.

"Huh?"

"The Bronx. New York," he said, licking his lips. "I'm here on a basketball scholarship."

"Oh, nice," I said, shaking my head. "How often do you get back home?"

Before he could even respond, Nika walked up with her heels in her hand. "Girl, I was in the damn club still looking for your ass! You mean to tell me that you've been out here booed up all this time?" she snapped with Jorell following her.

"Yeah. Derrick was just out here keeping me company until you came. That's all."

Nika rolled her eyes then turned around to give Jorell one final goodbye kiss for the night. Meanwhile, Derrick took that opportunity to get my phone number.

"It was nice meeting you, Derrick," I said.

"All my pleasure, sweetheart," he said, kissing me tenderly on the cheek.

As I watched Jorell and Derrick walk away, the smile I had been trying to hide all night slowly crept across my face.

"Bitch!" Nika yelled out. I turned to look at her, and she had her lips pursed to the side. "'It was nice meeting you, Derrick,'" she mocked in the most girly voice imaginable, hand gingerly pressed up against her chest while dramatically batting her eyes.

"Yo, shut up. I ain't even sound like that," I said, rolling my eyes.

"And just that fast," she said with a snap of her fingers, "your ass done went back to sounding like a nigga." We both fell out laughing because it was so true. Not once the entire night did I curse or use slang. I even crossed my legs the whole time I sat down, which was totally rare for me.

As we eased into the car, Nika glanced over at me. "Girl, I thought you came out tonight to get Plus to notice you."

"I did."

"So are you gonna call Derrick then?"

I kept quiet for few seconds, pretending to mull the question over in my mind before looking over at her. "Hell yeah! Did you see how fine that nigga was?" We slapped hands and laughed before I cranked up the car to head back to the hotel.

Chapter 18

Plus

Perri didn't call me until three o'clock in the morning to let me know she'd made it in after the club. Between worrying about her and Tasha snoring like a damn grizzly bear all night, I swear I didn't get a wink of sleep. Even still, I told Perri that I wanted to spend the morning with her and Camille before they left to go back home. Our next break wasn't for another couple of weeks, and I needed some more time with my li'l momma to hold me over.

"Where you going?" Tasha rolled over in the bed and asked, eyes squinting from the morning sun.

As I sat on the edge of the bed putting on my Tims, I looked back over my shoulder at her. "I'm going to go spend some time with Camille before they go back."

"Camille or Perri?" I could hear the attitude laced in her tone.

After releasing a sarcastic snort of laughter and running my hand down my face, I turned around to face her. "Both of them, Tash. Now if we gon' keeping going through this dumb shit about Perri every single time she's around, then we need to figure out what the fuck we even doing. Perri is family, and furthermore, she's the mother of my daughter. She ain't going nowhere. Now you can either get with the fucking program, or we can just do this co-parenting shit." I stood up from the bed and grabbed the keys to my new Accord from the nightstand. "Ball is in your court, shorty."

Heading for the door, I heard Tasha yell out, "Plus, wait!"

I turned back to look at her, immediately seeing just what an object of beauty she was. The mere sight of her dark brown shoulders nakedly peeking from beneath the sheets and all of her long black hair tossed wildly across her head made my dick jump. Even with sleep in her eyes and her lips completely dry, she was gorgeous to me. Just that quick, I had to remind myself that I was supposed to be mad at her. If I didn't, I knew it would only be a matter of time before I jumped right back in the bed with her for a morning fuck.

"I'm sorry, Plus. You know this baby has my emotions all over the place these days," she whined.

"Yeah, a'ight," I said before leaving, slamming the door behind me.

Tasha was only three months pregnant, and I swear she was already getting on my last nerve. It seemed like she blamed every stupid thing she said and did on her being pregnant. I never went through any of that shit when Perri was pregnant with Camille. Besides Perri being a little horny, she was the same one since day one. She never whined or even complained. In fact, my mother told me that even in the delivery room Perri was a trooper, birthing my baby without an epidural. I could only imagine how dramatic Tasha's ass was going to be.

When I finally reached the hotel that morning, I walked into the lobby and saw Perri sitting down, holding a sleeping Camille in her arms. She didn't see me coming in, so I slowly crept up on her, watching the two of them from a distance. Perri was still just as attractive as she was the night before at the club, just more beautiful because she was holding our daughter. Her long, silky brown hair was still straightened and thrown over one of her shoulders. She wore a tight-fitting jogging suit that had the word "Pink" displayed on the jacket, and although her caramel face was bare without a single trace of makeup, she was pretty.

"Yo, you ready?" I asked, catching her off guard.

She looked up at me from where she sat, showcasing those pretty amber eyes. "Yeah, I'm ready." When she stood up from her seat, I grabbed the diaper bag from her arms and gave her a kiss on the forehead. Looking down at her face, I was met with the same closed-lip smile she'd offered me since she got here.

As soon as we got to my whip, I took Camille and placed her in the car seat Tez got for me when he gave me the car. After carefully strapping her in, I jogged around to the driver's side while Perri got in the passenger seat of the car. "IHOP?" I looked over and asked while starting the engine.

"You already know that's what I want," she said.

I let out a light chuckle because she was right. IHOP had been our favorite breakfast spot for as long as I could remember. Perri always ordered the Rooty Tooty Fresh 'N Fruity while I always ordered the Big Steak Omelette. Neither one of us ever deviated from that because we just weren't that explorative when it came to our food.

"So, how was the club, Miss Three A.M.?" I asked jokingly, turning down the radio.

She laughed and shook her head. "It was straight."

"Just straight? I mean, it had to have been more than that for you to stay out all night long."

She let out another light laugh. "I mean . . ." She paused, shrugging her shoulders. "I had fun."

"Umm hmm. So who tried to kick it to you?" I cut my eyes over at her while we were stopped by a red light. "I know somebody did, the way you was looking in that dress," I said, biting down on my bottom lip recalling the image of her last night.

"Nobody."

"Nobody? You sure about that?" I asked again, tapping my fingers on the steering wheel.

She shook her head, then stared out the window. For some reason, I didn't believe a word she was saying. I'd bet my last dollar that every single nigga in the club had glanced Perri's way at least once last night, because she was just too pretty to ignore. Inwardly, I laughed at myself and the way I was questioning her. Seeing her all sexy-like last night in the club stirred up something inside of me I had never really felt before.

Yes, she was my ace and my best friend. Hell, she was practically family, but the way that dress showed off her body . . . I'm talking curves I didn't fully realize she'd even had were on display. And that long, pretty-ass hair. Damn! Just the thought of another nigga sliding up in that tight little pussy of hers, a secret place that had only been reserved for me, had me feeling some type of way.

When we got to IHOP, the line was out the door. Luckily, I knew the manager. He was a huge Georgetown fan and just about every Sunday he would let me and my teammates come eat for little to nothing. With Camille in my arms and Perri right behind me, we walked past the people trying to get inside. Smelling nothing but coffee, pancakes, and maple syrup, we approached the hostess's podium.

"Yo, Josh. You got me," I said to one of the waiters I knew.

"Yeah, I got you, man. Just give me like two minutes," he said, putting two of his fingers up before walking away.

As Perri and I stood waiting, Camille started to cry. "Here," Perri said, passing me a bottle of milk from the diaper bag hanging on her arm.

While feeding Camille, I cradled her in my arms in an attempt to soothe her. I noticed that she was wolfing the milk down like she hadn't been fed in months. "When was the last time she ate?"

"Three hours ago. Why?"

"She's acting like she starving," I said.

"She always acts like that when it's time to eat." A few seconds of silence passed between us before she said, "Ahmad?"

"Yeah, P," I said, instantly recognizing the fact that she called me by my real name.

"How are you going to handle all of this when Tasha has the baby?"

Letting out a deep sigh, I mulled over the same question that had been constantly replaying in my mind. "I'on know," I started to say, but before I could finish, Josh came back over to us with two menus in his hand.

"You ready?" Just when I nodded my head, he turned away and said, "Follow me."

After propping Camille up in her car seat carrier, I slid into the booth and sat across from Perri. I let out a light chuckle watching her scan the menu.

"Nigga, whatchu laughing at?" she asked.

"I'm laughing at you. You know damn well you gon' get that Rooty Tooty bullshit like you always do," I told her, shaking my head.

Closing the menu, she rolled her eyes and allowed the corners of her mouth to turn up into a smirk. She knew I was right, which was exactly why she didn't say shit. When the waiter came over shortly after, I handed him our menus and immediately placed our orders. Just as I opened up my mouth to finish the conversation I needed to have with Perri, I was interrupted by the babbling sounds of Camille.

Hearing her little coos, I instantly looked down at her in her seat. She was only 3 months old, but it sounded like she was already trying to talk. Just seeing her big, bright brandy-colored eyes staring back at me caused my heart to swell with pride. From the moment I laid eyes on her in the hospital, I was in love. It's crazy to say, but I didn't know if it was even possible to love another person, or another baby for that matter, as much as I loved Camille.

"I'm trying to figure it all out, Perri. I think Tasha's going to move out this way when the baby comes, though," I said, peering down at Camille playing with her feet.

"I see," Perri said lowly.

Just from the sound of her voice, I knew that Perri wasn't pleased with what I had just told her. Removing my eyes from Camille, I glanced over at her and saw that she now had tears pooled in her eyes. "What's going on, P? Talk to me," I said.

"It's nothing." She looked away and pretended to engage in something else in the restaurant, but I knew better.

"It's definitely something, yo. Just tell me what's wrong."

"You think this shit is easy for me, Ahmad?" She raised her voice, catching me a little off guard. "You think I want my baby to grow up without her father around? Meanwhile, you, Tasha, and your new baby will all live together like one big-ass happy family." Quickly she wiped her eyes before a single tear could slip down her cheeks, which were flushed from emotion.

"Damn," I muttered, thinking about how that shit would look. "I didn't even look at it like that," I admitted.

"Tasha's baby will get to see you on a daily basis, yet Camille will get to see you every other month? Or when you get time?" she hunched her shoulders and asked rhetorically.

"I woul—"

"It's whatever, Ahmad. Just forget about it," she said, cutting me off.

After we sat in an awkward silence for what felt like a lifetime, the waiter finally came over with our food. While he set all of the plates down on the table, I saw Perri's cell phone light up from an incoming call. Glancing down, I instantly recognized the name Derrick that popped up on the screen. Before I could even speak on it, Perri picked up and answered the call.

"Hello," she said, tucking a piece of her long hair behind her ear. "Oh, heyy."

Just that quick, I watched her lips, which had been pursed into a frown, curl up into a natural smile. Her light eyes widened and somehow became brighter in that split second. When she got up from the table without even excusing herself to have a private conversation, I found myself growing agitated. I didn't know if it was my teammate Derrick or some other nigga with the same name, but either way, she was taking time out from spending with me to entertain another nigga. I didn't like that shit at all.

Quietly, I sat back and observed her where she stood by the front door of the restaurant. Even being that far away, I could see that she was blushing. She was throwing her head back and laughing every other second like this nigga was really that fucking funny. Every so often she'd twirl her finger around the length of her hair, which was by far some of the girliest shit I had ever seen her do.

After a few more minutes, she wrapped up the call and made her way back over to the table, face completely lifted and attitude on some sort of natural high as she slid back into the booth across from me.

"The fuck was that?" I let out.

"What are you talking about, Ahmad?"

"Oh, I'm still Ahmad?" I asked. Just to keep myself calm, I let out a sarcastic snort of laughter, pinching the bridge of my nose. "Who the fuck is Derrick?"

"It wa—"

"And don't even fix your lips to tell me that was my fucking teammate," I said, cutting her off.

"Yes, that was Derrick, your teammate. We exchanged numbers last night after the club. Why?" Her face was all balled up in anticipation like she was ready for whatever comeback I might have.

"Perri, you are my baby's mother. That's why. You can't just be out here fucking with my homeboys and shit," I spat.

"Baby's mother?" she questioned before letting out her own sarcastic snort of laughter. "I thought I was your 'homie.' Like one of the guys," she mocked. "Ain't that what you be saying about me?"

"You know what the fuck I mean, Perri!"

"No, I don't know what the fuck you mean! You think you can go parade around with Tasha's birdbrain ass all day and I'm going to be stuck in the house by myself? Ha!" She shook her head. "You think I can't get a man since, let you tell it, I act so much like one!"

"Perri, calm down," I said through gritted teeth. She was getting so loud that Camille had started to cry and people were actually beginning to stare. "That's not what the fuck I meant. You are my best friend, and yes, I've always looked at you like my homegirl—"

"Cool, I'm your homegirl then. Got it!" she said, folding her arms over her chest. "Are you ready to go now?"

I looked down, seeing a table full of uneaten food, and shook my head. "Fine," was all I said. After placing money down on the table, I picked up Camille and walked out behind Perri, who was walking a mile a minute. Besides the little baby sounds Camille made, the car was completely silent on the drive. When I finally pulled up to the hotel, I got out of the car and unstrapped Camille from the back seat. I kissed both of her chubby cheeks and whispered in her ear that I loved her and that I'd see her soon. Without uttering even a single word after, Perri took Camille from my arms, turned, and walked away like a stranger.

Chapter 19

Perri

It was almost midnight on a Thursday when I found myself in Walmart, cruising down the empty aisles. There were no squeaky carts or crowded paths in sight as I slowly made my way. I told my father a little white lie, leading him to believe that Camille was completely out of diapers. In all actuality, we could have made it another day, possibly two, but really I just needed a moment to myself. I just knew that I couldn't bring Camille out this time of night and he would keep a listening ear out for her while I was gone.

One week had passed since I'd last seen or spoken with Plus, and although I hated to admit it, the silence between us was slowly killing me. Sure, my heart was shattered to pieces when I'd heard that Tasha was pregnant, but the fact that she and the baby were actually moving there to be a family rocked my soul to its core. Everything he had been planning with Tasha these past few months was all I could only dream he would one day plan with me. But as the days went by, the realization of what we truly were to one another was slowly beginning to hit home. Plus was simply my best friend, nothing more than a childhood crush, and I needed to come to terms with that shit.

When I finally found the makeup aisle, I searched for the Maybelline mascara Nika told me to get. She said that I really didn't need to wear makeup but that a thin coat of mascara and a sheer layer of lip gloss would enhance my look. As long as I kept my wild, bushy-ass eyebrows in check, that was. Nika was naturally beautiful without even trying, so I trusted her opinion on the matter. The fact that I had gotten so much attention from my mini-makeover that night at the club made me want to keep up my new look. Of course, I wasn't into wearing heels and dresses every day, but the rest I thought I could actually manage with her help.

While looking at the mascara as I held it up in my hand, I felt my phone suddenly vibrate. I reached down into the pocket of my black basketball shorts and pulled it out. "Whaddup," I answered, not even looking at the number.

"Am I calling too late?" Derrick asked. His deep, raspy voice sounded tired and completely drained.

"No," I said, shaking my head, trying to immediately soften the tone of my voice. "It's not too late." Although I knew I sounded a bit too eager, I couldn't resist the smile from forming on my face, followed by some sort of happy wiggle dance that only a girly girl would do.

It was almost as if he could see me, because in that very second, he let out a small snort of laughter on the other end of the phone, causing me to immediately stop and stand still. After peering over my shoulder to make sure he wasn't actually around, I tucked a piece of hair behind my ear and swallowed. "What's up with you though?" I asked, trying to sound proper and regain my composure.

"Ain't shit. Had a long-ass day and I just wanted to hear your voice before I went to sleep."

"Well, it's . . . it's really good to hear from you." As soon as the words left my lips, I smacked myself on the forehead for just hearing how lame I sounded. Again, his light chuckle that followed caused me to cringe. Derrick and I had been texting like crazy for the past week, but we hardly ever talked on the phone. Other than talking to

Plus, TK, and Jamal over the years, I never talked to boys on the phone like that. So even at the age of 19, I didn't know how to carry a suitable phone conversation.

"So what you doing?" he asked.

"I'm in Walmart."

"Walmart? This time of night?"

"Yeah. I just needed to get out for a moment. I couldn't sleep so . . ."

"I feel you," he yawned.

"You sound really tired," I said, hearing every bit of the exhaustion in his voice.

"I am. I had a long-ass day between practice, class, and studying for this damn physiology exam."

"Well, get some rest and just call me tomorrow." Inwardly, I didn't want our conversation to end, but I could tell he was beat.

"What are you doing next week for break?" he asked.

"Shit, pro'ly . . ." I easily said, instantly covering my mouth. Derrick rarely, if ever, heard me cuss, because I was trying to keep my tomboyish ways under wraps. "I mean, probably just kicking it with Camille. Why?"

After letting out another light chuckle, he said, "We renting a house out in Ocean City. You trying to roll with the kid?"

"Sorry, but I have Camille," I said lowly, feeling a little disappointed.

"Bring her," he suggested with ease, almost as if he had been prepared for my response.

"I don't know." I sighed. "For how long?"

"Just three days. Next Thursday through Sunday."

Keeping quiet, I allowed the scenario to play out in my mind, asking myself question after question to help make the best decision. Did I really know Derrick that well to go out of town with him? What would the sleeping arrangements be? Would Plus be okay with me taking Camille?

"Plus is supposed to be spending the break with Camille," I said more to myself than Derrick.

"If I'm not mistaken, I think that nigga going too," he said.

"He is?" I asked in surprise. Let Ms. Tonya tell it, Plus was spending all of his break with Camille because he just missed her sooo much. Now come to find out he was going to Ocean City with his boys. "Is Tasha going?" I instantly asked, trying to hide the slight attitude in my tone.

"Yeah, I think so. I think Rel supposed to be asking your girl . . . What's her name?"

"Nika," I said lowly, still thinking about the fact that Tasha's stupid ass was going too. It was as if he could tell my mind was racing, because he didn't respond.

Before too much time had passed, I knew I had to break the silence that I had created. "Yeah, sure, I wanna go," I said. At that moment, I wasn't exactly sure if I'd made the best decision, but I didn't want to give it too much thought. Even though we'd only known each other for a week, I liked Derrick already, and if he was the chosen one to help me get over Plus, then so be it.

"Damn, shorty, you just made my night. I just knew you were gon' tell a nigga no," he said with a light laugh.

"So do I need to get my brother to take me up there?"

"Nah," he chuckled. "I'm gon' come pick y'all up. You ain't gotta worry about nothing."

With the phone tucked between my shoulder and ear, mascara in hand, I continued to walk around the store. We talked another thirty minutes or so before we said our goodbyes and hung up for the night. Just talking to Derrick so freely made me feel like he was an old childhood friend of mine and it completely lifted my mood.

After doing a self-checkout for a single pack of Pampers and a tube of black mascara, I left Walmart with a closed-lip smile on my face. There would only be four more days until I got the chance to see Mr. Derrick with his fine ass, and I couldn't wait.

It was finally Thursday morning, and I was zipping up my suitcase for our trip to Ocean City. I had to give it to Plus, because he really did spend a lot of time with Camille these past few days. She'd spent just about every night with him at Ms. Tonya's house, and I thought he even took her to the park. Not that she could actually run around and play, but I guessed he was trying, at least. He even tried to kick it with me one night, asking if I wanted to come over and play a game of dominoes and smoke a little something. Seeing as how I was still in my feelings, I told him no and avoided him as much as possible.

After packing up my bag, I began my walk over to Ms. Tonya's house. Immediately, I spotted Mr. Ronnie hanging out on the corner, surrounded by a bunch of the neighborhood crackheads. Even from a distance, I could tell that he had lost a significant amount of weight, to the point where his clothes didn't even fit as good. Ronnie was always a big man, standing at about six foot three inches tall and weighing close to 300 pounds. Shaking my head, I silently prayed he wasn't on that shit before continuing on my path. When I finally stepped up on the stoop, seeing the front door open wide, I pulled back the rickety storm door and walked inside. Immediately I smelled the scent of lavender Fabuloso and heard "Reasons" by Earth, Wind & Fire blaring from the large box speakers in the living room.

A smile instantly swept across my face as soon as I saw Camille. She was sitting in a small rocking chair that sat on the top of the kitchen table where Ms. Tonya was sitting. Her bright, brandy-colored eyes beamed with delight as soon as she took in the sight of me. "There goes Mommy's sweet girl," I cooed, unstrapping her from her seat and immediately scooping her chunky little body up in my arms. She was so happy to see me that she was literally bouncing up and down in my arms like a baby kangaroo on the loose. When she did stuff like that, I swear happiness was forced on me no matter what mood I was in or what I was going through personally.

"Yes, there goes your momma, chile," Ms. Tonya said, shaking her head at the way Camille was reacting to me.

"Why you ain't got her dressed?" I asked, noticing that Camille was barefoot and still in the plain white onesie from the night before.

"I figured you kids needed a break. Just let her stay here with me this weekend, and y'all go on to Ocean City to have some fun. Who's this Derrick boy I been hearing about anyway?"

"Just a friend. One of Plus's teammates I met when we went up to Georgetown the other week," I explained.

"Hmm," she said, taking a sip of her coffee.

"What's that supposed to mean?" I asked.

"Nothing." She paused and smirked. "You not trying to make Ahmad jealous now, are you? I mean, I see that you've been straightening your hair and you've done plucked those eyebrows—"

"Waxed," I corrected her, cutting her off.

"Well, waxed . . . Whatever, chile," she said with a flick of her wrist. "You been dressing a little differently too." Judging by the silly smirk on her face, I knew she thought she had said something.

I simply rolled my eyes, trying hard to disguise the fact that she was calling me out on my shit. "Just trying something a little different, that's all. Doesn't have shit to do with Plus," I told her.

"Mmm," she muttered, taking another sip.

"What doesn't have shit to do with me?" Plus said, walking into the kitchen wearing nothing but gray sweatpants and a bare chest as he took Camille out of my arms. I could tell that he must have just jumped out of the shower, because his curly hair was wet and the fresh scent of Irish Spring fanned past my nose as he began taking steps toward the table. My eyes lingered over the brown muscles of his back, which were now more developed than ever. When he turned around to take a seat, my eyes couldn't help but dart to his arms and chest. Slowly I licked my lips, allowing my eyes to travel down even farther to the bulging print in his pants.

When I started to feel my mouth water, realizing that I was not only staring but probably drooling by now, I swallowed hard and cleared my throat. "I'll be back sometime Sunday morning to pick her up, and I'll be sure to call you when we get there," I told Ms. Tonya, ignoring Plus's question altogether.

I walked over and leaned down to where Plus was holding Camille in his lap before placing a kiss on the top of her head. After feeling Plus's hand gently graze the tips of my long hair, which had loosely fallen over my shoulders, I looked up at him. With dark brown eyes peering back at me and lips that had turned up into a natural smirk, he shook his head.

"What?" I said, standing up.

He let out a low snort before licking his lips. "You did all that shit to impress a nigga." He pointed at me up and down. "And can't even be yo'self," he said, referring to my new look.

I stayed quiet for a few seconds, noticing the so-called disappointed look on his face. "You're right," I said, taking a step back. "I did all this to impress a nigga who has yet to notice me."

Catching just a glimpse of the confusion that had suddenly etched across his face, I looked over and locked eyes with Ms. Tonya. She gave me a silent wink. And with that, I turned to head out of the front door, not speaking another word.

Chapter 20

Plus

As I was driving down Route 50 headed toward Ocean City to meet up with the crew, thoughts of Perri flooded my mind. Initially, I was pissed when I found out that Perri was going to Ocean City with Derrick. Not only was she my best friend, but she was my baby's momma, so in my eyes, she was completely off-limits to my friends and the people I hung with. Sure, I knew that perhaps one day she'd find somebody. Possibly. But I didn't know how emotionally unprepared I was for that shit until I saw Derrick's number flash across her screen that morning at IHOP. Then there was the fact that she was changing the way she looked and carried herself. I had to admit that Perri was beautiful as fuck, but I no longer recognized her, and honestly, that shit scared me.

I always envisioned us grabbing a beer after work, maybe watching a game of football or two on Sundays as we grew old. Hers would be the place I'd escape to whenever my wife got to nagging and shit. But never in a million years did the thought of truly having to share her with another man cross my mind. Up until lately, I'd always just looked at her as my best friend. Sure, we had a deeper connection than what I had with TK, Jamal, or even Jorell for that matter, which was why I took it there with her in the first place. I just didn't think I'd be feeling so . . . jealous right now.

"Baby, I can't wait until my appointment next week. I hope it's a boy," Tasha said, disrupting my thoughts.

"Yeah, me too, Tash," I looked toward the passenger side and told her, trying to sound excited.

Of course, I'd handle my business as a man and take care of my child, but did I really need another baby right now? Hell no. I wasn't excited about this pregnancy in the least, but I knew I needed to do what was right. Camille was all I really needed at the moment, and if I was being completely honest, she was all I wanted. However, to keep from hurting Tasha's feelings, I kept my comments to myself. When she threw the whole moving to Georgetown thing on me, I immediately wanted to object, but she had already gotten accepted to the university, gotten a part-time job, and found us a place to live together, saying that she'd pay the first month's rent and deposit. At that point, I really didn't have a leg to stand on, so I just rolled with it.

After another hour, we finally pulled up to our destination. Driving up the red brick-paved road, I was captivated by the large white home that sat right there on the bay. Four huge white columns barred the large front porch, which had five green planters hanging from its ceiling. It looked similar to those plantation-style houses built in the early 1900s. Although I hated to admit it, the place was still nice as hell. As I drove up closer to the front of the house, I could see the water out back, neighboring piers, and boats docked all around as sailboats cruised right on by. I got excited as hell just thinking about how much fun we were about to have.

I didn't have much money other than my leftover scholarship money and stipend, which I regularly sent to Camille, but Tez always hooked me up, so this was my way of rewarding myself for making straight A's this semester.

After parking the car, we got our bags out of the trunk and walked up to the front of the house. Feeling the April air whip across our faces and hearing the distant sounds of waves, we stepped up on the porch. I used the rental key I had to let us inside, knowing that we were the first ones there. Immediately, we took in the whitewashed hardwood floors that led to an open living room and kitchen combination. The white marble countertops sparkled, along with the windows of the double French doors that led out back. After setting our luggage down, Tasha was the first one to look out at the view, pressing her nose up against the glass. In the backyard, there was a covered pool, Jacuzzi hot tub, and basketball court all surrounded by the bay.

"Damn, this place is beautiful," I said, coming up from behind and wrapping my arms around her waist.

She laid her head back on my chest and stared up at me. "It really is. This is our first vacation together, babe," she squealed.

I leaned down and kissed her neck, allowing my hands to slide up the front of her shirt. Hearing a soft moan escape her lips immediately caused my dick to jump in my pants. Right when I was about to unbuckle her jeans, I heard the front door open.

"What it do, playa?" Jorell hollered, coming through the door. I looked back, seeing Nika following him as they both dropped their bags to the floor.

Sliding my hands from Tasha's waist, I walked over and dapped him up. "Y'all finally made it I see."

"Hell yeah, mane. It's beautiful out here, fa real," he said, taking the Braves cap off his head. Dreads wild and desperately in need of a re-twist, he pushed them back with his hand before placing the cap back on his head.

"Hey, Jorell," Tasha came over and said, giving him a hug.

While they rapped, I made my way over to Nika. "What's up?" I said, giving her a half hug. "So you really getting serious with this country-ass nigga, I see," I joked, pointing back at Jorell.

"We'll see," she said, cutting her eyes over at him with a smile.

"Yuh. whatever," he said, gold teeth showing through the crack of his lips as he grinned. "That's my la' baby right dere. Why you playin', gul?" he asked, making her laugh.

When she and Tasha finally looked at each other, neither one parted their lips to speak. Instead, Nika grabbed Jorell's hand so that they could go tour the rest of the house. As soon as they were out of sight, Tasha snaked her arms around my neck and kissed me, slipping her tongue inside my mouth. Instinctively, my hands slid down to her plump ass, and within seconds, I could feel myself getting hard all over again. Just as I ground against her and released a slow groan into her mouth, the door flew open again. I pulled back, breaking our kiss, only to see Perri and Derrick standing in the foyer.

Looking over, I quickly noticed that the expression stamped on Perri's face was practically one of disgust. Nose scrunched up and lips twisted up into a nasty scowl, she eyed the two of us. I wasn't exactly sure if she was disgusted by me, Tasha, or both of us. Rather than debating it in my mind, I walked over to her and gave her a hug, followed by my usual forehead kiss. It wasn't a big deal, but feeling her body somewhat relax in my arms gave me hope that we could somehow get our friendship back on track.

Before I could even pull back, Derrick stepped in close to us. "You did your thing, man. This is a nice-ass spot you picked out," he said, extending his hand.

Even though I really wasn't dealing with that nigga like that because he was trying to push up on my baby's mom, I sucked it up and took his hand. "Thanks," I said dryly, refusing to look like a little bitch in front of everyone.

"Where's Nika?" Perri asked, looking around.

"She and Jorell went upstairs," I told her.

"Come on, we need to find where we're sleeping at anyway," Derrick said, taking her hand.

Instantly, I grew pissed hearing him say that shit. I was going to have a serious conversation with Perri because I'd be damned if she was going to give up the goods after knowing that nigga for all of two weeks. I must have shown my anger on my face because Tasha grabbed me by the arm as I watched the two of them head up the steps.

"What's wrong, baby?" she asked.

"Nothing," I lied. "Come on, let's go find us a room before all the good ones are taken."

Just as we started for the steps, the door opened again with TK, Jamal, and Shivon all walking through it. "Let's get this party started!" TK shouted, dancing with his hands up in the air.

I shook my head at his crazy ass and walked over to dap them all up. It was rare that I saw them these days with me being away at Georgetown, but this was my crew since day one, and I would be lying if I said I hadn't missed them. That's why I planned all of this months ago in hopes of bringing my new crew and my old one together. However, had I known Derrick would be here kicking it with Perri, he wouldn't have been invited. I didn't even tell Perri about this trip because I knew there was tension between her and Tasha. Now that everyone was here under one roof, I could only pray things stayed drama free for the next three days.

"What's going on, man?" I said, dapping up Jamal.

"I don't know. You tell me, Mr. Georgetown," he joked.

While TK ran to go look at the view out back, Shivon and Tasha hugged and immediately started their gossiping.

"All right, y'all, come on, let's go find us some bedrooms. Everybody else is already here," I said.

"Everybody like who?" Shivon asked with her hand on her hip.

"Girl, Perri's manly looking ass and her girlfriend," Tasha whispered like we couldn't hear her.

"Don't start no shit up in here, Tash. I'll take yo' ass back to PG real quick," I cut my eyes over at her and said.

She rolled her eyes before going up the stairs with Shivon.

"I thought you said you weren't inviting Perri," TK questioned, coming back over to where we were.

"I wasn't but—"

"But what?" Perri asked, coming down the stairs. Clearly, she'd heard what TK said judging by the hurt in her eyes. A wave of guilt instantly washed over me as I grew speechless, not knowing how to respond.

As if on cue, Derrick came down the steps behind her. "What's wrong?" he asked, looking down at her then back toward us.

"I'm not wanted here," Perri said before rushing back up the stairs.

"Damn, Perri looks . . . different," TK muttered, widening his blue eyes.

"Yo, what the fuck is going on? What she mean she's not wanted here?" Derrick asked with his face all balled up.

He walked down the rest of the steps and came over toward us, standing directly next to TK. While they were both tall, standing at about six foot four, Derrick had more weight and muscle on him than TK did. He had a thick New York accent and rough demeanor, which intimidated most people but not me. Up until this point, he was cool, but I didn't like how he was getting in my and Perri's business.

"Plus wasn't going to invite Perri because of the drama with her and Tasha. So what happened? How did she get up here?" TK asked.

"She's my guest," Derrick explained, pointing back to himself with his thumb. "I invited her to come kick it with me." He squinted his eyes and looked at me. "Nigga, I thought you told me that there was no beef between her and your girl. You told me it wasn't like that between you and Perri because she was your best friend. So, what's up?" He shrugged. "What's the beef?"

"Man, Tasha been jealous of Perri since high school, and them having a baby together didn't make that situation any better. And now that Perri's looking like that"—TK pointed, shaking his head and letting out a light chuckle—"she for damn sure jealous."

"No disrespect, but that's her problem. I paid my money just like everybody else, and Perri is my guest. I'on want her to feel no type of way, ya feel me?"

"Damn," I muttered lowly, thinking of how bad Perri must have felt overhearing that shit. "Let me go check on her."

Derrick held his hand up to my chest to stop me. "Nah, man, I got her. Go take care of your shorty, and I'll take care of mines."

I jerked my neck back and narrowed my eyes because he caught me off guard with that comment. However, being in the spirit of the break, I bit my tongue and didn't say shit. As he walked back up the stairs to go check on Perri, I shook my head. Not knowing whether to be mad at this nigga or angry at my damn self for letting shit get this far, I let out a deep sigh. All the while, both TK and

Jamal just stared at me with confused looks on their faces.

"So who the fuck is that nigga? That's Perri's man now?" Jamal asked, exposing the gap between his two front teeth.

"I don't know. He's one of my teammates," I said, shrugging my shoulders. "When Perri came out to see me play a couple of weeks ago with my moms and Camille, a bunch of us went out to the club that night. That's where they met."

"And she already taking trips out of town with the nigga?" TK asked, raising one of his eyebrows.

"Same shit I said." I ran my hand down my face, feeling stressed over the whole situation.

Chapter 21

Perri

"Can you just come get me? Please?" I practically begged Tez over the phone. "I just wanna leave."

"You killing me right now, P. I got some shit I gotta handle today," he said.

"Fine," I sighed, hanging up the phone.

Just as I disconnected the call, I looked over to see Derrick standing in the doorway of the bedroom. He was dressed simply in a white tee with the sleeves cut off, navy blue basketball shorts, and a navy blue Yankees cap, which he'd turned to the back. He wore a thin gold chain around his neck and diamond stud earrings in his ears. As he walked closer to me, the scent of his Jean Paul Gaultier cologne invaded my nose. Just after he sat next to me on the bed, I couldn't help but lean my head on his shoulder. I was too tough to cry, but I needed some comfort at the moment.

"So you leaving me?" he asked, his deep, raspy tone coming through as he spoke lowly. "You just gon' let these niggas run you off?" He ran his hand up and down my back in an attempt to console me, resting his chin on the top of my head.

"Yeah. I don't wanna be anywhere I'm not welcome."

He lifted my chin just so he could look me in the eyes. "I want you here, ma."

Looking up at him, I took in every handsome feature of his angular face. Piercing dark brown eyes that showed nothing but the utmost sincerity behind them and then his lips. Full dark pink kissable lips he always licked right before he spoke. With my chin still in his hand, he leaned down close to where I could feel the warmth of flesh on my face. Just as my heart started to race and knots began to form in my stomach, I closed my eyes, awaiting what I just knew would be our very first kiss.

"Ahem." I heard someone clearing his throat. I opened my eyes only to see TK standing in the doorway with nothing but his swim trunks on. His bright bluish green eyes lit up with a sneaky smile as he stepped one foot inside the bedroom. "We 'bout to put some food on the grill and get in the hot tub. Y'all coming?"

Derrick looked at me with hopeful eyes. Smirking with those dimples of his embedded in each of his cheeks, he stood and reached to pull me up with him.

"Fine." I sighed, rolling my eyes. "I need to change, so get out!"

After they left and shut the door behind them, I threw on a Georgetown T-shirt with some basketball shorts and black Nike slides. I then put my hair up in a messy bun because I knew Nika didn't want to spend her whole break flat ironing my hair. I glanced at myself in the mirror that hung on the wall, inspecting my face for blemishes then checking my teeth before heading out the door.

As I walked down the steps, I could hear "Thong Song" by Sisqó being played. The sounds of loud chatter and laughter filled the area downstairs. When I reached the bottom steps, I saw Tasha, Shivon, and even Nika dancing to the music in two-piece bikinis. All the guys were shirtless, wearing nothing but swim trunks, taking shots and slapping hands. Suddenly, I felt out of place in my T-shirt and basketball shorts. I'd never owned a bathing suit, and up until now the thought of buying one had never even crossed my mind.

"I guess some of us aren't getting in the hot tub," Tasha said snidely as I made my way farther into the room.

"Tasha!" Plus stated firmly, glaring at Tasha, who just rolled her eyes.

As Derrick walked over to me, Plus and I locked eyes. Just by the look on his face, I could tell he was sorry, and not that it took away the hurt I felt, but I knew I'd forgive him in time.

"Where's your bathing suit at, ma?" Derrick asked, whispering in my ear.

"I . . . I don't have one."

He looked back at everyone before turning back and scratching his head. "Come on, let's go take a walk."

"Where are we going?" I asked.

"You trust me?"

I didn't say anything at first, but after a few seconds, I nodded my head. Once he threw back on his T-shirt, we started for the front door.

"Can put a nigga in a dress all you want, but at the end of the day, she's still a nigga," I heard Tasha say behind me. I started to turn around, but Derrick firmly grabbed my hand to hold me in place.

"Bitch, shut the fuck up," I heard Nika say just as the door slammed behind us.

As we trekked down the waterside holding hands, I noticed a bunch of shops with swimming and fishing equipment nearby. As soon as I saw one with bathing suits displayed in the storefront window, I knew exactly what he was doing.

"Come on, let's go in here," he said, pulling my hand.

"Derrick, you don't need to buy me a bathing suit, really. I just won't get in the hot tub."

"Nah, I just wanna see you in one," he said, winking his eye at me. His eyebrow with the two nicks bounced as he pulled me farther inside the store.

I shook my head, and against my better judgment, I followed his lead. While we were in there, he pulled several two-piece bikinis from the rack. All of which I told him I would not be wearing. Instead, I grabbed a conservative royal blue one-piece swimsuit off the stand, costing only 15 dollars, and handed it to him. "I'll take this one," I said.

Watching his face as he looked it over, I noticed the disapproval in his eyes. "If this is the one you want then . . ." he said, letting his voice trail off.

"It is," I stated firmly.

"Can you do me one favor though before we leave?"

"What's that?"

"Just try on this one right here for me," he said, holding up a red two-piece bikini. "If you hate it, then we'll leave the shit right here, but if you like it," he said, winking his eye at me again, "I'll buy this one for you too."

I wanted to object and firmly hold my ground, but there was something about the excitement in this nigga's eyes that made me weak. No man had ever looked at me like that before, not even Plus, and I liked it. I loved the way Derrick looked my body over like he just wanted to devour it. It made me feel sexy and like a woman.

Rolling my eyes as if I didn't want to try it on for him, I snatched the bikini from his hand. I went into the dressing room and quickly put it on. When I looked myself over in the mirror, I couldn't help but admire my beautiful figure. Nika told me that I had a video girl's body, but of course I didn't believe her. Now as I stood here observing myself, I could see what she was talking about. I had full, perky breasts and wide, curvy hips. Even after having Camille, my stomach returned flat, and my waist was small.

Feeling myself, I twirled around in the mirror to get a better look before doing a happy dance. Abruptly, however, there was a knock on the door, causing me to jump out of my skin.

"You ready, ma?" Derrick asked on the other side of the door. "Let me see what it's looking like."

Slowly I turned the doorknob and stepped out so that he could see me. Nervously standing there with my hands clasped behind my back, I waited for him to say something. However, he didn't utter a word. Instead, I watched his dark brown eyes slowly travel up my body, inspecting every inch and curve. He bit down on his bottom lip as he closed his eyes and shook his head before letting out a small snort of laughter.

"What's wrong? You don't like it?" I asked, rocking back on my heels, feeling completely awkward.

"You just don't know how beautiful you are, ma. I swear," he started to say. He put his fist up to his mouth as if he were trying to stop himself from saying all he truly wanted to.

"Thank you," I said lowly, suddenly feeling a little shy.

"If you want that blue thing, I'll get it, but I'm definitely buying you this one too," he said.

I was going to change back into my basketball shorts to leave the store, but Derrick asked me to leave the bikini on. He bought me a white cover up to put on over it in addition to the royal blue one-piece that I originally wanted.

As we walked back to the house, he lifted my hand to his lips and kissed the back of it. "I swear, ma, you are the prettiest girl I have ever laid my eyes on."

"Thanks," I said, turning away to keep him from seeing me blush.

When we got back close to the house, I could smell the scent of smoked barbecue lingering in the air, and

I could hear the thumping of loud music coming from inside the house. I opened up the door and saw Nika and Jorell sitting at the kitchen bar, taking shots of tequila. Assuming that everyone else was outside, I made my way over to them with Derrick behind me.

"Where y'all been at?" Nika said with a little attitude. I knew she hated that I left her there alone with Tasha and Shivon.

"We went to the store. Why aren't y'all in the hot tub with everyone else?" I asked.

"You knew I wasn't going in there by myself with them bitches," she said, tossing back another shot.

I laughed and shook my head. "Well, are you ready?" I asked.

"Hell yeah. Come on, Jorell," she said, standing up from the barstool.

After pulling the cover-up I was wearing up over my head, I tossed it on the loveseat in the living room.

"Damn, gul," Jorell muttered, looking me over.

"Nigga, don't make me hurt you," Nika snapped.

He laughed and made his way over to wrap his arms around her from behind. "You know I only got eyes fa you, la' baby," he said, kissing her on the cheek.

"But you do look sexy, Perri. I see you, boo," Nika said.

After opening up the French doors to go out back, I saw TK and Plus standing by the grill. Both were shirtless, one with the skin of chocolate while the other a pale shade of vanilla, as they turned our way. As soon as Plus saw me, his eyes temporarily bucked and his mouth slightly dropped. Slowly he scanned my body over from head to toe, similar to the way Derrick had done back at the store. And just that quick, I felt a surge of butterflies fluttering around in my stomach. I tried my best to ignore his gaze, but it was so obvious, not only to me but to everyone around us. Derrick placed his hand on my waist almost in a territorial manner, and when I looked at Tasha, she had her face all balled up.

"Plus, is the food ready or what?" she asked, snapping him out of his trance.

He pulled his eyes away from me and looked down at the grill. "Almost, but not yet," he said, flipping the meat over.

Derrick and Jorell got into the hot tub first, both reaching for my and Nika's hands so they could help us in. I tried to sit next to Derrick, but he immediately pulled me down onto his lap and snaked his arms around me. Feeling his hardness beneath me caused goosebumps to rise to the surface of my skin. Almost instantly, I could feel that same pulsation between my thighs. If I hadn't already been sitting in a tub full of hot water, I was pretty sure my bikini bottoms would have been soaked.

"I'm sorry, ma," he whispered in my ear. Hearing almost a hint of a smile cutting through his low, deep tone, I turned my head back to look at him. I closed my eyes, feeling his low-cut beard lightly prickling my skin as he softly latched onto the lobe of my ear for a subtle suck.

I let out a little laugh and shook my head before opening my eyes. I didn't even have to ask what he was sorry for because I knew he was talking about that monster I could feel underneath me. It was damn near jumping to the beat of the music, trying to fight its way out of his shorts as he held me firmly in place. Looking back over my shoulder, I noticed Plus's eyes damn near burning a hole through the both of us. As much as I wanted to get out and ask him what was wrong, I didn't. I stayed put, enjoying the feeling of Derrick's strong arms wrapped around me.

"Aye, let's get this party started," TK hollered over the music, waving one of his hands high up in the air. He walked over with a tray full of Jell-O shots, all in assorted flavors. Each of us in the hot tub grabbed two shots apiece and sucked them down while listening to the music.

About twenty minutes later, the food was done, so we all got out to go eat. I had to admit that Plus did his thing on the grill. We ate grilled chicken, hamburgers, and hot dogs, which were all cooked to perfection. Of course, we didn't have any sides other than chips, beer, and liquor, but it was all good. For the first time in a good little while, I found myself happy and having a good time.

After partying all night, dancing, singing, playing cards, and drinking, Derrick and I began making our way upstairs. As I walked up, I could literally feel Plus's eyes zoned in on us, so I looked back down, and sure enough, he was staring right at me, leaning back on the couch with his legs cocked opened wide. I watched as he took a swig of his beer without ever taking his eyes off of me. Somewhere between sadness, disappointment, and anger was how his facial expression read.

"Good night," I mouthed quietly to him.

Without even a hint of a smile, he chucked his chin up at me before taking another swig of his beer. I turned back and continued up the steps with Derrick directly behind me. For some strange reason, I began to feel guilty. Guilty because I was suddenly feeling Derrick the same way I had been feeling Plus since I was 15 years old. The fact that Derrick made my body feel things that I had only felt with Plus didn't help.

When Derrick and I got to the bedroom, he closed the door behind us. He sat down on the floral-print loveseat that was in the corner of the room and patted the seat next to him with his hand. "Come rap to me, ma," he said, licking his lips. As soon as I sat down next to him, he placed his hand on my knee. "So you gon' tell me what's up with you and that nigga Plus?" he asked, cutting his eyes over at me.

"What do you mean?" I asked, already knowing full well what he was talking about.

"I mean, that nigga couldn't take his eyes off of you tonight, and he was looking at me like he wanted to kill a nigga."

I shrugged my shoulders. "I don't know," I said, shaking my head. "Maybe he was just being overprotective. I mean, Plus and I are like family, and we've been the best of friends since we were four years old," I tried to rationalize.

"Nah, that wasn't it. I got a little sister, so I already know what that shit looks like. That nigga's in love with you."

I coughed and damn near choked at his choice of words, immediately shaking my head. "No, he's definitely in love with Tasha. I'm like one of the guys to Plus," I said, finally catching my breath.

"You were like one of the guys until you came in wearing this shit." Pulling his bottom lip between his teeth, he pointed to the red bikini I was wearing. "So let me ask you something," he said, squinting his eyes. "How do y'all even have a baby together? I mean, if y'all are just best friends like you say, and you supposed to be just like one of the homies, how did that shit even happen?"

"Prom night," I said lowly. "He didn't want to go to Georgetown a virgin, and I was okay with losing mine to him, so we . . . we just did it," I explained, cutting my eyes over at him to see his reaction.

A few moments of silence fell between us before he finally spoke. "Do you love him?" he asked, his baritone voice so low and full of worry as he peered at me with the most serious of expressions on his face.

Taking a deep breath, I sighed, already knowing that I didn't want to lie but didn't want to push him away either. I liked Derrick, and for some reason, I could actually see us being together. "Yes. He's my best friend, and he's also Camille's dad," I said, telling the truth.

He grabbed me by the chin and looked me in my eyes. "Are you in love with him?"

I swallowed hard, and without taking too much time, I shook my head and said, "No." Deep down I knew I was lying, but I didn't want to end things with Derrick before they even got a chance to get started.

Sliding his hand up my thigh to place a firm grip on my waist, he pulled me in close and leaned down to kiss my lips. It was our very first kiss, and sure enough, it was everything I dreamt it would be and more. As our tongues intertwined, soft moans could be heard exchanging between the two of us. The way his hands roamed all over my back, hips, and thighs caused my body to shiver under his touch. And although I knew it was way too soon for sex, I couldn't deny that the temptation was there and that it was strong.

When I felt his hand glide down between my legs, skimming my most sacred place, I pulled back to catch my breath. "I can't," I said, just above a whisper.

"I'm not trying to take it there with you tonight, ma. I know it's too soon," he said, licking his lips. "Your body is just . . ." Pausing, he lustfully looked me over as though he was trying to find just the right words to describe me. He bit down on his bottom lip and shook his head before letting out another light snort of laughter. After standing up from the couch, he grabbed the back of his neck and twisted his lips into a sexy smirk. "Come give me a hug good night," he said.

I stood up and wrapped my arms around him, placing my head against the muscles of his chest. When I looked up at him, he leaned down and placed a simple peck on my lips before exiting the room. Earlier, he'd told me that he was going to sleep downstairs on the couch, so

I assumed that's where he was headed. As soon I closed the door behind him, I let out the breath I had been holding for that last few minutes and smiled. With my back leaned up against the door I sealed my eyes. Savoring the last taste of his tongue that was left behind on my lips, I whispered, "Good night, Derrick."

Chapter 22

Plus

After tossing and turning all night dreaming about Perri, I woke up feeling more confused than ever. I was beyond pissed when I saw Derrick follow Perri up the stairs last night. Sure, I knew she wasn't my girl, but the thought of her fucking someone else, especially someone I knew, made a nigga sick to his stomach. Part of me didn't want to see Perri get hurt, because I had been around Derrick long enough to know he had some doggish ways. The other part of me just wanted her for myself. Selfishly, I was content with having Tasha on my arm as my girl while still being able to kick it with Perri, fucking her from time to time.

Besides my mother and sister, Perri and Camille were the most important people in my life. Perri meant the world to me, and I was starting to see that shit more and more these days. We had been through so much together over the years, and she was the only one who knew everything about me, from my deepest, darkest secrets to my biggest fears. Up until this point, I hadn't even realized the woman she had become. She was beautiful in more ways than I could even count and now I was perplexed. I was terrified of losing her to another nigga.

"You about ready?" Tasha asked, standing in the doorway across from where I sat on the edge of the bed.

"Yeah, I'm ready," I said, looking her over. "You look good, shorty."

She had on a pair of dark blue skinny jeans and a yellow snug-fitting blouse. Even at four months pregnant, Tasha hadn't really gained any weight. The only reason I knew for sure she was pregnant was the fact that I made her pee on the stick for me two more times after that night at the hospital. Her long black hair was pulled up high in a ponytail, and her dark brown lips were shiny from the clear gloss she put on.

"Do I, now?" she teased seductively, making her way over to straddle my lap.

"Good enough to eat, shorty," I said into the crook of her neck, palming her ass with my hands.

Instantly she started gyrating her hips, causing my dick to swell beneath her. As I placed wet kisses to her neck, I could begin to hear her moan.

"Do you think we have time for a quickie?" she whispered.

Just as I was nodding my head, our bedroom door came open. When I looked up to see who it was, I was met with Perri's wide amber eyes staring back at me. I slid Tasha off of me and quickly stood up from the bed.

"What's up, P?" I asked, attempting to fix my pants. I was hard as rock, so I knew she saw my dick sticking out.

"Yo, everybody's ready downstairs. Y'all coming or what?" she asked. The slightest hint of an attitude could be heard in her voice as she spoke.

"Come on, Tash, let's go," I said.

After making our way out of the house, we walked down the pier to hop on a large fishing boat. It wasn't quite eighty degrees outside, but the sun was shining bright. The entire time on the boat, my eyes stayed fixed on Perri and Derrick. It was like I just couldn't help but look at the two of them. Today she wore some black basketball shorts, a Nike T-shirt, and some black high-top Nikes on her feet. Her hair was thrown up in a messy bun, and her face was bare other than maybe some Chapstick.

Even with her looking the way she did, like a tomboy, Derrick didn't seem to mind. I watched as he protectively stood behind her, helping her reel in a big fish and being so attentive as though the two of them were in their own little world. When she finally pulled the fish up out of the water, she turned around to hug him and I caught a glimpse of the huge smile on her face. He pushed back the wispy hairs framing her face that were blowing in the wind before leaning down to kiss her cheek. She really liked this nigga, and the more I was a witness to it, I found myself burning up inside.

"Plus, look at my pole," Tasha said, pointing to the tip of her rod, which was wiggling.

"Yeah, you definitely got something."

"Well? Can you help me pull it up?" she asked.

I grabbed the pole and began to reel it in fast. Sure enough, there was a large silver croaker squirming on the hook. When I finally got it all the way up, Tasha jumped up and down while squealing and clapping her hands. Before I could even get the fish off the hook, she grabbed the pole from me and stood it straight up, making the fish dangle in the air.

"Now!" she said childishly, looking over at Perri. "I caught one too."

Perri looked over both her shoulders to see who she was talking to, then back at Tasha, cocking her head to the side. "You talking to me?" Perri asked. Her voice was hard, almost like a nigga's, as she scrunched up her nose with Nika sniggering behind her.

"Well, you just caught a fish, didn't you?" Tasha sassed with her hand on her hip.

Perri squeezed the body of the fish she'd caught, holding down its fins, then freed its mouth from the hook. She wiped one of her hands down the front of her shorts, removing the tiny bit of blood that had gotten on her fingertips.

"Now, let me see yours," Perri said with the flailing fish in her hand.

Judging by the way Tasha balled her face up and flared her nose, I knew she was disgusted. "I swear you are such a nigga," she said, shaking her head. Then she slowly cut her eyes over at Derrick, who was standing at Perri's side. "And these the type of bull-dike bitches you like?" she said, pointing her finger toward Perri.

"Ahh shit," Jorell and TK murmured almost at the same time.

Before I could even choke Tasha's ass up myself, Perri rushed over and pushed Tasha to the ground. Without notice, Perri jumped down on top of her to where she was straddling her body. Although Tasha had her hands covering her face to block the blows, it was no use. Perri was getting her good with the wild punches she was delivering, talking shit in between. The rest of the crew all gathered around the scene and were yelling for them to break it up.

"I got your bull-dike bitch," Perri spat as Derrick and I both pulled her up off of Tasha. Even after Derrick had a good grip on her, holding her firmly around the waist, she was still cussing, kicking, and fighting. "Bitch, I told you to stop fucking with me, didn't I!" she yelled aggressively, clapping her hands for effect.

While I knew Tasha was in the wrong, it pissed me off that Perri was trying to fight her knowing she was pregnant. "Perri!" I yelled, causing her to immediately calm down a bit. I took that opportunity to kneel down and check on Tasha. When she removed her hands from her face, I saw blood. Her bottom lip was busted, and her nose had already begun to swell. "The fuck, yo!" I said, looking back at Perri. "She's pregnant!"

In that very moment, Perri's eyes grew wide, and all the fussing and fighting she was doing came to a sudden halt. "My bad, yo," she said weakly, holding her fist to the top of her head. "She just keep fucking with me." I looked up and saw that Perri now had tears pooled in her amber eyes. "I been trying to keep my cool, act like a lady and a perfect mother, just like you want," she said, looking down at me, her voice weakening with every word spoke. "But she just won't stop."

When I lifted Tasha from the ground to stand her up on her feet, she was crying. "This is who you call your best friend? Someone who tries to kill your child, Plus?"

"Come on. Let me go get you cleaned up," I said, wrapping my arm around her shoulder.

I didn't even want to acknowledge the questions she was asking me, because she was right. Just when I thought I actually might have deep feelings for Perri, deeper than I'd ever imagined, she pulled some crazy shit like this.

Last night I dreamt that I had finally made it to the NBA, and shockingly, Perri was my wife. I had come home after a basketball game, and Perri was in the kitchen cooking by the stove. Camille was a little toddler, and as soon as she saw me, she came running over to give me a hug. After scooping her up in my arms, I walked over and greeted Perri with a kiss on the lips. With Camille still up in my arms, I then went to go look for my son, who I assumed was the son I'd soon be having with Tasha. I swear it seemed like I checked every single room in that big-ass house, but I could never find him. And that's how the dream ended, with me panicking and waking up in a cold sweat.

Later that day, after we'd come back off of the boat, I took Tasha to a little clinic down the road from where the house was at. Other than her face being a little fucked up, it turned out that she was completely fine and the baby's heartbeat was still strong. It's crazy because I didn't even realize how much I wanted this baby until after the risk of losing it smacked me in the face. Once Tasha got all cleaned up and checked out of the doctor's office, we headed back to the house.

Immediately hearing everybody outside, we cut through to the backyard instead of going in the house. All the guys were on the basketball court playing, while Perri, Nika, and Shivon all sat to the side. When we walked up, Perri looked over at us with a guilt-ridden face. Tasha sucked her teeth in response and strolled past the girls without even acknowledging them.

"I'm sorry, Tash—" Perri started to say.

"Save it, bitch! You lucky my baby's okay or else I would beat yo' ass," Tasha snapped, interrupting Perri's apology.

Letting out a sarcastic snort of laughter, Perri simply shook her head.

"This bitch really is crazy if she thinks she can actually beat yo' ass. I mean, look at her fuckin' face," Nika said, failing to whisper.

Tasha cut her eyes back hard at Nika and attempted to walk toward her, but I grabbed a hold of her arm just in time. "Don't start no shit, Tasha. Bring yo' ass on," I said.

We sat down on the bench a few feet away from the rest of the girls, watching Derrick and Jorell play a game of two on two with TK and Jamal. Both TK and Jamal couldn't play worth shit, so it wasn't really a competition. Jorell and Derrick were dunking on those niggas left and right.

"Yayy! That's my baby!" Nika cheered when Jorell made a three-point shot.

He ran over to the side, puckering up his lips to give Nika a kiss, but she turned her head. "You stink, babe," she whined.

"A'ight, it's like that? Don't be trying to kiss me later either, gul," he teased.

"Y'all niggas ain't even playing fair," I said, standing up from the bench. "Yo, Mal, pass me the rock."

Jamal passed me the basketball, then came over to sit next to Shivon, who had gradually eased her way back over to sit next to Tasha.

"Ah shit, it's going down now," TK said, already talking shit.

"I'on give a fuck. I'll still beat yo' ass with or without Plus on your team," Derrick said. I knew that nigga was probably just showing off in front of Perri.

"Less talk, more action, nigga," I said, dribbling the ball.

As soon as the game got started, I took it to the hole for a quick layup. You would have thought TK made the basket himself the way he was walking like J.J. Evans down to the other end of the court, saying, "Dyn-o-mite!" Derrick, however, didn't waste any time retaliating. He quickly made a three-point jump shot, then backpedaled hard down the court, preparing to defend me. That nigga met me at every twist and turn I took. He was literally on my ass like we were playing in the championship game. Having no other choice, I hurriedly passed the ball to TK. When he tried going up for a simple layup, Jorell rebounded the ball off the backboard, then quickly ran down to dunk it in the hole. Dropping down from the rim, Jorell awkwardly planted his feet on the ground and somehow twisted his ankle.

"Ahh fuckkk," he wailed, grabbing his lower leg. After a minute or two, he was able to actually stand up, so we knew his injury wasn't severe. He hopped off to the side and sat down on the bench before telling Nika to run and get him some ice.

"So what you want to do? Y'all want to quit playing or nah?" I asked.

Derrick cut his eyes over at Jamal, his other option, and shook his head. "Yeah, let's call it a game," he started to say.

"Perri can play," Nika shouted out, causing Derrick to look in her direction.

Releasing a throaty groan, Perri pushed Nika on the arm. "Gee, thanks," she said sarcastically.

"You play, ma?" Derrick asked, surprised. I guessed that nigga didn't really know as much about her as I thought. When she nodded her head, that nigga smiled damn near ear to ear. "Come on, shorty. Come be on my team."

When she got up from the bench, adjusting the drawstring of her shorts, I sucked my teeth. "Man, let's just play another time," I said, waving her off. I knew that in most people's eyes I was discrediting her skills by doing that, but Perri was actually a decent ball player. Better than decent.

While everyone ignored my remark, Perri walked over to stand with Derrick. I watched as he put his arm over her shoulders and leaned down to whisper in her ear. She nodded her head up and down to whatever he was saying before he turned around and threw the ball at me. "Check," he said.

Even though I was pissed at Perri for fighting Tasha, I found myself hating the fact that she was playing on that nigga's team even more. Throughout the years, she had always played on my team whenever we played games of two on two. This was all new territory for me. With Derrick guarding me, I dribbled the ball left then cut hard to right, before pulling up to make a three-point shot. I watched the ball go into the hoop with ease before backpedaling down the court.

Perri carried the ball back up the court and faked left on TK before pulling up for a three-point shot of her own. Nothing but net.

"Damn, shorty, you got skills. That's what I'm talking 'bout," Derrick praised, giving her a high-five then a pat on the ass.

"Get 'em, girl!" Nika said.

"The fuck, TK? Get your head in the game, nigga!" I yelled.

After waving me off, TK dribbled the ball back down the court. Perri was defending his ass close, not giving him any room to shoot the entire time.

"Pass the ball, nigga! Pass the ball!" I yelled, feeling myself getting all worked up.

When he finally passed me the ball, it was as if Derrick had been waiting for it. Right as it floated in midair, he stole it and carried it down the court, only to slam-dunk it in the hoop.

"Yesss!" Perri cheered.

The same bullshit went on for the next thirty minutes or so, until TK and I finally lost the game 22-37. "Scrub-ass nigga. That's why I don't play wit' yo' ass," I fussed at TK, walking off the court. Meanwhile, Derrick picked Perri up and spun her around like they had just won the NBA championship.

Chapter 23

Perri

Once the game was over, we all showered and ate dinner, each in our own separate little cliques. Of course, Jorell and Nika hung with Derrick and me in the kitchen while Tasha and Shivon remained somewhere joined at the hip. The Three Musketeers, Plus, TK, and Jamal, all hung outside for the rest of the night, distancing themselves from everybody else. There was so much tension in that house that I honestly couldn't wait to leave. I contemplated calling Tez again, but after begging him to come get me the last time, I knew he'd be annoyed.

Later that night around ten, I found myself in the bedroom alone, surrounded by complete silence. I had just gotten through talking to Ms. Tonya to check up on Camille, and now I was lying back in the bed. Continuously, I threw my ball up in the air and stared toward the ceiling when suddenly a knock sounded at the door. Too lazy to get up and open it, I yelled, "Who is it?"

"It's Derrick, ma," he said.

"Come in."

When Derrick walked in, he had a hesitant look on his face. My eyes immediately zeroed in on his smooth caramel chest and arms, which were garnished in tattoos. His lower half, however, was covered in gray sweatpants with white socks on his feet. Approaching the side of my bed, he scratched the top of his head. "You want some company?" he asked lowly.

Truthfully I didn't, but something about the look in his eyes made it hard for me to turn him away. When I nodded my head, he came and sat down on the bed, nudging my thigh for me to slide over. Feeling the warmth of his exposed skin against mine as he lay back on the other half of my pillow somehow gave me comfort during a time I was feeling lonely and confused.

"You good, ma?" he asked, his voice deep and raspy as he lifted his arm to cradle me.

After tossing my basketball to the floor, I laid my head on his smooth, brawny chest. Noticing the light sprinkles of freckles that surrounded the tattoos on his arm, I explored each with a trace of my finger. "I'm good. It's just been a long day, and I'm . . . I'm just drained," I said.

"Yeah, I feel you. Why didn't you tell me you could ball though?"

I shrugged my shoulders, letting out an emotional sigh. "I don't know."

"I mean, shorty, you play so good that I thought you would be playing in college or some shit right now."

"I would have but I . . . I got pregnant with Camille. I had to give up my scholarship and stay home." I shrugged.

"Damn," he muttered.

Listening to the pity in his voice made me realize the huge sacrifice I had made. Sure, I wanted to go off to college and live on campus like the rest, but if I had to choose between that and Camille, I'd make the same decision a million times again. She was my constant peace and somehow a connection to my mother.

"So are you and Tasha straight now?" he asked, trying to change the subject.

"No, and Plus hates me too," I all but whined.

"He doesn't hate you. I'm sure he's just frustrated by the whole situation, but he'll come around," he said. Letting out a light chuckle, he said, "To be honest, I really don't know how the nigga is even doing it. Being around his two baby mommas at the same time? Shit is crazy." He shook his head before dragging his hand down his face as if he were placing himself directly in Plus's shoes.

"Well, I guess that's why I wasn't invited," I said lowly. Just the thought of Plus choosing Tasha over me once again made me want to cry.

"You were invited. By me, remember?" he said, leaning down to place a soft kiss on my forehead. That simple gesture alone reminded me of the Plus I loved so much.

After talking for another couple of hours or so, I could hear the sounds of Derrick's light snores dancing around the room. I glanced over at the digital clock that sat on the nightstand beside us and saw that it read 12:36. Deciding not to wake him, I softly slid out of his arms and climbed across his body so that I could cut off the lights. I decided that before I joined him back in bed I'd go downstairs and get a glass of water.

Tiptoeing down the dark, narrow hall, I began to hear the murmurs of voices in the distance. As I reached the bottom step, the voices became a little bit clearer, and although they were whispering, I could tell it was TK and Tasha in the kitchen. Still on my journey to get one final glass of water for the night, I planted my foot down on the floor from the staircase. However, I stopped dead in my tracks hearing Tasha say, "Why didn't you come check on me?"

"I knew you were straight, Tasha. All she did was hit your face," TK said. It was completely dark in the house, and although I couldn't see them, I could hear their voices fairly well now.

"But who knows what could have happened to my baby, TK? That bitch jumped right on top of me and you laughed like that shit was funny," she snapped.

Sucking his teeth, he said, "Man, Tasha, it wasn't even that serious."

"You see? That's the reason I won't break up with Plus," she whispered.

That's when my ears perked up and I tiptoed a little farther toward the kitchen. Hearing the hardwood floors squeak beneath me, I froze in place. The room grew silent, and just when I thought I had been made, I heard TK say, "You don't have to tell him. I'll just cut you off." His voice was lower than before, almost as if the two were about to share an intimate moment, but I couldn't see anything. "Is that what you want?" he asked.

The next few torturous moments were filled with complete and utter silence, until I heard the sounds of kissing and heavy breathing. I couldn't believe my ears. Not so much that Tasha was cheating, but more so about TK. He was like a brother to Plus, and it broke my heart just hearing how foul he was doing him. Just when the chunks of vomit started to rise within my throat, Tasha let out a loud, seductive moan.

"Ahhh . . . mmmm," she wailed.

"Shh, girl, you making too much noise," he whispered.

I turned around and headed back upstairs, tiptoeing the entire time in hopes they wouldn't hear me. Trekking down the long hall past the bedroom I was sleeping in, I turned right to go down the next corridor. After reaching the third door on the left, I came to a halting stop. My heart was beating so fast within my chest, I could nearly feel its vibration in my throat as I stared at the brass knob. Like releasing air from a balloon, I slowly let out the breath I had been holding in before opening up Plus's bedroom door.

When I saw him lying there on his back, naked as the day he was born, I couldn't help but feel sad for my best friend. While Tasha's snake ass was doing him dirty right up under his nose, he was in here sleeping like a baby. A glowing moon provided light through the windows as he lay in bed with nothing on but a thin white sheet draped loosely across one of his legs and his privates.

"Plus! Plus!" I said, shaking him from his sleep.

Squinting and slowly peeling one eye open at a time, he looked at me. "The fuck you want, P?" he groggily asked, rubbing the side of his fist against his eyes.

"You need to go downstairs, Plus. Now!" I said. My heart beat wildly inside of me as I tugged on his arm.

"For what?"

"It's Tasha."

"What's wrong? Is she okay? Shit, the baby," he panicked.

I rolled my eyes. "She's fine, Plus. More than fine, trust me. Just go and see—"

He sucked his teeth, cutting me completely off before I could even finish my sentence. "Man, don't start no bullshit, Perri!" he said, waving me off with his hand. "Leave Tasha the fuck alone. She's pregnant, and we don't need no more of your drama right now. Matter of fact . . ." He paused, running his hand down his face. "Matter of fact, get the fuck out. I'm not fucking with you like that right now anyway."

I cocked my head to the side. "You can't be fucking serious," I said in disbelief.

"As a mu'fucking heart attack. Now bounce!" he said.

Jerking my neck back, I took a good look at the asshole sitting before me and didn't even recognize him. No longer was Plus the vulnerable guy who would climb into my bedroom window in the middle of the night, answering riddles and math problems until we'd both fall asleep. The boy who would stand for me and with me, against just about anything or anyone, for that matter. The boy who actually named our daughter Camille after my deceased mother because he knew just how much it would mean to me. Instead, he had morphed into this cowardly man sitting in front of me. A selfish, senseless, and undesirable stranger.

When I walked out of the room, I made sure to slam the door hard behind me. With every step I took toward my room, I could feel tears starting to build. Just as I was about to turn the corner, Tasha approached. She saw me and jumped a little, either because she wasn't expecting to run into me or because she knew she had been doing something she wasn't supposed to. After pointing her chin up toward the ceiling, she attempted to walk past me.

"I know what you and TK been doing, bitch," I let out.

"What are you talking about, little boy?" she sneered with her arms folded across her chest.

"Oh, you know!" I shouted, pointing my finger. "You know exactly what I'm talking about." Closing the space between us to the point where our noses were practically touching, I lowered my voice to just above a whisper and said, "You's one foul-ass bitch, Tasha, and believe me, the truth will come out. And soon!"

With that, I walked away. As soon as I reached my room, I jumped back in bed with Derrick, who was on top of the covers with his sweatpants on and his socks still on his feet. When I buried my face into the center of his bare chest, he woke up and wrapped his arms around me.

"What's going on, ma? What's wrong?" he asked in a sleepy tone.

With my face still pressed up against him, I shook my head, not wanting him to see me cry. He must have felt the wetness of my tears on his skin though, because he lifted my chin for me to look up at him. That same light of the moon provided me just enough light to see the genuine concern on his face. Cupping my chin, he thumbed away the tears that had begun to flow freely down my cheeks.

"Tell me what's wrong, sweetheart?" he asked. The sound of his voice grew clearer and more serious as he firmed his grip on my chin.

"I . . . I just want to go home, Derrick," I whispered.

Chapter 24

Perri

Late Summer, 2004

"You sure you're ready for me to meet your family, babe?" I asked, looking over at Derrick. It was Labor Day weekend, and we were in his car driving up to New York. In the past four and a half months, Derrick and I had come to grow very close, and just last month we had finally decided to make it official. Yep, just as he had predicted the very night we'd met, I was his lady.

"More than ready, ma. You gon' love my momma," he said, leaning back far in his seat with only one hand on the steering wheel.

After another forty-five minutes on the road, we got stuck in bumper-to-bumper traffic and Camille, who was in the back seat, started to cry. I removed a diaper and a bottle of milk from her diaper bag that was on the floor beneath me before hopping over in the back seat. Although I had just changed her an hour ago at the rest area, I leaned down to smell her then slipped my finger inside her diaper to check.

"Well, you're dry. Are you hungry, sweet girl?" I cooed.

"Fuck, man," Derrick muttered, beating on the horn.

"Yo, calm down and stop all that cussing," I said, placing the bottle in Camille's hands.

"My bad, ma, I just hate all this damn traffic." He paused then said, "You're one to talk. Shorty, you cuss like a sailor."

I smiled. "But I've been getting better," I said, knowing good and well I was lying.

"Give my baby just one more year and she's gon' be cussing like crazy being around her foulmouthed momma."

"Shut up. I don't be cussing like that around her," I said.

"Shiidd!" he said, causing me to laugh. It was true. Although I was working on it, I still had a ways to go.

Once the traffic began to flow, we made it to New York within thirty minutes. We pulled up beside an old, dingy gray sign that read WELCOME TO MILL BROOK HOUSES. Looking up, I took in the tall red brick buildings that sat behind a low black iron gate. A few purposely placed trees were scattered across the fractured parking lot, which was filled with various groups of people.

"I'm home, baby!" Derrick exclaimed, grinning widely like a kid in a candy store as he put the car in park.

When we got out of the car, he scooped Camille up in his arms and started to lead the way. As we walked, I watched the neighborhood kids play outside while the fire hydrant flooded the front streets with water. Tossing footballs and listening to loud rap music, they enjoyed the last days of summer.

"Yo, D-man! D-man!" they all ran over and shouted, looking up at Derrick like he was some sort of local hood celebrity. They were throwing questions at him, like when was he going into the NBA, how long was he going to be home, and was I his girlfriend. Seeing the deep dimples pierce the sides of Derrick's face when he dapped them all up and rubbed the top of their little heads made me smile. When all the children finally ran away to continue playing, I caught a glimpse of one dusty-looking little boy. He couldn't have been more than 10 years old. Wearing dingy, cutoff jeans for shorts and hair in desperate need of a cut, he stared at Derrick with admiration in his eyes.

"What up, Josh," Derrick said, dapping him up.

"That's your baby?" the little boy asked, pointing up at Camille.

Derrick cut his eyes at me before giving a little smirk. "Mind ya business, young'un," he said, gently pushing the little boy in his head.

"When you going to the NBA?" the little boy asked, following us as we walked.

Derrick shrugged his shoulders. "We'll see, young'un. But look, we 'bout to head inside and check out Ma Dukes and shit. I'll be around for a few days, so I'll holla at you," Derrick dapped him up one more time. "And, Josh? Stay out of trouble," Derrick finally said, mushing the little boy in the head.

Just as the little boy turned around and happily ran away, we walked through a heavy red door. Dirty cream-colored linoleum floors and the scent of urine greeted me as soon as we stepped inside. After we entered the rickety elevator, I watched Derrick push the button for 12. When the elevator came to a stop and the metal doors opened, my feet clung to the sticky floor.

"Come on, shorty," Derrick said, rushing me along. If I was certain about anything at that moment, it was how excited Derrick was to be back home. His dimples seemed to be permanently inserted in each side of his face as we walked down the hall.

When we got to the apartment door that read 1277, Derrick knocked on the door before turning the knob. The tiny, smoke-filled apartment smelled like fried chicken, which immediately made me think of Ms. Tonya and Plus. Before we could even make it out of the entryway, a heavy-set, light-skinned lady with freckles covering her entire face appeared. She had pink curlers in her hair and wore a pink floral housecoat with dingy pink slippers on her feet.

"Well, don't just stand there, nigga. Come give your momma a hug," she said, planting her hands on her hips.

Derrick passed Camille over to me before walking over to give his mother a tight squeeze. Although his mother had to have been well over 250 pounds, he lifted her body up off the ground as if she were a small child. When he pulled back from their embrace, she looked him over from head to toe.

"You been eating like you supposed to, Derrick?" she asked with a raise of her brow. "Taking your vitamins?"

"Yes, ma'am," he said. "Oh, Ma, this is my girlfriend, Perri, I was telling you about."

Smiling, I walked up to greet her with Camille in one of my arms and her diaper bag hanging off of the other.

"Perri, this is Ma Dukes," he said. "And this here . . ." Smiling, he paused and took Camille out of my arms before giving her a kiss on her chubby cheek. "This here is my baby. Camille."

"Yo' baby? Hmm," she muttered, rolling her eyes. "Well, it's nice meeting you two. What you say your name was again?"

"It's Perri," I said, extending my hand for her to shake.

Instead of shaking my hand, she turned and walked away as though she didn't see it. "Come on in here and have a seat," she said.

I cut my eyes hard at Derrick because already I didn't like the vibe I was getting from his mother. He shrugged his shoulders and grabbed the back of his neck out of frustration. Not once did she truly acknowledge Camille, and that shit didn't sit well with me at all.

When we entered the living room, I saw two burnt-orange sofas sitting across from one another. Surrounding them were wild plants whose vines had grown up each of her walls. A coffee table was in the center of the room, and on it were two open cans of Colt 45 and an ashtray that was full of ashes and cigarette butts.

Before I took a seat on the sofa that was closest to the door, she looked me over, and I could have sworn I saw her nose slightly flare like she was disgusted. "You into the boyish ones now I see," she mumbled.

I had on my favorite pair of black basketball shorts and a white "Just Do It" Nike T-shirt. My hair was in a simple French braid that hung past the middle of my back, and of course I didn't have on any earrings. Not a single drop of makeup was on my face, not even Chapstick. Derrick was cool with me being just me, so since we were traveling, I left all that extra shit at home.

Derrick let out a light snort at his mother's commentary before shaking his head. "Don't start no shit, Ma," he said.

"I'm not," she sang, holding her hands up in surrender and pursing her lips. "Well, I made fried chicken, mac and cheese, white rice, green beans, and biscuits. You hungry?"

"Hell yeah, I'm starving," Derrick said, looking over at me.

I nodded my head because I was hungry too and the food sure did smell good. Ms. Scott, or "Ma Dukes" as

Derrick called her, got up to go to the kitchen, leaving Derrick, Camille, and me in the living room alone. Looking over at him bouncing Camille on his knee, I wondered if I should mention how rude his mother was to me. Instead, I got up and started looking at some of the family pictures that were hanging up on the walls and set on stands.

There was one with Derrick and, I assumed, his little sister when they were probably around 7 or 8 years old. Derrick had a little afro, and he was wearing a light blue polyester shirt with a butterfly collar. Holding the picture in my hand, I let out a light laugh.

"A li'l nigga was fly, wasn't he?" he asked with a smirk on his face.

"Yeah, you was fly all right. Superfly," I said, laughing. "Is this your sister?" I asked, looking at the cute little light-skinned girl in the picture. She had a face full of freckles and two puff balls sitting on the top of her head.

"Yeah, that's Shay. She's on her way."

I didn't know why but all of a sudden, I felt nervous. If Shay was anything like his mother, I knew today was going to be a long one. Right off the bat, I could tell that his mother didn't like me, and I prayed that with his sister I'd have a different experience. As I looked at more pictures, some of him playing basketball, others of him and his mother, I came across one of what looked to be his high school prom. Derrick looked fine in an all-white tuxedo, and next to him stood a gorgeous slim-framed girl. Judging by her light-buttery complexion and long, silky black hair, she had to be of Hispanic descent.

"That was Derrick at his prom, and that's my baby Mia," his mother said, entering the room.

I looked back over my shoulder and saw that she was wearing an ugly little smirk on her face. Cutting my eyes over at Derrick, who seemed to be ignoring his mother's commentary altogether, I cleared my throat. He looked up at me and winked as if nothing were wrong. Rolling my eyes, I walked past that picture and looked at some more before I came upon another one with Derrick and ol' girl. The two of them were smiling cheek to cheek, and I could tell that she was sitting in his lap.

"That one was right after graduation," his mother said. "Mia graduated with honors that day, and now my baby's off to become a lawyer," she bragged.

"Wow! You two sound really close," I said with a hint of sarcasm in my voice.

"Oh, we are. The closest any mother and daughter-in-law could possibly be," she said proudly.

"Daughter-in-law?" Just as I was about to address the label she had put on her relationship with Derrick's ex, the apartment door flew open.

"Where he at?" a girl with blue hair shouted, rushing in and letting the apartment door slam behind her. "Oh, my gahh! Big bro," she shouted when her eyes landed on Derrick.

With Camille still in his arms, he stood up from the sofa and held his arm out to give her a hug. "Damn, Shay, let a nigga breathe," he said.

When she loosened up the tight bear hug she put on him, she stepped back to look him over then let her eyes fall on Camille. "Ooh, she's pretty," she said, touching Camille's little hand. "Whose baby is this?" Just as she was asking, she looked over in my direction. "Hello," she hesitantly said.

"Shay, this is my shorty, Perri. Perri, this is my sister, Shay," Derrick introduced us.

Shay walked over and surprisingly extended her hand to me. Almost immediately seeing the resemblance to

Derrick in her features, I shook her hand and smiled. When she let go of my hand, I walked over and took Camille out of Derrick's arm.

"And this is my daughter, Camille," I said.

"She's beautiful. Has your light, pretty eyes, too," Shay said.

"Thank you."

"I was just telling her about Mia," Ms. Scott interrupted.

"Are you serious right now?" Shay looked toward her mother and frowned. "This girl don't want to hear about no damn Mia, Ma. Mia up and left, took her little prissy ass all the way up to Boston. So just let that shit go and stop trying to start shit," Shay fussed.

"I'm not starting nothing. I was just explaining who she was on the pictures," Ms. Scott said, holding her hands up in defense. "That's all!"

"Don't none of that shit matter no way. I'm here with Perri, Ma. Not Mia. Now let's go eat," Derrick said, removing the Yankees cap from his head.

Later that evening, after we ate and spent a little more time with his mother and sister, we headed over to the hotel. Silently, I was thanking God that Derrick didn't suggest we stay at his mother's apartment. Not that I was too good or anything like that, it was just obvious that his mother didn't like me, and that made me feel uncomfortable.

After getting Camille bathed and down to sleep in her portable crib, I jumped in the shower. Having such a long day, I stayed under the hot, steamy water for at least twenty minutes. That was until I heard Derrick open up the bathroom door.

"Hurry up. I need to shower too, ma," he said.

"Oh, my bad. Give me like five more minutes."

As I stood under the showerhead a little while longer, I could hear him moving around in the bathroom. I didn't know what he was doing, but I knew he had to get in, so I needed to hurry up. Just as I started to lather up my washcloth with soap, I could feel a cool breeze coming from behind the curtain. I looked behind me, and sure enough, it was Derrick taking a peek.

"Derrick!" I squealed.

Even after four and a half long months, Derrick had yet to see me naked. Part of that was because he spent most of his time at Georgetown while I was still at home, but there was also another part of the equation. Part of me was holding back because I just didn't know if I was ready to physically give myself to another man. Sure, the temptation was there because Derrick was beyond fine, and there were plenty of times when we'd even fooled around, but not once had we taken it to the next level.

"You killing me right now. All this time in here and you just now putting soap on your rag, ma," he complained, still peeking through the curtain.

As I tried to hide my breasts behind the washcloth in my hand, he slid the shower curtain back farther and proceeded to step inside. He was completely naked, and although I told myself to close my eyes, they immediately disobeyed me. My eyes first scanned across his thick, muscular arms and broad chest, which were covered in tattoos. Dropping my eyes a little lower, I then took in the sight of his well-defined abs. The finest strand of hairs trailed just below his waistline, which was held up by a pair of strong bowed legs. Between them, however, was another form of art: a long ten-inch pole that hung damn near to his knees.

Derrick licked his lips and bit down into a sexy smirk. His eyes were dark and low as he grabbed the washcloth from my hands and turned me back around, coming up so close behind me to the point where I could feel his dick practically jumping on my ass. He then reached around in front of me and proceeded to bathe me. He ran one of his sudsy hands across my breasts then down the center of my stomach as he gently sucked on my neck. I then closed my eyes and enjoyed the feeling of his fingers strumming the front of my clit.

"Mmm," I softly moaned.

Derrick must have taken that as a green light to proceed, because he began grinding himself up against my ass. Before I could even catch my breath, I felt his fingers dip inside of me. First it was slow, matching the motion of his hips behind me, but then as the tension started building between us, his fingers picked up speed. The grip of his other hand tightened on my waist as I fought back the emerging explosion between my thighs.

Never had I wanted another man as bad as I wanted Derrick in that moment. Not even Plus. My body was hot for him, and at this point, his fingers were only a pleasurable tease. Turning around to face him, I looked down at that monster between his legs once more and felt my mouth instantly begin to water.

I had never given head before, and hell, I didn't even think I'd ever want to. However, seeing that thing of beauty that Derrick had been toting around in the flesh seemed to stir something up inside of me. Now don't get me wrong, Plus was working with everything Derrick had, and truthfully maybe even a little more, but the fact was Derrick wanted me. Like, he actually looked at me as if I were the most desirable woman in all the world, making me want to offer up my body to him in the most unimaginable ways.

As we passionately kissed, he grabbed my hand and slowly slid it down his abs. My fingers skimmed just the top of his hairs before he gripped my hand around his dick. "You feel this big mu'fucka?" he said, whispering in my ear. Panting from the arousal of his deep, raspy tone and his girth that was pulsating in my hand, I nodded. "Once I put this dick in yo' life,"—he roughly grabbed my face for me to look at him—"you mines, shorty." He slid his tongue into my mouth and kissed me deeply before pulling back once again. "You think you ready for all that?" he hissed.

Just as I was nodding my head, saying yes to all the nasty things he wanted to do to me, Camille started to cry. "Shit," I muttered.

He let out a little snort of annoyance. "Saved by the bell, ma," he said, running his hand down his face.

Without even cutting off the water, I hopped out of the shower and wrapped my towel around me. When I stepped inside the room, Camille was standing up, holding the edges of the crib. As soon as she saw me, she stopped crying, and for some reason, she began to giggle. Her bright golden eyes shined back at me almost as if she knew she had just ruined my moment with Derrick.

"Let me find out you cock blocking," I muttered, picking her up.

As soon as I kissed her chubby cheek and sat down on the edge of the bed with her in my lap, my cell phone started to ring. I let out a deep sigh when I glanced down and saw Plus's name flash across the screen. In the past four months or so, I could count on my two hands how many times we had talked. Although he came home from school every other weekend, we sadly only exchanged Camille by going through Ms. Tonya, only texting one another every now and then in between.

Ever since that night in Ocean City when he told me that he wasn't fucking with me like that, our friendship seemed to decline. Part of me wanted to tell him about Tasha and TK, but the other part of me wanted him to just find out on his own. I wanted him to finally see Tasha for who she truly was without thinking I was hating on her in the process.

Letting out another deep breath, I answered the call. "Hello."

"Perri, I need you," he said. His voice was hard yet sounding as if he was on the verge of tears. "I'm about to fucking kill this nigga," he cried in between the background noise that was filled with loud screaming and fussing.

"Wait, kill who?" I said, trying to understand.

I could tell he moved his mouth away from the phone before I heard him yell, "Bitch, shut the fuck up, dripping blood all over the floor and shit. How you fucking my nigga behind my back? Trifling-ass ho," he spat.

"Plus!" I yelled into the phone, trying to get his attention through all the commotion on the other end.

"You is a trifling-ass ho," he yelled. "Did you or did you not fuck my nigga? Did you?" he shouted, straining his voice.

"Please. Ahhhh!" Once Tasha's voice became clearer, I knew all shit was about to break loose. "Get off of him, Plus. Get off!" she yelled.

"Fuck nah! Back up, Tasha, before I choke yo' ass out too," Plus shouted. "I'm gon' kill this muthafucka."

Hearing the call disconnect on the other end, I found myself feeling hopeless and, even more so, guilty. The more I panicked, the more my hands began to tremble, causing Camille to cry. Here I was hours away from home and couldn't do a damn thing to help Plus in his time of need. If only I had told him that night in Ocean City, none of this shit would have even gone down. I just prayed he wouldn't do something stupid, something he'd later regret.

"What's wrong, ma?" Derrick asked, still dripping wet from the shower with a towel wrapped around his waist.

Letting one lone tear slip down my cheek, I said, "Sorry, but I really need to get back home."

Chapter 25

Plus

"One more push, Tash. One more," I said, coaching her along.

"Arghh!" she wailed, hunkering down weakly to push. After she unexpectedly went into labor three weeks early, we arrived at the hospital to find out Tasha was already eight centimeters dilated. She had now been in labor for the past hour with no epidural, and already I could tell she was starting to give up.

"You're almost there," I said, looking down at the head of my son crowning through.

After three more pushes, his little cry sounded off, and the doctor raised him up high in the air. The mere sight of his pale pink skin and head full of curly black hair stirred up familiar emotions. Although I remembered tears building up in my eyes when they first landed on Camille, that same sense of love for my son was there. When I cut the umbilical cord and the nurses took him away, I smiled. I never did get the chance to cut Camille's umbilical cord, so I was happy to have that moment.

"You did good, baby," I said, wiping the sweat off Tasha's forehead.

She looked up at me and gave a weak little smile. It was a slight, almost peculiar curl of the lips that I just couldn't read. However, when the nurse came back over to place our baby in her arms, her smile immediately widened, and her eyes lit up with love. Just as I was running my finger down one of his tiny little feet, another nurse walked inside the room.

"Oh, he's beautiful. Congratulations, you two," she said. "What are you guys going to name him?"

I looked over at Tasha, and when our eyes met, she gave me a slight nod of her head. "Ahmad Taylor Jr.," I proudly said.

After writing his name down on the clipboard she had in her hand, she and the other nurses all left the room. No more than a few seconds later, TK came rushing in. He was completely out of breath like he had been running, and yet when he entered the room, he stopped dead in his tracks. His eyes immediately enlarged at the first glimpse of my son before taking in the family picture of the three of us.

"Damn, nigga," I said, going over to dap him up. "I hadn't even gotten a chance to call my momma yet. How did you even know she had the baby?" I asked.

"Ms. Monroe called me," he said, referring to Tasha's mother.

"Ms. Monroe called you?" I asked, confused, my eyebrows immediately dipping in as I tried to understand.

When I saw him glaring over at Tasha, I noticed that his jaw was tightly clenched. He wore what seemed to be a pissed expression on his face, and I watched his hands gradually ball up into fists. In that very instant, I could feel the thick, quiet tension that had fallen upon the room. I glanced back at Tasha, who was oddly staring off, avoiding eye contact with both TK and me. Up until this point, I hadn't even thought about the fact that Tasha had yet to acknowledge TK's presence.

"You called your mother?" I asked, looking at Tasha.

"I sent her a text while we were on the way," she said, looking down at baby Ahmad.

"You need to tell him, Tasha," TK then said with a swell of his chest.

"Tell me what?" I asked, looking between the two of them.

Tasha began shaking her head back and forth, almost as if she was refusing to speak. For some reason, seeing tears slide down her face caused a gut-wrenching fear to creep over me. TK stepped up close beside us, and his eyes narrowed in on the baby.

"All right, guys, I need to take baby Ahmad with me to run a few tests," another nurse suddenly came in and said.

"Baby Ahmad?" TK asked. Bewilderment consumed his voice before he closed his eyes and pinched the tip of his nose. "Fuck nah!" he spat, shaking his head. "That's my fucking son!"

Just as I was about to ask that nigga what the fuck his problem was, my son's eyes opened for the very first time. Bluer than any sky I'd ever seen, they instantly rendered me speechless. But before TK could get another word out, my hands found themselves wrapped around that motherfucker's neck and I began dragging him to the floor.

"Sir, please. Please! You cannot do that in here!" the nurse yelled.

"Plus, stop! Pleeasse!" Tasha screamed at the top of her lungs.

"Call security now!" the nurse yelled out into the hall.

The last thing I needed was the cops called on me, so I punched that nigga as hard as I could one good time. Instantly hearing the crack of his nose was satisfaction enough, and with that, I hopped up and walked out of the room. Pacing the hospital floor, I reached into my pocket and grabbed my cell to call the first person who came to mind.

"Hello," she said.

I hadn't talked to her like that in months, yet I needed to hear the familiar sound of her voice. Thankfully, she answered on the second ring. I knew she was still mad at me for the way I spoke to her in Ocean City, and seeing how everything had played out now, I couldn't even blame her.

"Perri, I need you," I said, hearing my own voice crack as tears started to form. "I'm about to fucking kill this nigga." I grabbed my throbbing head and paced the floor in hopes of calming myself down, but that was no use. The burning anger I felt inside caused me to see red. My hands were literally shaking, and I immediately started having thoughts of homicide.

"Wait, kill who?" she said, trying to understand it all.

The next thing I saw was Tasha in her hospital gown, wobbling out of the room with TK following her.

"Plus, baby, let me explain," Tasha cried, pressing her hands together as if she were praying to the Lord Himself.

At just the mere sight of the two of them standing there side by side, I lost it. "Bitch, shut the fuck up!" I yelled. When she walked up close on me, I looked down at her with disgust. "Dripping blood all over the floor and shit. How you fucking my nigga behind my back? Trifling-ass ho," I spat. Spit violently flew out of my mouth as I stabbed her in the forehead with my finger.

"I'm so sorry," she cried. When she dropped down to her knees, the hospital gown she had on fell open, exposing her naked body.

"Plus!" I could hear Perri yelling through the phone, trying her best to get my attention through all the commotion.

Weeping loudly as the nurses all tried to pry her from the floor, Tasha continued to shake her head and plead her case. "I'm so sorry. I didn't—"

"Trifling-ass ho!" I yelled, cutting off her words. "Did you or did you not fuck my nigga? Did you?" I shouted again, straining my voice. Feeling a surge of anger rapidly take me over, I drew back my fist to hit her. But before I could even attempt to swing, TK rushed over and grabbed me by the arms. Blow for blow, we started going at it, right there on the hospital floor. And within just a matter of seconds, we found ourselves tussling on the ground.

"Ahhh! Stop!" Tasha screamed. "Get off of him, Plus. Get off!" she yelled, pulling on my shirt. I had just fought my way on top of him and was literally trying to choke the life out of his ass.

"Back the fuck up, Tasha, before I choke yo' ass out too," I spat, jerking my shoulder to get her off of me. "I'm gon' kill this muthafucka." Seeing his pale face turn bright red, veins popping from his neck, and tears forming in his eyes, I tightened my grip around his throat. "You supposed to be my nigga. My brother," I said lowly through gritted teeth. Squeezing so tightly around his neck, I suddenly began to hear him gasp for air.

Just as TK's blue eyes started to roll to the back of his head, I was lifted up by two men in black uniforms. You would have thought when they threw the handcuffs on my black ass I'd calm the fuck down, but no, I was too amped up to be powered off. They ended up dragging me away, still fighting, kicking, and cussing at the top of my lungs. The last vision I remembered before being thrown into the back of the police car was of Tasha. She was half-naked in a puddle of blood, kneeling over TK, who was curled up on the floor into a fetal position. Nurses and hospital staff in white coats and blue scrubs all gathered around.

The next morning, I found myself walking down the steps of the DC county jail. With my hand arched over my eyes, shading them from the bright morning sun, I looked down toward the sidewalk. Leaned up against Tez's black Acura with their arms folded across their chests were my mother and Tez. Perri stood off to the side of them, looking as though she had just rolled out of bed. Wearing gray sweatpants, an oversized white T-shirt, and a look of exhaustion on her face, she stretched her eyes. When our gazes finally met, she nervously smoothed back her frizzy hair with her hand.

I cleared my throat and stepped down off the bottom step. Tucking my hands deep into my pockets, I first approached my mother. Immediately, I could see the disappointment in her eyes.

"Ma—"

Before I could even explain, she cut my words off with a stiff slap to the face. The hard whack she delivered instantly brought tears to my eyes. And although the burning sting hurt pretty badly, the look of discontent on her face was punishment enough.

"Get yo' ass in this car, boy," she yelled, jerking me forward by my shirt. "You are lucky Tez knows somebody, or else your ass would have been charged and locked up. Not to mention your stupid ass would have gotten kicked out of school."

I looked over at Tez, who gave me a slight head nod then dapped me up. I guessed this was his way of letting me know he had my back. When I opened up the back door of his car, Perri jumped in ahead of me and slid over behind the driver's seat. Just as I dipped down to get in, I felt another hard smack to the back of my head.

"Ma!" I yelled, grabbing the back of my head.

"Ya big dummy!" she fussed. When we all got into the car, I thought she was done, but she still wouldn't let up. "I told your ass years ago to leave her little fast behind alone. But nooo. 'I need a model chick on my arm. Tasha so fine, Tasha's so this and Tasha's so that,'" she mocked. "Nigga, Tasha ain't shit!"

Running my hand down my face, I threw my head back and let out a loud sigh of annoyance. Hoping—no, praying—that she would just shut up already, I closed my eyes. Hearing my mother tell me what I'd already come to realize stressed me out even more. The only thing I could even think about at this point was burning one. I had known for some time now that dealing with Tasha's ass was a mistake, but before I could end things with her, she up and got pregnant.

"She was just trying to trap yo' ass because she knows you about to enter the draft," my mother said, turning around in her seat to look at me. "Dumb-ass nigga. I swear," she muttered, shaking her head.

Perri must have felt my frustration, because she reached over and grabbed my hand. Interlacing her soft fingers through mine, she glanced over at me with a look of pity in her eyes. She offered a closed-lip smile before turning her head back to stare out of the window.

"Where's my baby at?" I asked lowly, still hearing my mother fuss in the front seat as we drove along.

"She's with my dad," Perri said, continuing to look out the window.

"Yo, I really appreciate you coming, P. I swear you always got a nigga's back."

She turned back toward me and looked me directly in the eyes. Firming the grip she had on my hand, she said, "Always."

At that moment, I knew then that there were no apologies needed and no discussions to be had. Everything that we had gone through those past few months had been buried as though the friction between us never existed. Perri was family, she was my best friend, and no matter what happened between us, she always would be.

Chapter 26

Perri

Early Thanksgiving morning, Myesha, Ms. Tonya, and I were all working hard in the kitchen. The savory smell of turkey, stuffing, and honey-baked ham filled the air. Even though I couldn't cook a lick, I was bound and determined to learn a little something this holiday season. Despite the fact that this would be Derrick's and my first major holiday together, it was also our first family dinner at Tez and Myesha's new house. It was a large red brick home with five bedrooms and two and a half baths, all sitting on a half-acre lot right outside of Bowie.

"I am the official Thanksgiving taste tester this year," Plus came in and said. Bare chested, he slid across the kitchen floor with navy blue basketball shorts and low white socks on his feet. Coming up close behind me, he leaned over my shoulder to see what I was making. "Now you know yo' ass can't cook. What you 'bout to burn up in here?" he teased.

"Shut up," I said, continuing to peel the white potatoes for the potato salad.

"Perri is trying to become demasticated, Ahmad," Ms. Tonya said.

Myesha, Plus, and I all paused and looked at one another, replaying and confirming exactly what she had just said in our minds before erupting in laughter.

"Damn, Ma. I know you didn't go to college and shit, but come on. It's domesticated," he said with emphasis.

"Boy, shut up. I say it how I like to say it!"

He then turned his attention back to me. "And what you trying to do all that for? Who the fuck you trying to impress?" he asked, poking me in my side.

"Her boo thang. That's who," Myesha added.

"Boo thang? What, Derrick coming up here today?" he asked.

"Yeah," I muttered.

When I turned around to head toward the fridge, he placed each of his arms on the counter around me. He leaned in close, placing his cheek directly against mine, and whispered in my ear, "You give that nigga my pussy yet?"

It was true that Plus had no actual claims to my body, but I instinctively swallowed hard and allowed my eyes to shut. As much as I was falling for Derrick, being this close to Plus just did something to me. The vibration of his voice in my ear, the warmth of his skin against mine, and the faded scent of his cologne all caused my heart to race and my breath to shallow.

Peeling one eye open at a time, I leaned back and said, "None of ya business, nigga."

With his arms still trapping me, he bent down and shocked the hell out of me by gently placing a kiss to my collarbone. It was just a soft, subtle suck of the skin, which caused my knees to slightly buckle beneath me. His eyes narrowed into speculating slits before a cocky smile spread across his face. Both revealed that he already knew he was the only one to ever take pleasure in my body.

"Ahem," Myesha said, clearing her throat.

I glanced over, seeing the smirk on her face that confirmed she had seen Plus kiss me on the neck. When

I looked back up at him, he was still wearing that cocky little grin on his lips. There wasn't a doubt in his mind that I was all hot and bothered, so I tried my best to play it off. Shoving him hard in the chest, I rolled my eyes and pushed him out of the way before heading over to the fridge.

"You play too much," I said, watching him lick his lips and wink his eye at me. Plus played too many games, and this time I didn't feel like participating.

A few seconds later, the doorbell could he heard. "I got it," yelled Tez, coming up the stairs. He and my father had been downstairs in the basement with Camille watching TV, so he must've just come up.

"Hey, best friend," Nika sang, entering the kitchen.

I walked over and gave her a hug before taking the groceries out of her hand. She was contributing cranberry sauce, sparkling cider, and rolls to our Thanksgiving dinner. After giving out hugs to the rest of the family, she took off her coat and started helping me peel potatoes.

Leaning back with his leg propped up against the kitchen wall, Plus looked over at Nika. "You can cancel all that best friend shit you was talking, too. She only got one best friend, and that's me," Plus said.

"Whatever, Plus. I'm her best girlfriend. Is that better?" she asked with her hands on her hips.

Shrugging his shoulders, he said, "I mean, whatever. As long as you know."

"Anyway," Nika said, rolling her eyes at Plus before looking at me. "What time are Jorell and Derrick supposed to be here?"

"I think by three." I glanced at the clock on the microwave, and it was now quarter after eleven. I had just enough time to finish up in the kitchen and get dressed. My hair was in a bush ball on the top of my head, and Nika promised that she would flat iron it for me.

"Ooh, we gotta hurry up so we can get ready," she said.

As soon as Plus sucked his teeth, Myesha giggled and shook her head.

"Are y'all girls done with them potatoes?" Ms. Tonya asked.

I told her yes and took her the bowl of potatoes that Nika and I had peeled. After whipping up the sweet potatoes, eggs, and milk, mixed with a drizzle of vanilla and a dash of cinnamon and sugar, I filled up each of the pie shells. Aria walked into the kitchen and grabbed the mixing spoon out of the bowl

"Camille is downstairs crying," she said, licking the pie mix off the spoon. She was now 14 years old and looking like a full-grown woman. She had more hips and ass than Ms. Tonya and I put together, and Plus couldn't stand it.

I looked over at Plus, who had a piece of honey-baked ham hanging out of his mouth. "You got her, or you want me to go?" I asked.

"I got her. I know you gotta go get ready for yo' man," he said, smirking as he grazed past me and walked out of the kitchen.

"You two are a trip," Myesha said.

Raising my eyebrow, I looked over at her. "What are you talking about?"

"I mean, it's so obvious that he wants you."

"And she wants him just as bad," Ms. Tonya cut in and said.

I shook my head before looking back and forth between the two. "I have a boyfriend. Besides, y'all know me and Plus are like family. It's not even like that," I said.

"Sure, that's why y'all have a baby together, right?" Ms. Tonya said, rolling her eyes. "Because y'all are like family." Her voice dripped with sarcasm as she leaned down to check the baked macaroni and cheese that was bubbling over in the oven.

"It was our first time, and we were just experimenting," I said, downplaying all the emotions I felt for Plus the first time we made love.

"And what was it the second time?" Nika chimed in. Myesha's and Ms. Tonya's eyes grew wide as they both gasped in shock before giggling.

When I cut my eyes hard over at Nika and cocked my head to the side, she covered her mouth with her hands. Realizing the secret she had just revealed, she lowered her head in shame. Other than her and maybe Jorell, no one knew that Plus and I were together sexually more than once. I told her that in confidence and now here she was running her big mouth, telling all my business.

"Eww," Aria said, covering her ears. Although there was Camille, hearing that her brother and I had a sexual history must have disgusted her, because she scrunched up her nose and walked out of the kitchen.

Not wanting to further discuss the only two sexual encounters I had ever had, I said, "I gotta go get ready. Nika, come on."

After going up to one of Tez's guest bedrooms, which he had designated just for me, I quickly showered and dressed. I wore a charcoal gray sweater dress that clung to my curvy size-six frame. Wearing black leather knee boots and silver hoop earrings that sparkled, I looked myself over in the mirror. Thanks to Nika, my long brown hair was now silky straight, and my eyebrows were arched to perfection. Just like she had taught me, I added a thin coat of black mascara to my lashes and a sheer coat of pink lip gloss to my lips.

"Derrick is going to eat you alive when he sees you in this dress," Nika said, standing behind me in the mirror.

"You think so?" I smoothed down the front of my dress before angling myself in the mirror to get a different view.

"Oh, I know so. And Plus is going to die a slow death when he sees you hugging all over Derrick, looking as good as you look."

Smiling, I shook my head at her. "Plus isn't thinking about me. After that whole debacle with Tasha, his ass done already moved on to someone else."

"For real? Who?"

I shrugged my shoulders and turned around. "Some girl named Daysia is all I know. She's been calling his phone all week since he's been home from school. And every time she calls, he feels the need to step out of the room," I said, rolling my eyes.

Judging by the look on Nika's face, I knew I sounded like a jealous ex-girlfriend or baby momma. "Well, are you mad about it?" she asked. One eyebrow bounced up as a silly smirk graced her face.

"Of course not. I'm with Derrick. I just don't know how healthy it is for him to be jumping into another relationship so soon. I mean, Plus and Tasha had been together for almost four years, so no matter how I may feel about her trifling ass, I know he loved her. Not to mention she cheated on him with one of his best friends and had a baby by him. You don't just get over something like that after a couple of months."

Hearing myself speak on what happened between Plus and Tasha caused my heart to break for him all over again. After we left the jail that morning, he never mentioned Tasha's or TK's names again. I knew Plus was hurting, which was the underlying reason for his extreme partying and hoeing around these past few months. Even his grades had begun to slip. He actually brought home two B's this semester, which was totally unlike him. Plus had been a straight A student for as long as I could remember, so his grades were a clear indication that he was mentally and emotionally falling apart.

"Yeah, I guess you're right," Nika said.

Not too long after that, I heard the doorbell ring. For some reason, my nerves instantly took over, and my stomach started to churn. Derrick had already met my entire family, but that was just in passing. Today he would actually be spending real quality time with them, and that made me feel a bit uneasy. After only meeting Derrick three times in the last seven months, Tez talked a lot of junk about him already. And although Derrick and Plus were cool from being on the same basketball team at Georgetown, I knew it wouldn't take much for Plus and Tez to join forces. Somehow I just knew I was in for a real Thanksgiving treat.

When I walked downstairs, Derrick stood in the foyer with a bundle of red roses in his hand. He was dressed down in a pair of blue jeans, a navy blue sweatshirt, and his favorite Yankees cap on his head. Small diamond studs sparkled in each of his ears, and he wore a thin gold chain around his neck. He allowed his eyes to trace my figure from head to toe. Standing beside him was Jorell, who had his chin chucked high up in the air. His dreads hung freely and his gold grill was just shining through the crack of his dark, full lips as he proceeded to blow an air kiss at Nika, who was right behind me. Tez, Plus, and my father were all gathered around as if some sort of show were about to start, and in the background the light, girlish giggles of Ms. Tonya, Myesha, and Aria could all be heard.

As soon as I stepped into the foyer, Derrick didn't hesitate to open up his arms and greet me with a tight hug. Inhaling, I took in his clean Irish Spring scent and closed my eyes. Even though I wanted to linger in his arms just a little while longer and maybe even get a kiss, I knew several pair of eyes were on us. When he passed me the bouquet of roses, I smiled, giving them a quick sniff, and then I thanked him for the gesture. As I carried them into the kitchen to put them in water, I passed by Nika and Jorell. I shook my head at the sight of them all hugged up, kissing like they were the only two people in the room.

My father then walked over to Derrick. "How's it going, young man?" he asked, extending his hand.

Once I got into the kitchen, I grabbed Camille from Aria and watched from a distance. I could no longer hear them, but I could still see the interaction between the two. Derrick removed the hat from his head and shook my father's hand before walking over to Tez. Silently, I stood by the fridge and watched the two of them.

Tez pushed back his long hair, which was now in sandy brown locs instead of braids. Flipping his head from side to side, he cracked the muscles of his neck before proceeding to then crack his knuckles. Standing in a wide, protective stance, he stood directly in front of Derrick, chin chucked up high and hands clasped together like a typical gangster. Both stood with a swell in their chests, standing over six feet tall and staring each other down in some sort of silent war. Although a Thanksgiving feast had already been prepared, the smell of testosterone damn near overpowered the food in the room.

"You okay, girl? I know Tez is probably in there show-ing his ass with the whole overprotective brother act," Myesha touched my shoulder and said.

Although I nodded my head to say I was okay, I was actually shitting bricks. After another five minutes of their private conversation, Derrick came into the kitchen to join me. "Are you okay?" I immediately asked.

As soon as the words left my lips, Tez walked into the kitchen as well. "That nigga's a'ight. We ain't do shit to him," he said. After smacking Myesha hard on the behind, he then told her to fix him a plate.

"You hungry?" I asked Derrick as he greeted Camille by shaking her little hand.

Wearing a smirk on his face, he licked his full dark pink lips and nodded his head. "Yeah, I'm definitely hungry, ma," he said. Leaning down, he then whispered in my ear, "But not for no fucking turkey. I got a taste for something else if you know what I mean." He pulled back and winked his eye at me before licking his lips again. Blushing, I turned my head only to see Plus staring a hole through the two of us. I couldn't exactly read his expression. It was neither happy nor sad, not even angry, for that matter. His face was calm, but behind his eyes were these question marks. Now what had him puzzled, I wasn't so sure.

After feeding Camille and putting her to sleep, we all got the food together and sat down at Tez's long dining room table. My father and Tez each sat at the heads, while Nika, Jorell, Derrick, and I sat directly across from Myesha, Ms. Tonya, Aria, and Plus. A major feast, which included ham, turkey, stuffing, collard greens, baked macaroni cheese, sweet potatoes, and cornbread, was spread across the table in bulk. The sight and savory smell alone caused my stomach to growl.

Once Daddy said grace, we all dug in and ate like it was our last meal here on earth. Although I didn't do anything but peel the potatoes and boil the eggs, Ms. Tonya praised me for making the potato salad, which she had actually made herself.

"Damn, ma, you can cook, too?" Derrick leaned over and asked, causing all eyes to turn on us.

Just as I was smiling at the compliment he gave me, Plus and Tez both looked at one another before letting out several snorts of laughter. "Yeah, she can cook all right," Tez mumbled, shaking his head. "Milk and cereal."

I rolled my eyes and prayed he would just shut up, but as soon as he got quiet, Plus joined in too. "Remember that time you called yourself making cheese toast? You put a piece of bread and a slice of cheese down in the toaster together," he said, causing everyone at the table to laugh except for me. "Man, when that cheese started to melt, smoke was every-damn-where. And I think we was only like, what?" he said, looking over at me. "Like eight or nine at the time. Scared as shit when that damn smoke alarm went off."

I shook my head and finally laughed, recalling that day.

"And where was I?" Ms. Tonya asked, trying to remember.

"You was out following behind Ronnie's drunk ass, I'm sure," Plus said.

"Ahmad, don't make me slap the shit out of you in here," she said.

"Who's Ronnie?" Derrick asked.

"My no-good daddy," Aria chimed in.

"Ayo, remember that night after your sixteenth birthday party?" Tez looked at Plus and asked.

Plus and I locked eyes before falling out laughing. "Yeah, I remember that night." He paused, releasing a slight chuckle. "Perri got high as shit," he said with a smirk.

Letting out a loud gasp, my eyes widened to the size of quarters. I couldn't believe he had just outed me like that, and in front of my daddy and Ms. Tonya no less. "Nigga, you was high too. Stop frontin'," I retorted.

"We was all blazed that night. Plus pulled on that shit so hard," Tez shook his head and said. "Like he was trying to drink milkshake from a straw. You remember that shit?" Tez looked over at me. "Coughed up his right lung that night."

All three of us laughed while everyone else sat there amused.

"But you." Tez pointed at me, biting back the prideful smile from forming on his face as he remembered that night. "My nigga. My G," he said. "You smoked that shit like a professional. I was like, damn, baby sis been blazing all this time and ain't tell nobody."

"Is that right?" Daddy cut in. His eyebrow was raised and his stern voice dripped with discernment as he glared at me.

I held up my hand and shook my head. "It wasn't like that, Daddy. Really. We just tried it that one time."

Before the lie could fully roll off my tongue, Plus and Tez cut me off. "Shiidd!" they both shouted out at the exact same time. Everyone at the table erupted in laughter with the exception of my father and Ms. Tonya.

With the most serious expression I could muster up, I looked back and forth between Plus and Tez, silently telling them to shut the fuck up. No matter how much of a tomboy I was, I was still a daddy's girl at heart. And even if I was almost 20 years old, I never wanted him to be disappointed in me.

When Ms. Tonya cut her eyes hard over at Plus, giving him a similar look of disappointment, he nonchalantly shrugged his shoulders. "What? You was out chasing behind Ronnie's ass that night too! Remember?"

With her lips pursed to the side, she rolled her eyes and stuck another piece of cornbread in her mouth. There wasn't much she could come back with after that.

I personally hadn't seen Ronnie in a while, but I knew he still made his way over to their house every now and then because Aria would tell me. He had been stealing money and electronics from Ms. Tonya's for the past six months. Already knowing that Plus had too much on his plate with basketball, school, and the loss of Tasha and the baby, not to mention TK, I didn't have the heart to tell him.

Things around the table had suddenly quieted down with everyone having low sidebar conversations or simply eating their food. Suddenly, I noticed Daddy use the white cloth napkin to wipe the corners of his mouth before dropping it down on his empty plate. He leaned back in his chair, allowing extra room for his protruding belly, then cut his eyes over at Derrick.

"So tell me, young man, what are your intentions for my daughter?"

I had just taken a sip of red Kool-Aid, so I practically choked hearing my father ask him that. Meekly, I looked over at Derrick, who was taking rather long to answer the question. Praying that he would say all the right things to make this conversation end as quick as possible, I nudged him in the side.

"Truthfully, sir, I have the utmost respect for your daughter," he said then looked over at me. "She's talented, smart, and . . . you beautiful as hell, ma."

I, along with every other woman sitting around that table, cooed, letting out a series of "aww's" at the exact same time. But the subtle sound of teeth sucking could also be heard coming from Tez's and Plus's directions. I didn't even bother addressing them, because I was too wrapped up in Derrick's dark brown eyes, which had me in some sort of a trance.

"Sir," he said, slowly peeling his eyes off of me, "I believe I'm in love with Perri."

My mouth almost hit the floor.

"This nigga," Plus mumbled under his breath.

Squinting my eyes, I glared over to give him a look and a half.

"So let me ask you this," Tez said to Derrick.

"Y'all, please stop," I said, holding up my hand. "Daddy asked him a question, and he answered it. That should be good enough." I defended Derrick because I could already see the conversation turning ugly.

"It's a'ight, ma. I'll answer whatever," Derrick said, licking his lips.

"You love her," Tez stated, letting out a snort as he leaned back and crossed his arms over his chest. "But does she love you?"

Dropping my head down into the palms of my hands, I let out a deep sigh. I couldn't believe Tez was acting up like this. Not once after finding out he had a secret girlfriend did I hound Myesha, but here he was embarrassing the hell out of me. Sure, I knew big brothers were supposed to be protective, but this shit was overboard to me.

"Well, ma?" I heard Derrick say, cutting his eyes over at me.

When I removed my hands from my face, I looked up to see that he, along with everyone else at the table, was waiting for an answer. Even though my mouth hung slightly ajar, I really didn't know what to say. My mouth had suddenly gone dry, and I found myself completely speechless. "I . . . I . . ." I stammered.

"What you say, ma? I . . . I . . . didn't hear you, ma," Tez mocked, leaning forward with his hand cupped around his ear.

Plus and Jorell both laughed while Derrick only let out a snort, revealing just how irritated he was.

"That's something we can talk about in private," I said.

"Exactly!" Tez said, pointing at me with his finger. His lips were already twisted to the side in an "I told you so" fashion as he smirked. I rolled my eyes.

When Derrick mumbled, "Wow," and shook his head, I knew he was probably pissed, but I was only telling the truth. After only seven months, I wasn't ready to profess my love for him, especially not in front of everyone like this. I tried grabbing his hand underneath the table, but he quickly moved it away and avoided eye contact with me.

"Yo, look, I'm sorry, a'ight?" I leaned over and whispered in his ear.

He looked at me and softened the expression on his face before nodding his head. Grabbing my hand underneath the table, he nodded his head once more, letting me know that everything would be okay.

Chapter 27

Plus

Once the women in the family all started cleaning up, the fellas and I headed back down into the basement. Tez's basement was a full-blown man cave with a seventy-inch plasma TV and chocolate leather sofas. In the center of the room was a nice-sized pool table and in the back was a fully stocked bar. We had the football game playing on surround sound and had sat down to play a game of spades.

"Yo, Rel, you wit' me," I told Jorell. He nodded his head.

"Pops, you playin'?" Tez looked over and asked Mr. Phillip.

"No, you boys go ahead and play. I'ma just sit back here and watch this game," he said, nodding toward the TV. He laid the recliner all the way back before taking a swig of his Budweiser beer.

Glancing over at Derrick, Tez nodded his head. "I guess it's me and you then, homeboy."

"A'ight, that's what's up," Derrick said, twisting his cap to the back before pulling up a chair.

The four of us quickly sat down and began playing. When Tez fired up one of his blunts, I was waiting for Mr. Phillip to say something, but I guessed there wasn't much he could. Tez was now grown at 22 years old with his own home and his own money.

"I got four. What you got?" I looked across the table and asked Jorell.

"Two and a possible," he said.

Tez pulled on his blunt and rocked back in his chair, counting the books in his hand. After letting a thick stream of smoke escape his lips, he glared over at Derrick. "I got three."

"Hmm, well let's go ahead and lock it up, son. Put us down for seven," Derrick looked at me and said.

After all the cards had been thrown onto the table, Tez and Derrick had picked up eight books while Jorell and I had only made five. As soon as I saw Tez and Derrick slap hands, I instantly became annoyed.

"Damn, nigga. I thought you said you had three books," I fussed, glaring over at Jorell.

"Breh, I thought I did. I was hoping yo' ass had the ace and not one of them, mane," Jorell's country ass tried to explain.

Once I wrote down the score, I went ahead and dealt the next round. When I picked my cards up off the table, I saw nothing but a handful of trash. Not having one face card in my hand, I let out a deep sigh.

"Looks like we 'bout to run a yard on dem niggas, son," Derrick said cockily.

Tez cut his eyes over at me before removing the blunt from his lips and letting out a light chuckle. "Looks that way," he said, shaking his head. "You heard the man. Put us down for ten."

I put Jorell and me down for four, but honestly, I didn't feel confident that we'd get it. The first card Tez played was his little joker. Silently I was praying that Jorell had the big one, but that idea went completely down the drain when I saw the three of spades drop from his hands. After Derrick collected that book, Tez then threw out the big joker. "Shit!" I muttered, throwing my hands up in the air.

The game continued just like that for the next eight hands, until Tez and Derrick finally took the victory. "A'ight, A'ight. I see you," Tez said, slapping hands with Derrick.

When Derrick stood up from the table, he stretched out wide and yawned. "I guess it's time for me to get up out of here," he said.

"It's kinda late for you to be heading back to New York. Pops and Godma driving back home tonight, so I got room if you wanna stay," Tez offered.

My face unconsciously balled up, seeing that nigga Derrick's eyes light up at the suggestion. "Nah, nigga. Ain't gon' be no fucking in here tonight," I said. Although everyone had started laughing, I was dead-ass serious.

Derrick held his hands up in surrender and looked to Tez. "Nah, I wouldn't try to disrespect your home like that."

Tez let out a slight snort before glaring hard at Derrick. "I know fucking well you wouldn't, son."

After tapping a sleeping Mr. Phillip on the arm, Tez then helped him up from the recliner chair. "You sure you and Godma gon' be all right driving back tonight, Pops?"

"Yes, we'll be fine, son. You kids have fun," he said, then looked at me. "Y'all want us to take Camille back with us?"

"Nah, I want to spend some more time with her before I have to go back," I said.

"Well, I definitely understand that, son," he said, shaking my hand. He then walked over to Derrick. "It was nice talking to you tonight, young man," he said, shaking his hand. Then he placed one hand on Derrick's shoulder. "Listen, Perri's a tough nut to crack, but keep at it. Eventually, she'll soften up, for the right person that is. When she loves, she loves hard, and if you are ever so lucky to experience that"—he shook his head—"trust me, you'll be envied by almost every man." Mr. Phillip then turned back to look at me. "Isn't that right, son?"

While I nodded to agree with Mr. Phillip, Tez shook his head and let out a light laugh, which he hadn't expected anyone else to hear. For a moment, I just sat there pondering Mr. Phillip's words. Perri did love hard. She had been there for me more times than I could count, and never once had she asked for anything in return. We were connected in a way that was beyond any friendship. Hell, even beyond family for that matter.

After my mother, Aria, and Mr. Phillip left, Tez showed Derrick and Jorell to their rooms for the night. Nika, Perri, and Camille ended up all sharing one of the guest bedrooms upstairs, and since it was going on two in the morning, they were already asleep. Once Tez came back down in the basement, I looked up at him from where I was sitting on the sofa.

"I thought you would have already gone to bed. Myesha's still up waiting for me, so I'm 'bout to turn in myself," he said.

"Since when did you and that nigga Derrick get all chummy?" I asked somewhat out of the blue.

Tez's eyebrows gathered as he squinted in wonder. Slowly his eyes then softened, and the corners of his lips slightly turned up into a hesitant smirk. "I mean, why not? He's with my sister and really seems to care about her," he said, shrugging his shoulders.

I sucked my teeth and waved him off. "Man, she don't know that nigga!"

"Is there something about that nigga that I should know then?" he asked, cocking his head to the side. "I mean, is he out there at Georgetown making a fool outta her?" he spat, elevating his voice in anger. The way his chest broadened and his expression grew into an angry scowl, I knew I needed to speak up, and quick.

"Nah, man. Nah," I said, holding up my hand, trying to calm his crazy ass down. "I don't be seeing him around no other females like that. I mean, not now that he's with Perri anyway."

"So then what's the muthafucking problem?" he asked, confused.

I ran my hand down my head, then let out a sigh and shook my head. "Nothing," I said lowly.

Tez's frown turned back up into a grin once again. "Nigga, Perri's been in love wit' yo' ass since before your sixteenth birthday party. If it's anybody's ass in here I need to kick, it's yours." He pointed.

My eyes grew wide, and my mouth fell slightly open from shock, listening to what Tez just said. "For real? Yo, I swear I didn't know," I said lowly.

"You should have never slept with my sister if you didn't look at her like that, because that only magnified her feelings for you. And then y'all ended up with a baby together." He shook his head.

"Man, it wasn't like that—"

"Nigga, it wasn't like that to you." He pointed, cutting me off. "The only reason I never said anything was because she begged me not to. I was two seconds from fucking your ass up that day after graduation when I found out she was pregnant, but I didn't because of her. And now yo' ass sitting here acting all jealous and shit. Fuck that! Yo' ass ain't been wanting her. Talking all that best friend bullshit. You knew what it was when you took her virginity."

I dropped my head in my hands, listening to Tez cuss me out.

"Nigga, I was the one who had to dry her tears when you were all hugged up kissing Tasha that night at your sixteenth birthday party. I was the one who had to console her on prom night when we dropped y'all asses off at the fucking hotel" he yelled, pointing back at himself. "It was me, nigga, who watched her heart break when she found out Tasha was pregnant!" He shook his head. "And now you wanna sit here and be mad about the next nigga. Nah. As long as he treat her right, I don't give a fuck no more. She's grown and so are you," he said, finally lowering his voice.

"If you want her like I know you do, then you'll step up. It's time for you to finally see her as a woman and start treating her as such. If you can't already see, she done grown the fuck up! She's not one of your li'l homies no more, yo. She's the mother of your child, and if you ain't gon' treat her right, then let that shit go," he said, slicing his hand through the air. "Just co-parent and be friends."

"I know. I know," I let out, feeling completely ashamed and fucked up in that moment.

Tez walked over close to me and put his hand on my shoulder, causing me to look directly up at him. "'Cause next time, nigga, brother or not, I won't hesitate to fuck yo' ass up. And you know I don't make empty threats."

I nodded my head in clear understanding of his every word. It was rare when Tez showed this side of himself, but he'd been in the game long enough for me to know he wasn't nobody to play with. There had been mention of him catching several bodies over the years, but I never asked or even wanted to know for that matter. He was my brother, and in my eyes, that nigga could do no wrong.

After leaving Tez down in the basement, I made my way to the bedroom and lay back across the bed. Allowing my feelings for Perri to consume my thoughts, along with all the details Tez had just revealed, I stared up toward the ceiling. I knew I loved Perri, so that wasn't even a question, but now after realizing that I was actually in love with her, that shit scared me. I didn't know what to do with all those emotions because I had never loved another woman that way, not even Tasha.

If it was the last thing on this earth I did, I knew I had to make shit right with Perri. Not only did I owe it to her and myself, but I owed it to Camille. Maybe not tonight and maybe not even next week, but I was coming for my woman, and soon.

Chapter 28

Perri

2006

Sitting in the passenger seat of Nika's car, I blankly stared out of the window. We were ten minutes away from Georgetown where Derrick and I would be spending our very first Valentine's Day together. I hadn't seen him since Christmas break, so I was more than excited to spend some quality time together. He said that he had a lot planned for us, and I couldn't wait to see exactly what he had in store.

Since Thanksgiving break, it seemed as though Plus and I had gotten back tight again. Every day he'd call both me and Camille, and he'd come home from school more in the last three months than he had in the whole last year. He and I still acted as those same two kids from the Millwood projects, playing basketball at the rec and *Madden* on the PlayStation 'til the wee hours of the morning, and sneaking behind the house just to blow trees while everyone else was fast asleep.

"So what's Derrick got planned for you?" Nika glanced over and asked.

"I don't know. He's got something up his sleeve after the game though," I said, still looking out of the window.

"Well, I know one thing. Jorell had better have something big planned for me. Does Plus know you coming to town?"

Just the sound of my best friend's name caused an instant smile to form on my face. "Yeah, he knows." I looked back at her. "What?" I asked, seeing that her lips were twisted to the side.

"Nothing," she said with a little laugh, shaking her head. "So then what does he have planned for Valentine's Day?"

"I'on know," I muttered with a shrug, thinking about Daysia, Malika, and Sarah: all of the girls Plus currently called himself entertaining at the moment.

As soon as we pulled up to the Uline Arena and entered the parking garage, Nika put the car in park and grabbed her purse from the back seat. In exactly thirty minutes the buzzer would sound off to begin their game against Duke. We rushed inside the coliseum in hopes of moving quickly to our seats, but it was no use because fans were gathered from wall to wall. After twenty minutes of waiting in line and scooting through the thick crowd, we finally made our way to our seats only to see familiar faces.

"Hey, Perri, how are you?" Shay stood up in the aisle and said.

I gave her a hug and then waved to Ms. Scott. Surprisingly, she was all teeth when she leaned up and waved back, grinning as though they had already won the game. When she sat back in her seat, I noticed a gorgeous girl sitting beside her. With only seeing the back of her head, I could already call this girl "gorgeous." She had long, silky black hair, wore a sophisticated red pantsuit, and had long, manicured red nails that moved about on the tips of her fingers as she spoke.

After wrapping up the conversation she was having with the person next to her, she flipped her long hair back over her shoulders and turned around in her seat. Adjusting her red blazer, she sat up real prim and prop-er-like in her chair. It was only then that I realized it was Mia, Derrick's ex. The pictures of her in Derrick's mother's apartment did her no justice. In addition to the long, silky black hair on her head, she had long, curly eyelashes that seemed to be more than an inch long. The buttery-colored skin covering her face was without any flaws and complemented her doe-like dark brown eyes. With small lips and a pointed nose like a white girl, she sat there with her size-two frame.

Just as she crossed her legs, exposing the red pumps on her feet, Ms. Scott grabbed her hand. "This here is one of Derrick's little friends," she said, lazily pointing toward me.

Mia stood up from her seat and flipped back that long, silky hair of hers once more before extending her hand for me to shake. "Hi, I'm Mia. Derrick's girlfriend," she said matter-of-factly.

With my face in a sudden scowl, I looked down at her pale, bony hand then back at Nika, whose stance was already prepared for war. Letting out a small sarcastic snort of laughter, I turned back and decided to shake her hand. "Hi, I'm Perri. Derrick's girlfriend," I said, mimicking her tone.

She jerked her head back and balled up her pretty little face before looking over at Ms. Scott and Shay for a response. But just as Shay parted her lips to speak on the matter, the buzzer sounded off, and the two teams jogged out on the court. My eyes immediately searched for Plus. Wearing a navy blue sweatband around his curly black head of hair and long navy blue socks pulled up high on his muscular calves, he led the team out onto the floor. Then there was Derrick: big, light, bright, muscular nigga with tats all up and down his arms as he jogged out last on the court.

"Oh, it's game time, honey," Ms. Scott said, patting Mia's arm for her to sit.

We stared each other down for almost a minute it seemed before she finally sat her ass down in her seat. It was only a small victory, but a smile graced my face as I sat down after her and turned my attention toward the game. I tried my best to focus only on Derrick and Plus, but as the clock wound down, the fact that this bitch Mia was here claiming Derrick as her very own burned me up inside. From where I sat two seats down, I could hear her cheering and loudly yelling his name. For every assist or basket he made, she'd holler out, "That's my babyyy!" or "Yayy, Derrickk!" And each time, I couldn't help but to roll my eyes. When halftime came, I thought she'd try to step to me again, but instead she left with Ms. Scott and Shay right behind her.

"Yo, what the hell is up with that?" Nika nudged me and said.

"That's Derrick's ex, but why the fuck she thinks he's still her man, I have no idea."

"Look, I haven't whooped a bitch's ass since I left Connecticut, but I'm down for whatever if you need me," Nika said, rolling her shoulders.

Even though I laughed, I knew my girl was serious by the expression on her face. "Yo, I grew up fighting niggas three times her size in the hood. Do it look like I need any help beating a bitch's ass?"

"Well, I'm just saying," she said.

Just moments before the second half began, Mia, Shay, and Ms. Scott made their way back to their seats, looking like the Three Stooges. Even Shay with her two-faced ass. She hadn't spoken two words to me since the game started, and as much as she smiled in my face during my visit to New York, I couldn't help but feel some type of way.

Finally, there were two minutes left in the game and the score was tied 72-72. With just one look at Plus, I knew it was game time. It was the fire in his eyes that I had seen on so many occasions over the years, both on and off the court. As soon as he got his hand on the ball, he immediately took it down the court for a pretty three-point jump shot. With everyone on their feet, the entire arena erupted in a roar.

When number 24 from Duke ran back and pulled up for a jump shot of his own, Plus stole the ball midair and dribbled it back down the court. He did a quick chest pass to Jorell, who passed it right back. That only set Plus up for another three-pointer, which caused the crowd to go wild all over again. Duke tried their best to keep up, but at that point they were clearly no match for Plus and the team.

As the center, Derrick got the rebound for Duke's last failed attempt. He launched the ball clear down the court to Plus, who wasted no time hanging in the air for a Michael Jordan–style finger-roll. And just as the final seconds counted down on the clock, Duke desperately flung the ball up high in the air from the opposite direction of the court. They clearly missed the hoop just as the buzzer sounded off, indicating the game was finally over.

After the game, we all headed down to the hallway outside the locker room. Mia, Shay, and Ms. Scott all stood on one wall, while Nika and I stood across from them on the other. Mia and I were back to staring each other down, hatefully standing across from one another in clear contrast. She looked so pretty, soft, and sophisticated in her Lord & Taylor pantsuit. And then I, on the other hand, was dressed down in a gray Champion sweat suit with Plus's Georgetown jersey thrown over it. My brown hair was pulled back in a simple ponytail, and wheat-colored Timbs were on my feet as I leaned back on the wall with my legs cocked and my arms folded across my chest.

Plus was first out of the locker room, and as soon as we saw one another, we shared a smile, a hug, and our usual forehead kiss. Closing my eyes, I inhaled the fresh smell of soap on his skin and relished the familiarity of his touch.

"Ahem."

I opened up my eyes and looked across the hall to see a devilish smirk etched on Mia's face.

"Well, you must be Perri's boyfriend," she said, walking over to shake Plus's hand.

Before he could even put his hand in hers, I knocked it away and stepped in between the two of them. "No, bitch, this is my best friend and my daughter's father."

"Oh! Yo' baby daddy. That explains it," she said.

"Mm-hmm," I could hear Ms. Scott mumble under her breath.

"Look, I'm tired of—"

Just as I got in Mia's face to cuss her out, Plus grabbed me by the arm and pulled me back. "It's not even worth it, P," he said, cutting off my words. At the exact same time, Derrick walked out of the locker room, and judging by the expression on his face, he knew he had some explaining to do.

"Ahh, he . . . hey, baby," he stuttered, walking over to greet me. After wrapping his big, strong arms around me, he hooked his finger under my chin. He leaned down and placed a deep, passionate kiss on my lips that instantly sent shivers down my spine.

Although I initially was glad he did all that in front of Mia to put her in her place, when I pulled back and saw the strange look Plus gave us, I wished Derrick's approach had been a bit more subtle. Plus had seen us kiss plenty of times before, but never had I seen him look so uncomfortable and offended in all my life.

Removing himself from the awkwardness we both felt between us, he ran his hand down his head and said, "A'ight, I guess I'll catch y'all later then."

Just as he started to walk away, I yelled, "Wait!"

He looked back at me with his jaw slightly clenched and his lips tucked in. His eyes wore a confused state of defeat as he ran his hand down the top of his curls once more. "Sup," he said.

"Good game tonight."

"Thanks. And, P?"

My eyes widened with question.

"Happy Valentine's Day."

"Happy Valentine's Day, Plus."

As he turned back around and began to walk away, I couldn't help but feel that I should have been running right behind him. My heart was literally torn in that moment because there was a part of me that knew I was still deeply in love with Plus. And unless my eyes were completely deceiving me, he was now feeling something for me too.

Before too many more thoughts of Plus could consume my mind, Derrick walked over to give his mother and sister a big hug. He then came back over and put his hand around my waist, pulling me next to him. "Look, Mia, thanks for coming out and showing support for me tonight. That really means a lot to a nigga, but she's," he said, pointing over at me, "my girlfriend. I haven't heard from you in almost a year, and you just come back and expect shit to pick back up where it left off." He shook his head. "Nah, shorty. It don't work like that, ma."

"But we never broke up. How can you—"

"It's over, Mia," he said, cutting off her words.

"Oh, Derrick!" his mother let out.

Just as we turned to walk away, Mia spoke up again but this time with more hurt and anger lacing her voice. "So this is what you're doing now? Dating men? You a homo now, Derrick?" she yelled.

"Shorty!" he snapped, turning back to look her dead in the eyes. His face was cold while his eyes held an angry fire. "It's over! Just let that shit go, ma."

Just as he wrapped his arm around my shoulder and we began to finally walk away, I could hear Jorell finally coming out of the locker room. "Fuck is going on out here, breh?"

Derrick and I just kept moving, though, ignoring Jorell's question and leaving Nika behind to deal with her man. The sounds of Mia and Ms. Scott pleading their case to Derrick faded in the distance. Once we got to the parking garage, I leaned back against Nika's car and waited since I didn't have the key. Derrick hovered over me and stepped in close to where he was invading any and all of my personal space. Throwing my arms around his waist, I looked up into his piercing dark brown eyes.

"Yo, I thought I was going to have to fight you back there," I said with a little smirk.

"For what? I told you, I love you," he said, his deep baritone suspended over me as he came in a bit closer. Dropping his hands a bit lower to gently grab a handful of my ass, he strongly pressed himself against me. When he bent down to kiss me on the lips and slipped his tongue into my mouth, a soft moan escaped my lips.

I nearly jumped out of my skin when the car alarm went off, only to look over and see Nika and Jorell laughing.

"Y'all niggas nasty. Get a room, breh," Jorell said, locs pulled back in a low ponytail and gold teeth contrasting against his dark brown skin like always.

"That's the plan," Derrick replied lowly, biting down on his bottom lip.

Once we got in the car, I realized I had two missed calls from Plus and one text message. When I opened it up, it was a picture attachment of Plus and me, both kissing on Camille. The message above it read, Love you always, P. My heart sank into the pit of my stomach because I felt like it was Plus's way of finally telling me that he looked at me as more than just a homie. More than just the mother of his daughter and his so-called "best friend."

I wasn't oblivious to the fact that tonight Derrick would want all of me. It was our first Valentine's Day together, and although we hadn't had sex just yet, the sexual tension between us continued to make its powerful presence. In my heart though, I knew I needed to talk to Plus first. I needed to finally clear the air and tell him exactly how I'd felt all these years. I needed to find out if he'd ever felt just an ounce of what I had and to know if there was a chance, any chance at all, for us to be together. Because if there was, I knew I couldn't give away something to Derrick that didn't belong to him. Not without regret.

Once we parked the car right outside their dorm, I told Derrick that I would let him go get dressed while I ran up and talked to Plus right quick. I thought Derrick would object or be a little upset, but instead he gave me a peck on the lips and said, "A'ight."

Since Jorell and Plus shared a dorm room, I rode the elevator up to the eleventh floor with Jorell and Nika. As soon as we entered the hall, loud rap music blared behind several doors while the faint smell of weed and funk invaded my nostrils. Just as we were two doors down from their room, another one of their teammates by the name of Red peeped out his door.

"Aye yo, Rel. C'mere, let me holla at you for a minute," he said. Nika tried to keep walking along with me, but Jorell pulled her back by her waist.

When I finally got to Plus and Jorell's door, I closed my eyes and exhaled a deep breath. In my mind, I had rehearsed everything I needed to confess and every question I needed answers to. Nerves were starting to get the best of me as the bubbles in my stomach rolled, but I knew there was no turning back. I wasn't leaving without getting everything off my chest.

Taking another deep breath, I gave a quick knock to the door and slowly turned the brass knob. Cracking the door faintly open, I noticed that the room was dimly lit, and I could hear Dru Hill playing in the background. "You dressed?" I said, pushing the door farther open. When I stepped inside, I found Plus sitting on the edge of his bed with his pants down around his ankles. And down on her knees, in between his legs, was some girl giving Plus head.

"Oh, shit!" Plus looked up at me.

"Uh, my bad," I said lowly, stepping back out into the hall and closing the door. I could hear Plus yelling for me to wait, but I couldn't stop my legs from running. Tears had begun to form in my eyes, but I fought hard to hold them in. I had made a fool of myself once again over Plus, and I refused to cry.

When I ran past Jorell and Nika in the hall, she grabbed me by the arm. "Where you going? Did you talk to Plus?" she asked.

"He's busy," was all I could get out before the chunks of vomit rose up in my throat. I covered my mouth and tried to take deep breaths, but it was no use. I threw up right there in the middle of the hallway. Feeling even more embarrassed, I ran as fast as I could down the corridor, leaving Nika, Jorell, and my puke on the floor behind.

Chapter 29

Perri

When I got down to Derrick's room on the tenth floor, I immediately had to calm myself. There was no way I could go in there crying over another nigga. Not when he had professed his love for me time and time again and had even put his ex, Mia, in her place. I quickly wiped away the tears from my eyes and took a deep breath before knocking on his door.

"Who is it?" he yelled.

"It's me."

When Derrick came to the door to let me in, I could see sprinkles of water lightly scattered across his bare chest and arms. Wearing nothing but a white towel wrapped around his waist and black shower shoes on his feet, he led me inside. The fresh smell of Irish Spring soap filled the small room, which was somewhat on the junky side. Both twin beds were unmade and small piles of clothes were dispersed evenly across the floor. An open box with two slices of day-old pizza sat on top of the desk, while soda cans and paper balls were among the other decor.

"Wow, you cleaned up for me," I said with a little laugh and sniff.

"I see you got jokes. But nah, this is all my roommate's junk," he said.

"Mm, sure," I mumbled, going inside his bathroom to rinse out my mouth.

Once I returned, I sat on the edge of his bed. Allowing my eyes to wander around the room once more, I took in the posters of Buffy the Body and Gloria Velez that were hanging on the wall. I had only been to Derrick's room one other time, and I didn't quite remember it being in this condition. His gold chains hung from one of the knobs of his dresser while an old picture of him and Mia sat on top.

He must have seen my eyes zeroing in on it because he picked it up from where he stood. "This shit ain't nothing," he said.

"Are you sure? I mean, you claim that I'm the one you love, yet I don't see any picture of me hanging up around here," I said, feeling myself become emotional. I didn't know if it was because of the picture of Derrick and Mia or the image of Plus getting head that was still embedded in my mind.

Derrick tossed the picture in the trash, bending his wrist as though he were shooting a ball through a hoop. "See? It's gone, ma," he said.

I shrugged my shoulders and chewed the corner of my lip. "Maybe we should just do this another night," I said softly.

He cocked his head to the side and scrunched his eyebrows in confusion. "I know you not gon' let some bullshit-ass picture from three years ago ruin our first Valentine's Day together."

"It's not just the picture. I just have—"

"Is everything all right with you and that nigga Plus?" he asked.

"I mean . . ." Shrugging, I let my voice trail off. "What does that have to do with anything?"

"Because whenever shit ain't right between you and your baby daddy, you take it out on me. That ain't fair, ma," he said, sitting down next to me on the bed.

"Everything between me and Plus is fine," I lied. "It's the fact that you're still holding on to the last bitch that has me heated," I snapped.

Honestly, I didn't know if Plus and I were okay. I had no reason to be mad at him other than my love for him was obviously greater than the love he had for me. He wasn't my man, so I had no right to be angry at what he did with the next woman. Yet I was. Seeing Plus's pleasure-filled face as the girl sucked the skin off his dick infuriated me. A physical pain shot through my chest and shortened my breath to the point where I thought I wouldn't even be able to breathe.

"I just threw that picture in the fucking trash, and not even an hour ago I told that bitch to her face that I was with you." He pointed to my chest. "What else do you need me to do to prove that I'm here for you, huh?"

I covered my face with my hands and shook my head because he was right. He had bent over backward to prove his loyalty and devotion to me. Yet, I kept pushing him away. Just as I opened up my mouth to say that I was sorry, he quickly shut me up with a kiss to the lips. Wrapping my arms around his neck, I felt the tip of his tongue slide across my cheek then down onto my neck.

"What I gotta do, ma?" he whispered into the crook of my neck.

My eyes closed as I felt the coolness of his hands slide up underneath the sides of my sweatshirt, then up and around my back. When he unsnapped my bra, my skin grew hot and my pussy pulsated with anticipation. I hadn't had sex in a long time, and my body was more than ready.

He pulled the sweatshirt up over my head and quickly tossed it to the floor. My bra fell off my shoulders and hung loosely around my arms, exposing both of my breasts. "Damn," he muttered, taking his bottom lip between his teeth, lustfully looking me over.

When I tried to pull the bra up to cover myself, he pulled it back down and tossed it to the floor as well. Wasting no time, he took one of my breasts into his mouth, sucking and lowly groaning with excitement. I looked down toward his lap to see that his towel had risen up high into a tent. When he noticed what I was staring at, he gently grabbed my hand and wrapped it around his length, allowing me to feel its girth as I closed my eyes again.

"You feel that?" he asked in between kisses to each of my breasts.

"Yes," I whispered. My eyes were still closed tight as I enjoyed the connection between his mouth and my flesh.

"This big muthafucka right here, it's all yours, ma," he said against my skin. He lifted his head and cupped my chin with his hand before looking me directly in the eyes. "Never forget that shit, a'ight?"

Nodding my head, I kissed his lips once more. He stood me up in front of him and slid my sweatpants down to the floor, all the while planting soft, wet kisses to my breasts and stomach. As I stood there before him, wearing nothing but a simple pair of purple satin panties, he looked up and admired everything in his sight. Simply flattered by the look in his eyes, I quickly turned my head away and blushed.

"Don't be shy now, ma," he said.

He unwrapped the towel from his waist, greeting me with that anaconda of his, which I had already met once before. Long, hard, and wet at the tip, it eagerly stared back at me. The mere sight of this nigga's dick had my mouth salivating and my pussy aching from within. I closed my eyes tight and gasped when he slipped two of his fingers inside of me. My panties were still on and pulled to the side as he plunged his fingers in and out of me with ease.

"Ahh," I moaned, holding on to his muscular shoulders.

His fingers began to pick up speed, and the grip he had on my ass tightened as he continued to suck on my breast. Just as my mouth fell open and I could feel that explosion coming near, he said, "Look at me!"

I opened up my eyes and looked down into his handsome face as he repeatedly drove his magical fingers deeper inside. It seemed as though my hips had a mind of their own because they started to grind and buck back in the very same rhythm. Before I knew it, the tension that had been building up between my thighs released hard. Right there on his fingers.

"Ahhh, Derrickk," I wailed out in pleasure. Glancing down, I saw a satisfied smirk etched across his face before he popped his fingers in his mouth, thoroughly sucking each one before slowly pulling them out. "Mmm. You taste good as fuck," he groaned, eyes low as if he were high yet filled with nothing but lust.

In a matter of seconds, he flipped me over on the bed and slid my panties all the way down. After he parted my legs, he buried his head face-first in between my thighs. Thank God I'd shaved. The feeling of his slick, wet tongue slithering up and down my folds was like nothing I had ever experienced. Goosebumps had risen up to cover my entire body as I listened to the sound of his wet mouth against me. Within a matter of seconds, I could feel that same tingling sensation arise, causing me to clench the sheets. Not able to take much more, I gripped the back of his head and let out the loudest moan imaginable. "Arrgh! Fuckk!" The most powerful of orgasms had ripped right through me like a lightning bolt, triggering a seizure-like effect.

I was still in a state of orgasmic pleasure when Derrick got up and put the condom on. He continued to take charge and wedge himself in between my thighs. Feeling the tip of his hardness patiently awaiting at my entrance, I wrapped my legs around his muscular frame and pushed him inside.

"Fuck, ma," he groaned. When his eyes closed and he bit down on that bottom lip, I knew I had him. As he worked himself in and out of me, winding his hips for effect, I tried my best to keep up, bucking and grinding my hips back to match his every stroke. With one hand gently gripping my neck, he kissed me deeply and maneuvered his way deeper inside. Nothing but the sensual sounds of our light moans and wet bodies colliding filled the room.

"Ohh, Derrickk," I moaned, feeling another orgasm build within the pit of my stomach.

"What's my name, ma?" he asked against my lips.

"Derri . . . Oh, Godd!" I cried.

"Nah, I'm not God, ma," he whispered. I could hear almost a hint of a smile in his voice as he hovered over my lips.

When he slid his hands down and took ahold of my waist, my body finally surrendered. Grinding those hips, he went deeper and deeper until I just couldn't take it anymore. "Fuckk!" I wailed, releasing everything I had pent up inside of me.

Just when I thought it was over, allowing my body to go completely limp, he flipped me over on my stomach and slid in from behind. He wrapped my long hair around his hand for a tight grip, causing my back to instantly arch. While his other hand softly fondled my breast, he slowly drilled into me from behind. My body had never felt so much pleasure. I had already had two orgasms, and from the way he was working me over, I knew another was just around the corner.

"Shiitt!" he hissed. Once his stroke picked up speed, I knew we were finally cumming together. "Aargh!" he groaned, finally releasing into the condom.

Completely spent, both of us collapsed down onto the mattress and looked up toward the ceiling. Breathing heavily and panting, we tried hard to regain our composure. We were both in a state of euphoria and coming down off of what seemed to be a natural high.

He looked over at me and interlaced his fingers through mine. "Damn, ma, had I'd known you were gonna be that easy, I wouldn't have made reservations for dinner and shit," he said with a light chuckle.

"Shut up," I said, hitting him in the arm.

He rolled over on his side to face me. "Nah, but for real. I had a lot of shit planned for us tonight. It's our first Valentine's Day together, and I really wanted tonight to be special."

"And it was," I said, lifting up a little to peck his lips. "Besides, you can make it up to me and take me out tomorrow. Okay?"

"A'ight bet," he said. Sitting up in the bed, he brought my hand up to his mouth and kissed the back of it. "Oh, and I got you something, too."

I smiled and shook my head. "Derrick, you didn't have to." I felt a little bad because I hadn't gotten him anything.

"I know, but I wanted to." Once he slipped on his boxer briefs, he got up from the bed and went over to his closet. He pulled out a large red gift bag with the head of a teddy bear peeking out from the top. When he walked back over, he proudly smiled and set it down next to me on the bed.

"Go ahead and open it up," he said. A tinge of excitement filled his eyes.

I was completely confused when I pulled out the teddy bear and underneath it was an old, used Spalding basketball. When I spun the ball around for a closer look, I saw that it had been signed by Dwayne Wade. My mouth nearly dropped to the floor, realizing the treasure he had just given me. "Oh, my . . ." I said, covering my mouth.

"Yeah, I know you like that nigga so . . ." He shrugged like it was no big deal.

"But how did you—"

"Don't worry about all'at. Just know I got it especially for you," he said with a wink.

I shot up from the bed and wrapped my arms around his neck before kissing him more passionately than I ever had before. When I pulled back from his lips, I stared up into his dark brown eyes. "I love you, Derrick," I admitted for the very first time.

"I love you too, Perri. Happy Valentine's Day, ma."

"Happy Valentine's Day."

That night, Derrick and I ordered pizza and stayed locked up in his dorm room since his roommate was out of town. We talked about everything under the moon, from his relationship with Mia to my dreams of one day coaching a college basketball team. All thoughts of Plus had been temporarily erased for the night, and I was thankful. Deep down, I knew that Plus would never love me the way I loved him. I needed to move on. Derrick was everything I could ever dream of in a boyfriend: handsome, romantic, and loyal. So from that moment on, I decided that I would let Derrick love me the way I knew I deserved to be loved.

Chapter 30

Plus

Today was finally the day of Perri's graduation from Prince George's Community College. Derrick, Jorell, and I all got up early and drove back home from school together just for the occasion. For the past few months, Perri had been the happiest I'd ever seen her, and I knew it was all because of Derrick. Those two were definitely in love. And despite the fact that I too was in love with her and wanted her all to myself, I decided to just let her be. In all honesty, I knew that if she and I were meant to be together in the future, then eventually we would be.

Just before we entered the Millwood projects, I glanced out of the backseat window as we rode past Tasha's home. Parked right there in the driveway was TK's old, beat-up Cavalier. I watched as he dipped down in the back door to pull out the baby I had once believed to be my own son. He held him high up in the air before holding him firmly in his arms. Up at the house, standing in the door waiting, was Tasha, still just as beautiful as she was the night of our senior prom.

"There go that bitch Tasha right there, mane, and that sucka-ass nigga TK," Jorell pointed out.

"Yeah, I see them," I said. Even through the pain, I was able to smile at the scene, forever thankful that I had dodged that bullet.

"I swear we should just go run up on that nigga right now, breh," Jorell said, getting hype.

"Nah, he got what he wanted. I'ma let him have that." And that's exactly what I meant. True, Tasha was beautiful, but she was more of a nuisance than anything. There's no way our relationship would have lasted, and I knew eventually she would have turned out to be the baby momma from hell.

As we turned into the Millwood projects, I swear nothing had changed. Bad-ass kids were running around and several days' worth of trash were still littering the streets. Only difference were the new young black faces that stood on the corners. Seeing the dope boys wiggling their fingers at each and every car that rode by brought back memories of Tez, Perri, and me when we were younger. Shaking my head, I remembered how Tez started out there hustling on the streets, and now that nigga was a young kingpin, living out in the "burbs."

After we parked the car in front of Perri's house, we all got out and walked up to knock on the door.

"Who is it?" Aria's grown butt yelled from the other side.

"Girl, you better open up this gah damn door," I said in a joking manner.

When she opened it up, she smiled and so did I. Every time I came home from school, we acted like we hadn't seen each other in years. I pulled her in for a tight hug then kissed her on the cheek. My sister had grown up to be a beautiful young lady. At 16 years old, she had long, curly black hair that framed her heart-shaped face. Her curvy size-eight frame made me cringe a little each and every time I saw her. All the little niggas in the neighborhood were damn near beating down our door trying to get with her, and with me being away at school, there wasn't a damn thing I could do to stop them. Too bad Ronnie's deadbeat ass wasn't a better father.

When I finally got inside the house with both Jorell and Derrick on my heels, my eyes instantly scanned the room for Perri. Instead, I saw Tez, Myesha, and Nika sitting in the living room, watching TV. Jorell instantly went to go sit by Nika, while Derrick and I stood.

"What's going on, man," Tez said, standing up to greet me. He dapped me up before pulling me in for a brotherly hug.

"Ain't shit. Where everybody at?" I asked.

"Perri and Pops still getting dressed and shit," he said, sitting back down on the couch. "Godma said she's on her way over with Camille though."

"Oh, a'ight."

While Derrick sat down on the couch and waited, I ran in the back to Perri's bedroom. I did a quick knock before opening the door. And there she was, standing in front of her floor-length mirror, twisting to admire herself in the dress she wore. If ever there had been an angel to fall from heaven, it would have been Perri on this day. The white dress she wore clung to her curvy figure, and her long brown hair cascaded down her back in big, loose curls. Her pouty lips had been painted a glossy shade of pink, and when she looked at me through the mirror, her bright amber eyes beamed.

"Damn," I muttered to myself.

"Oh, hey, Plus," she said, putting in her earrings.

"Damn, shorty. You look . . ." I simply shook my head because the words just wouldn't come out.

"I look what?" she asked, appearing confused.

I shook my head again, and without even thinking, I walked over to her and boldly spun her around. Holding the small of her back, I pulled her in close and pressed my lips against hers, catching her completely off guard. Although I hadn't been this close to her in over a year, our chemistry just felt right. My body was responding to missing hers like never before. My dick was jumping uncontrollably in my pants, and when I deepened our kiss, I unconsciously groaned inside her mouth.

She pulled back, slowly peeling one eye open at a time. "What are you doing?" she asked.

I just stared at her for a moment, trying to read her expression. She could deny it all she wanted, but the way she kissed me back was all the proof I needed to know she was still feeling me. "Look, P, I'm tired of fighting this shit. Tez told me how you felt about me back in the day and—"

"Tez," she mumbled, cutting me off. Her face became more annoyed with every second that passed, as she chewed the corner of her lip.

"Look, I love you," I said, taking both of her hands in mine. "And I'm ready to be yours and only yours, shorty. That is, if you'll have me."

She sighed and slowly shook her head. "I can't—"

"P, I don't give a fuck about that nigga Derrick," I said, cutting off her words. "You, me, and Camille, that's all a nigga cares about, shorty."

Narrowing her eyes, she looked at me as if to ask where this was all coming from. "But we're best friends, right? I'm like one of the guys," she said, shrugging her shoulders.

I let out a small snort because I knew she finally wanted me to make shit crystal clear. "You'll always be my best friend, Perri. Always. But for the record, I love you, and I'm in love with you." I pointed to her chest.

"But why now?"

Just as I was about to answer, a quick knock sounded at her door and in came Derrick's cock blocking ass. I noticed that he looked down to where I was still holding both of Perri's hands. He chucked his chin up a little and tucked his hands in the pocket of his pants. "Y'all 'bout ready?" he asked with a look of uncertainty in his eyes, staring more at Perri than at me. "Everybody's in the living room, waiting," he said.

Quickly, Perri pulled her hands back from mine and walked over to Derrick. "Yes, I'm ready," she said, giving a small smile. Perri sorrowfully peered back at me with confusion etched across her face.

"And by the way, you look beautiful, ma," he said, leaning down to kiss her lips. When he looked back and hit me with a head nod, I instantly knew that nigga was trying to send a message.

Seeing the two of them so affectionate with one another after everything I had just revealed burned me up inside. A nigga's heart was literally hurting like hell as they walked out together hand in hand. Trying to collect myself, I stood there for a minute before walking out to the living room where everyone was. As soon as I came in, I saw Derrick standing there with Camille in his arms and Perri at his side. The three of them looking like the perfect fucking family.

"Da-da, Da-da," Camille said, reaching for me.

I walked over and grabbed her from his arms. "C'mere, baby girl," I said. Perri did all she could to avoid looking at me, but when our eyes finally locked, I knew she'd seen the disappointment on my face. Nevertheless, I kissed Camille's chubby little cheek and took her over by the door.

"Everybody ready?" Mr. Phillip said, causing everyone to get up and head toward the door.

After loading up in the cars, we all headed over to the coliseum for Perri's graduation. Thousands of family members were in attendance, sitting in the stands and awaiting the graduating class of 2006. There were over 500 graduates that day, seated down in the center of the coliseum floor. While the ladies wore white caps and gowns, the men all wore navy blue.

I swear I was so proud when they called Perri's name and handed her her diploma. She had gotten her associate's degree in sports management. With Camille still in my arms, I stood up and cheered as loud as I could, whistling through my fingers in between. Perri had come a long way from that little tomboy from Millwood projects who just barely made C's. She had now morphed into this beautiful, educated woman right before my very eyes.

After the ceremony was over, we drove over to Mo's seafood restaurant where Tez had made reservations. To say the tension between Perri and me was thick would have been an understatement. Other than thanking me for the flowers I bought her, Perri hadn't said two words to me the entire night. When we sat down at the table, Derrick and Perri sat on one end while I sat with Tez down at the other.

Once all the crabs, shrimp, and oysters came out, and the drinks got to flowing, everyone appeared to be having a good time. Tez stood up and tapped a spoon against his glass. "I just want to say to Perri that I'm proud of you, sis. I always knew you were meant for greatness and this here is just the first step to being all you can be."

"Nigga, she ain't joining the army," I said, causing everyone at the table to laugh.

"Yo, shut up and let me finish," he said with a light chuckle. "But for real though, I know you had your heart set on going to a four-year college and that shit got put on hold. But just know that everything happens for a reason, baby girl," he said, pointing and winking at Camille. "Whatever you need to reach that next point in your life, whether it be a four-year university or getting a job, whatever, I got you."

"Thank you," she said, standing up to come down and hug his neck.

Once Tez had sat back down at the table and Perri was getting ready to sit too, Derrick stood up. "Nah, stay right there, ma," he said, placing his hand on her hip. As he turned toward the rest of us with a nervous look on his face, I wondered what the fuck this nigga could possibly say. If anyone should have been standing up to give a speech about Perri, it should have been me. Not some New York nigga she had only known for a year.

"I just want all of you here to know that Perri is very special to me," he said, clearing his throat. "Being around this family for the past year and getting to know Camille," he said, turning toward my baby girl with a smile, "has been without a doubt one of the best experiences I've ever had. To connect with this little one right here," he said, pointing to her. All the ladies around the table let out a series of "awww's," while I just sucked my teeth and took a drink of my soda.

"Y'all, I have loved this woman from the very first moment I laid eyes on her. Tell 'em, ma," he said, looking at Perri. "What I tell you that night? If it was the last thing on this earth I did, I was gon' make you my lady."

When that nigga dropped down on one knee in front of her, everyone, including Perri, gasped while I damn near choked to death on the soda I was drinking. In total disbelief, I stood up from my seat to see how all this shit was going to play out. Mouth slightly ajar and heart beating rapidly within my chest, I watched him take her by the hand.

"Will you do me the honor, Ms. Perri Daniels, of being my wife?" He reached into his pocket and pulled out, from what I could see down at the other end of the table, a decent-sized rock.

Perri covered her mouth and immediately looked over to Tez. When Tez's eyes bounced toward me, Perri turned around in her seat and looked at me as well. I shook my head. "Don't do this, shorty. Please," I begged lowly.

"Ma," Derrick called, gaining her attention again. "You know I love you, right?" he asked, stroking her cheek with his hand. She nodded her head. "A nigga's about to go to the NBA, and I need you, ma. I need my wife by my side."

"Perri!" I shouted.

She looked back at me and bit down on the corner of her lip. Although her amber eyes held confusion in them, I could also see what looked to be pity or maybe even an apology reflecting back at me.

"Ma, look at me," Derrick said, causing her to look back down at him. "I love you," I heard him say.

My ears had to be deceiving me when I heard her say, "I love you too," just above a whisper. I swear a nigga just wanted to scream hearing her say that shit, but the lump that formed in my throat wouldn't allow me to speak up.

"Will you do me the honor?" he asked again.

Silently, I prayed when Perri looked at her father and then back at Tez again. He slightly shrugged his shoulders and held both of his hands up as if to say leave him out of it.

I took in the deepest breath I could take and listened carefully to hear all the way down at the other end of the table. Perri turned back to face Derrick, who was still down patiently waiting on one knee.

"Yes, Derrick, I'll marry you."

To Be Continued . . .